DEATH OF AN

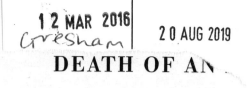

DEATH OF AN AIRMAN

CHRISTOPHER ST JOHN SPRIGG

With an Introduction by
Martin Edwards

This edition published in 2015 by
The British Library
96 Euston Road
London NW1 2DB

Originally published in 1934 by Hutchinson

Cataloguing in Publication Data
A catalogue record for this book is available from the British Library

ISBN 978 0 7123 5615 2

Typeset by IDSUK (DataConnection) Ltd
Printed and bound by CPI Group (UK) Ltd, Croydon, CR0 4YY

CONTENTS

INTRODUCTION

Death of an Airman is an enjoyable and unorthodox whodunit from a writer whose short life was as remarkable as that of any of his fictional creations. On first publication in 1935, the novel was greeted rapturously by no less an authority than Dorothy L. Sayers, creator of Lord Peter Wimsey and then the crime fiction reviewer for the *Sunday Times*. The story, she said, "bubbles over with zest and vitality in describing the exceedingly odd goings-on at a rather oddly managed Aero Club." Sayers had previously enthused over Sprigg's *The Perfect Alibi,* prompting him to write her a letter of appreciation. It must have seemed that a distinguished career beckoned for him in the field of crime fiction.

Fate intervened, however, and Sprigg's detective novels have languished in obscurity for almost eight decades. Their extreme scarcity has made the prices of first editions in well-kept dust wrappers rise faster than any of the airships in which Sprigg took a special interest. In years of searching, I could not find a copy of this book for sale anywhere; finally, I managed to read it, thanks to the generous loan of a copy from one of England's leading collectors. I was as impressed as Sayers, and happily the British Library has stepped in to make *Death of an Airman* available to present-day readers, most of whom are unlikely to be familiar with Sprigg's work.

When an aeroplane crashes, and its pilot is killed, Edwin Marriott, the Bishop of Cootamundra in Australia, is on hand. In England on leave, the Bishop has decided to learn how to fly, but he is not convinced that the pilot's death was accidental. In due course, naturally, he is proved right. The Bishop and

Inspector Bray of Scotland Yard make an appealing pair of detectives, and ultimately a cunning criminal scheme is uncovered. To say too much about the story would risk spoiling some of the surprises, but many readers will agree with Sayers' verdict that Sprigg offers "a most ingenious and exciting plot, full of good puzzles and discoveries and worked out among a varied cast of entertaining characters."

Christopher St John Sprigg is a name that sounds like a pseudonym, but it was real enough. He was born in Putney in 1907, but left school at 15 after his father lost his job as literary editor of the *Daily Express*. The Spriggs moved to Yorkshire, and Christopher started working for a local newspaper. Interested in aviation and writing, he catered for both passions by becoming involved with an aeronautics publishing business, and in 1930 he published *The Airship: its Design, History, Operation and Future*. This was followed two years later by a book titled *Fly with Me: an elementary textbook on the art of piloting*, and later by *Let's Learn to Fly*. No wonder the background of *Death of an Airman* impresses as authentic. His debut crime novel, *Crime in Kensington* (retitled *Pass the Body* for US publication) appeared in 1933, and introduced Charles Venables, an amateur detective. Like Bray, Venables is a character whom Sprigg employed more than once.

Sprigg's youth and dynamism were typical of many detective novelists of his era. He wrote six more whodunits, as well as editing a book of classic "uncanny stories" by the likes of Sheridan Le Fanu and M.R. James. For good measure, he tried his hand at short stories, experimenting with science fiction, and with a female sleuth faintly reminiscent of Miss Marple.

Writing fact and fiction was not enough for Sprigg. He adopted the pen-name Christopher Caudwell for much of his serious literary work, quickly establishing a separate reputation as a poet. He also became a passionate convert to Marxism, offering a Marxist critique of poetry in *Illusion and Reality. Studies in a Dying Culture*, published posthumously, included an introduction by John Strachey, a fellow Marxist who later became a minister in Clement Attlee's post-war government. Strachey shared Sprigg's interest in mysteries, and is credited with coining the phrase "the Golden Age of detective fiction". Sebastian Faulks has pointed out that Sprigg's enthusiasm for flying was not diminished by his shift to a hard-line political stance and membership of the Communist Party: "Flying was seen as a feasible form of heroism and individual self-assertion that survived the degradation of the infantry slaughters on the Western Front." Unfortunately, slaughter in wartime had not come to an end. In late 1936, Sprigg joined the International Brigade and travelled to Spain. He trained as a machine gunner, but was killed in action on 12 February 1937. He was not quite thirty years old.

At about the same time that Sprigg became a Communist, so did a fellow poet who dabbled in detective fiction. Cecil Day-Lewis, however, decided not to fight in the Spanish Civil War, and he survived until the 1970s, long enough to form a rather different view of politics He became Poet Laureate, married a beautiful actress, and had a son who became an Oscar-winning actor. Sometimes there is only a hair's breadth of difference between longevity and oblivion. Sprigg does not, however, deserve to be forgotten, and although he fell out of love with detective fiction in the last months of his life, he was young enough to have seen the error of his ways, had he lived. He was a talented writer, of whodunits and much else besides, and this reissue of *Death of an Airman* provides a welcome reminder of a worthy life, cut short as cruelly and prematurely as those of his fictional victims.

Martin Edwards
www.martinedwardsbooks.com

CHAPTER I

ARRIVAL OF A BISHOP

A YOUNG woman with a reddish face and horn-rimmed glasses appeared suddenly out of a door marked "Manager, Baston Aero Club".

"Well, young man, what do you want?" she asked sharply.

The middle-aged man in grey flannels who was standing in the club hall looked round to see who was being spoken to, and then perceptibly started when he realized that it was he who was being addressed.

"Are you the manager of the Baston Aero Club?" he asked.

"Manager and secretary. In fact, I run the place," she answered.

"I see." The speaker, though obviously not shy, had not quite recovered from the surprise of being addressed as "young man" by a woman some years his junior.

"The fact is, I want to learn to fly. That is," he added diffidently, "if I am not too old for that sort of thing." His diffidence contrasted with a certain deep richness of voice—the kind of voice which inevitably suggests public speaking.

The young woman beamed. "Don't you worry! We'll teach you if it kills us—or you." She rummaged over a table in the hall which was littered with papers and picked out a form.

"We'd better make you a member before you lose your nerve. Are you a British subject? We're not particular, but if you aren't British we don't get a subsidy for teaching you, so we charge you more."

"I am an Australian."

The red-faced young woman peered at him anxiously from behind her glasses. "I hope you don't get fighting drunk? Our last Australian smashed every glass in the place the day he went solo."

The stranger cleared his throat deprecatingly. "I think it unlikely that I should do the same. I am the Bishop of Cootamundra."

For the first time the girl looked a little disconcerted. "Well, I'm ... I mean how odd!" She looked at him critically. "You have got a *bishopy* air now one looks for it, and that sort of creamy clerical voice. But why haven't you a doodah round your neck and the obbly-gobblies on the legs?"

"You refer, I fancy, to the Roman collar and episcopal gaiters." The Bishop's stiff manner was contradicted by a twinkle in his clear blue eyes. "I am at the moment on leave. In any case we are less rigid about these formalities in the Commonwealth. The spirit quickeneth, you know."

"Talking about spirits," said the young woman vaguely, "I must close the bar. It's gone three. Those damned soaks will lose me my licence if they can. Excuse my language, by the way. We haven't many bishops here."

"Don't let me detain you."

"That's all right," the girl answered with quiet determination. "I'm going to get your signature on the dotted line before I leave you!"

While she spoke, the manager was rapidly filling up the form, and now she handed it to him. He signed it and took out his cheque-book. "I see the entrance fee is two guineas and the subscription another two guineas; that is four in all. To whom shall I make out the cheque?"

"My dear old soul, nobody takes any notice of the entrance fee—only the disgustingly rich ones. Make it out for two guineas to the 'Baston Aero Proprietary, Ltd.'"

"Oh, thank you." The Bishop completed and signed the cheque.

The manager glanced at the firm clear signature.

"Edwin Marriott," she read. "I thought you signed yourself 'George Canterbury', 'Arthur Swansea', and so forth."

The Bishop smiled. "I'm afraid not. Edwin Cootamundriensis sounds a trifle unconvincing, don't you think?"

She folded the Bishop's cheque with a caressing gesture. "This ought to be a good cheque—for a change," she said with an air of relief. "We should christen it with a quick drink really, shouldn't we? Oh, of course, I was forgetting. You probably don't drink. You know it will take a bit of getting used to, your Bishop line," she went on confidentially, "but it will be first-rate publicity when you take your 'ticket'. *Exchanges mitre for flying helmet*, you know."

The Bishop shuddered perceptibly at this remark.

The girl handed him a booklet and some leaflets and made a shooing gesture. "Pop out on the tarmac, there's a dear, and have a squint at the flying. I'll join you in a jiffy, and introduce you to your instructor and so forth."

The Bishop, hazy as to what the "tarmac" might be, walked out through the door in front of him and came out on to a concrete expanse. Chairs and tables were scattered *al fresco*, and to the right of the wooden club-house from which he had emerged was a gaunt shed which he supposed housed the club's aeroplanes. Before him, obviously, was the aerodrome, for even as he watched an aeroplane was running rapidly across it.

"Taking-off," he murmured with satisfaction.

The manager joined him later, looking still more reddish and dishevelled. Evidently this was the effect of attempting to close the bar.

"I'd better introduce myself first," she remarked briskly. "Sarah Sackbut, but everyone calls me Sally—or worse."

"How do you do?" said the Bishop politely.

"I suppose you're a lordship?" she went on. "I'm a little vague about the Australian Church?"

"I'd rather not. Few of my flock in Australia do so, and when I hear it over here it always makes me feel not quite real. I prefer Doctor Marriott. Or, as a fellow club member, call me Bishop— American, perhaps, but more familiar to me."

The Bishop's gaze wandered to a slim figure in white overalls and flying helmet which was standing near them. The portion of face which the Bishop could see was very attractive, and it was also faintly familiar, but he could not see enough to put a name to it.

A word from Sally made the girl turn. "This," Sally told her, "is our new member—the Bishop of Cootamundra. No non-sense about him—hail-fellow-well-met—the world's Bishop." Sally smiled at Dr. Marriott. "I suppose you recognize *her*? Face creams, you know. '*Lady Laura Vanguard, Society's leading beauty, uses Blank's Skinfude exclusively*,' and so forth. She's worth pounds to us in publicity, aren't you, Laura?"

"Well, why are you always worrying about my silly account?" asked Lady Laura plaintively.

"Hard cash is more than coronets," answered Miss Sackbut grimly.

"How too right!" Lady Laura flashed a smile at the Bishop. "Appallingly pleased to meet you. Is it one of Sally's silly jokes or are you really the Bishop-thing?"

"I really am," admitted the Bishop, feeling more unreal than before.

"What do you want to learn to fly for? Nearer my God to Thee sort of thing?"

"Don't be blasphemous, dear," said Sally.

"Better than being profane," replied Lady Laura. "I am sure you've terrified the Bishop with your language already."

"My ambition is quite earthly," interrupted the Bishop hastily. "It takes several weeks to travel from one end of my diocese to the other by the present primitive means of transport. The diocese has offered to buy me an aeroplane, but funds do not permit me to employ a pilot. I propose, therefore, to pilot myself."

Lady Laura murmured something, but her attention was on the aeroplane now climbing steadily into the blue afternoon sky.

Miss Sackbut strolled forward and the Bishop followed her. His attention was attracted by a woman in a black leather flying-suit who was standing in the attitude of determined isolation adopted by well-known persons in public places.

The features, pretty at a distance but on closer inspection some-what aged and battered, were still more familiar to the Bishop than Lady Laura's classic profile.

"Bless my soul!" he exclaimed. "Isn't that—yes, surely it's Mrs. Angevin, the transatlantic flyer! Dear me, quite an honour for the club!"

Miss Sackbut laughed sardonically, and the Bishop wondered whether his remark was inappropriate.

"Transatlantic flyers!" The girl snorted contemptuously. "The place is lousy with them! That tall fellow over there talking to our ground engineer is Captain Randall. He's flown both Atlantics both ways now. Having a crack at the Pacific this year. He's giving Dolly Angevin a bit of a dirty look, isn't he? They're as jealous as chorus girls, half these famous pilots. Still, he's a pilot and she isn't."

"I don't understand?" ventured Dr. Marriott. "Surely she flew the machine to New York? Wasn't she alone?"

"Oh, she can fly from A to B all right," admitted Miss Sackbut unenthusiastically, revealing the depths of disdain of the flying world for its public heroes, "as long as her engine turns round, but she's hamhanded."

"Poor girl! What a deformity!"

"Good lord! I only mean it figuratively," exclaimed Sally. "It means she's clumsy, if you follow me. And then didn't you see her *rumble* into the aerodrome just now? She always does."

"Really? I must say I heard no noise," answered the Bishop in surprise.

Miss Sackbut laughed. "Surely you understand English, Doctor Marriott? To 'rumble' is to sneak in near the ground with bursts of engine until you reach the aerodrome. Then you flop in. What you should do, of course," she added in lofty explanation, "is glide in from a height without using your engine. Rumbling is fine until the engine refuses to play. Then you drop into the street and they scrape you up."

The Bishop was a little staggered at this explanation, which made matters considerably more obscure.

"Dear me, how unpleasant! I must remember to avoid *rumbling* at all costs when I come to fly." The Bishop laughed. "Really, the word is quite apposite when one comes to think of it. What a lot I have to learn! You seem almost to speak a different language."

"Talking of language," said his informant, "what in hell's name is Furnace doing with that babe Vane?"

Miss Sackbut was staring at the aeroplane which the Bishop had seen take off a little earlier. He followed her gaze.

The gay red-and-silver aeroplane looked quite steady to the Bishop. It seemed to be climbing steeply and effortlessly, with the tail low down. But as he watched it, something terrible happened. It was all so quick that the Bishop found difficulty in grasping what really occurred. The aeroplane tilted sideways with a flick, the front dropped, and the contraption was whirling like a devilish top earthward, while the tail beat the air violently in a giddy spiral.

Miss Sackbut's voice rose in irritation. "Furnace is spinning. He oughtn't to do that on the kid's fourth lesson. Particularly with Vane, who's qualifying as our worst pupil. It'll scare the life out of him."

It was only now that the Bishop understood that this alarming manœuvre was intentional. Rotating with the attractive precision of a top, the aeroplane still fell. Its wings flashed alternately silver and red as now the under and now the upper surface caught the sunlight. The Bishop could see in the cockpits two black heads, absurdly small, which appeared and disappeared as the aeroplane revolved.

The spin ceased abruptly; the tail seemed to drop, and there was the machine flying again as before. He heard a rising drone, and the aeroplane climbed. Then the drone died down again, and the aircraft glided over the hangars, landing in front of them with a swinging swish of the tail.

It stopped, turned rockingly and lolloped over the aerodrome back to the hangar. Sally walked up to it when it arrived and the Bishop followed her.

Furnace jumped out of the front cockpit. He was flying without goggles or helmet, with a pair of ear-phones and speaking-tube mounted on a headpiece. The Bishop looked at the instructor with curiosity.

Furnace seemed to be near the forties and might have been a handsome man had not a scar run diagonally across his face from one temple to the opposite jowl. Each feature was distorted where the scar traversed it and his mouth was twisted in a perpetual lop-sided grin, which made his real expression enigmatic.

"An aeroplane fire. He got chucked against a red-hot wire," whispered Miss Sackbut, as she saw the Bishop's eyes rest on the scar.

The propeller stopped suddenly and a muffled object crawled clumsily out of the rear cockpit. This, the Bishop gathered, was the pupil. He was dressed in a bulky leather coat, enormous scarf, and large woolly gloves. He wore a flying mask, usually only adopted for high altitude or winter flying, which gave him a sinister appearance. The man looked portly, but when the coverings were peeled off he revealed himself as one of those lanky jockey-like youngsters, who might be any age between thirteen and thirty-five. At the moment there was rather a depressed expression on his peaky white face.

"All right, George," said Miss Sackbut to Furnace, "XT can be put away. There's no more instruction to-day."

"A good job too," answered Furnace irritably. "In my young days we used to go solo in two hours. Now everyone seems to want about twelve hours. In another ten years they'll take a fortnight. By that time I'll be in a lunatic asylum."

He shouted to a thin red-headed man in dirty and tattered overalls: "Here, Andy, put XT away." He muttered something to Miss Sackbut that the Bishop could not catch.

"I want you to meet a new pupil," said Miss Sackbut, introducing him to the Bishop.

"I am afraid I shall fulfil your worst fears," remarked the Bishop diffidently. "I know in advance I shall be a bad pupil."

The malicious grin widened. The Bishop gathered that this time Furnace was really smiling. "Oh, don't be frightened by my remark," the pilot said more graciously. "Some of my best pupils are your age. You won't learn quite so quickly as a youngster, but you'll be all the sounder as a pilot. I don't mind slowness in learning; but I've come to the conclusion, Sally, that Tommy knows what he ought to do and is just too lazy to do it."

The Bishop supposed that the muffled figure was Tommy.

Furnace bent the headpiece of his ear-phones backwards and forwards with a nervous gesture.

"I put him into a spin suddenly, and he got the machine out of it, and competently too. I'll swear he knows more than he pretends."

"How odd," remarked the Bishop politely.

Furnace stared at him gloomily. "Pupils are odd. I taught a certain transatlantic flyer to fly. I was amazed at her aptitude. Honestly, I thought she was a miracle. I used to go everywhere boasting about it. Then Tarry Bones, of Aberdeen, came down here one day, and it all came out that she had already learned to fly up there with him under an alias."

The Bishop was baffled by this elaborate mystification, and Furnace saw it.

"Don't you see the idea? It would have appeared in all the papers: 'Woman learns to fly in two hours.' Good publicity! She's never forgiven me for spoiling it."

The Bishop had seen Furnace's eyes rest malevolently on Mrs. Angevin while he said this, and guessed she was the woman referred to. He began to feel sympathetic towards her.

Furnace pulled off his ear-phones. He seemed exasperated. The Bishop might have taken it for a normal mood of the man, but he saw that Miss Sackbut was looking at him a little anxiously.

Tommy Vane now joined the group, having got rid of his outer garments after a prolonged struggle.

The young man smiled oddly at Furnace. "I say, Major, I don't like this flying business at all! What was that quick one you pulled on me just now? I didn't know whether it was me or the earth?"

"Is that the first time you've been spun?" asked Furnace suspiciously.

"You ought to know," answered the youth. "All the flying I've ever done has been with you. And just now I thought we should die together. 'They looped together and they span together and in death they were not divided.'" The youth chuckled happily to himself.

Furnace's expression was hard to fathom.

"You put on opposite rudder quick enough when you saw you had to get her out yourself."

"I saw that in an article," announced Tommy cheerfully. "'How and Why in a Spin.'" He prodded Furnace in the stomach. "Anyway, you old devil, if you wanted to scare me you did all right. My tummy heaved about like an oyster. A large brandy is what I need— quickly. I think you ought to speak to him about it, Sally."

Throwing one end of his gaudy muffler over his shoulder, he started to walk off, a queer little figure with rounded shoulders and trailing trouser-legs.

"The bar's closed," shouted Miss Sackbut after him.

Tommy turned and placed one rather dirty finger beside his nose with a wink. "This is illness. What's wrong with the first-aid chest? I know where it is."

"If he does pinch the brandy out of my office again, I'll wring his dirty neck," muttered Miss Sackbut fiercely.

"What does Dolly want?" she exclaimed a moment later.

It appeared that Mrs. Angevin had had enough of splendid isolation. She now walked over to the party, a welcoming smile on her face.

She looked appealingly up at her former instructor and slapped Furnace gently on the arm with her gauntleted gloves. "Well, Instructor mine, what have you been doing? Poor Vane looked positively green. You've probably frightened him off flying for life. You didn't let *me* spin until after my first circuit."

Furnace turned to her. He still smiled his artificial grin, but the Bishop noted that the hand in which he held his ear-phones whitened at the knuckles.

"Kindly keep your observations about my instructing to yourself before strangers," he said in a shaking voice. "They may not realize what anybody in aviation knows, that you're the worst woman pilot in this age and country, which is saying something. One day you may make as good a pilot as Sally here. But not until you stop making every decent person's gorge rise by turning yourself into a cheap circus."

Mrs. Angevin flushed brick-red. For one moment the Bishop, embarrassed beyond all words, and yet unable to get away inconspicuously, thought she was going to strike Furnace across the face with her gloves. Perhaps she was. But at that moment a clear and languid voice interrupted them. Lady Laura was behind him.

"I really think that instructors should never meet their pupils again, don't you, Bishop?" she murmured. "They're so used to cursing and swearing at them while they're learning to fly that they can't get out of the habit afterwards. You wouldn't believe the things George says to me when he forgets himself."

Furnace looked at her for a moment with an oddly hurt look in his eyes. He seemed about to speak, then he walked abruptly away without another word and disappeared into the club-house.

"Well, I never!" gasped Miss Sackbut. "He'll be terribly sorry about this to-morrow, Dolly. I simply can't understand what's come over him."

"I can," said Mrs. Angevin violently. "These unsuccessful pilots who think they ought to be at the top of the tree, and aren't, all go the same way. Drink. Drink and jealousy. The man's hardly sane."

She dragged on her gloves with a snort, nodded to Lady Laura, looked curiously at the Bishop, and walked away.

"Bitch!" remarked Lady Laura, directly she was out of ear-shot—or, the Bishop thought, probably a little before. "Still, I've never heard George flare up like that before."

She turned to the red-headed man in tattered overalls, who was climbing into the cockpit of XT preparatory to taxying it into the hangar.

"Get my Leopard Moth out will you, Andy? I'm going back to Goring this afternoon."

"Oke," said the ground engineer.

Miss Sackbut, accompanied by the Bishop, strolled thought-fully back to the club-house.

"I'm most awfully sorry this has happened," said Sally dis-mally. "What will you think of our club? Mrs. Angevin was right; George oughtn't really to have given Tommy practice in getting out of spins. Tommy's very slow, and he's still on straight and level flying after two hours' instruction. Still, George probably had some good reason. What I can't understand is his losing his temper like that. He's always been a peaceable cove."

"Mrs. Angevin had an explanation," said the Bishop dryly. He looked at Miss Sackbut with a steady gaze which she found a little disconcerting.

"Oh, that was a beastly thing she said! He's never been at all like that. It certainly is galling for a man of his war record—and his piloting ability, for they don't always go together, guts and skill—it must be infuriating to be instructor at a low-down joint like our club, and to see people like Dolly and Randall making fortunes. But it's all luck, that kind of thing, and George has always laughed at it. He's always been as cheery as anything, and awfully popular with his pupils."

"He struck me as not at all the type to lose his temper," admitted the Bishop.

"He's one of the best," said Sally warmly. "But, to be perfectly frank, something has been getting him down during the last fortnight. He's been brooding and quite different to his usual cheery self. I'm afraid he's got a crush on Lady Laura, poor fellow, and if so I'm sorry for him. The Lord knows why I'm rambling on, telling you all this."

"The experience is not strange," said the Bishop. "Evidently there is something in my face, of which I am unaware, which invites confidence. Well, I should like to start my instruction, if it is convenient, at noon to-morrow."

"Certainly. I'll book it. Get fitted up with a helmet, goggles, and 'phones in town if you can. Merrivale's are the best people. It's better than borrowing them, although we can lend them to you if you haven't time. I'm glad the scene to-day hasn't put you off."

"Good gracious me, no! I've taken quite a liking to Furnace. Is that Lady Laura who took off so gracefully just now?"

"Yes, she always takes off in a climbing turn. And that means she won't die in bed," added Miss Sackbut grimly.

CHAPTER II

CREATION OF A CORPSE

"Good morning, Miss Sackbut."

"Good morning, Bishop. You look magnificent in your flying helmet. At the same time, I shouldn't wear it when you are not flying."

The Bishop had rather fancied the figure he made in a black helmet. He bowed his head and accepted the rebuke in Christian meekness.

"I'm a little annoyed with George," went on Miss Sackbut. "He's taken XT and he's still up." She waved at a shadow fleeting across the thin clouds. "I don't know why. He knows you are coming. I didn't see him go up or I'd have ticked him off."

"Don't trouble. I can wait." He dropped into a large chair on the club veranda.

Sally called to the red-headed ground engineer.

"Andy! Did Major Furnace say how long he would be up for?"

The ground engineer shook his head. "Just said he'd sweep the cobwebs out of his head, and then took her up. There he goes!"

The frail shadow nosed up in a loop and rolled off the top of it. It seemed speeding straight for the aerodrome when the wings flashed silver in a vertical turn.

Sally snorted. "Getting rid of that morning-after feeling, I suppose! He must have a thick head! If he doesn't come down soon I'll borrow Dolly's kite and wave him down."

"Please, please!" expostulated the Bishop, smiling. "I have all the morning, and this is delightful to watch."

"Oh, you'll be able to do all that after fifty hours," said Sally airily. "Now he's spinning."

Once again the scarlet-and-silver wings flashed and flickered as they had done yesterday, but this time the Bishop was not disturbed.

"I thought the machine was in terrible difficulties yesterday," he admitted. "What a delicate touch it must need to perform those swift evolutions."

Sally laughed. "Good lord, he's not moving the controls! The aeroplane does it automatically."

The Bishop, when she spoke, had turned his head towards her. She looked a little abstracted.

She was nervously tapping the side of the chair in which she was sitting. He suspected that this four-square, self-reliant young lady with the calm eyes and masculine manner was a good deal more nervous than she liked people to suppose. And now there was definitely something on her mind.

The Bishop looked sharply at Furnace's aeroplane again. It had lost a lot of height since they had first seen it. It was flickering down towards a bank of trees. It fell still lower.

The Bishop heard a gasp beside him. Sally jumped to her feet, her face contorted with sudden alarm. "Here, George!" she said in a low, urgent voice. "Don't leave it so late!" Then her face paled. She gave an agonized cry that lived for ever in the Bishop's memory.

"*For God's sake use your rudder!*"

Separated by thousands of yards of clear air, inhuman, remote, the flickering toy vanished behind the trees. There was no sound, no wisp of smoke, but only the empty air, and the silence. ...

Sally turned abruptly, without a particle of expression on her face. "Quick, the ambulance!"

But Andy had forestalled her. There was a whir and a clatter, and straight out of the hangar sped the battered olive-green Ford which was at once fire-engine and crash tender.

The Bishop saw the engineer, his face set, clinging on to the wheel as the car bounded over the uneven surface.

The Bishop started to run towards the crash. Sally held him back. "You'll never get there in time. Tommy's with Ness," she said, pointing to the gaudy scarf and huge leather coat of Ness's companion, as the tender plunged across the aerodrome. "They'll get him out. It's no use running and winding yourself. Better come in the car. It's over in front of the club-house."

As they walked hurriedly towards it, the Bishop saw in another corner of the aerodrome a man jump into a low green sports car parked beside a scarlet and yellow hut. The sports car was bumping across the aerodrome almost before the crash tender had vanished behind the trees at the scene of the crash.

"That's Randall, I think," said Sally with forced calm. "He's dashing across in Gauntlett's Alfa-Romeo. He'll know what to do."

The Bishop was not deceived by her matter-of-fact voice. There was a dazed look on Sally's face. It was rigid with self-control. "George, of all people!" she said, as if to herself, in a profound surprise. She looked at the Bishop. "The controls must have jammed," she went on, almost as if asking his reassurance. "It couldn't have happened otherwise, not possibly!"

"It's no good, I can't stay here! I must do something! Come on. We'll go over." They got into her battered four-seater car.

Lady Laura, her face white, came running out of the club-house, and without a word jumped into the back seats.

They tore across the aerodrome, leaping from bump to bump, through a gap in the hedge that was a rutted cattle track, over more fields, down a long steady slope, until at last they came to rest beside the Ford.

The Bishop saw the golden head of Captain Randall bowed over an outstretched figure beside which he was kneeling. Standing beside him, their heads also bare, were Andy and Tommy Vane. Tommy's hands were bleeding unregarded over the saw he held in them, the saw with which they had extricated Furnace. . . .

Randall placed his handkerchief over the dead man's head. As Sally came towards them he met her and put his hands on her shoulders. There was a deep pity in his regard.

"He was killed immediately, Sally," he said gently. "The safety-belt must have broken on the impact, and his forehead was thrown against the dashboard." His eyes met hers. "He must have died instantly," he repeated. "Almost before he knew what had happened."

They put the limp figure in the ambulance. . . .

"If any of us could choose the manner of our death," said the Bishop gravely to Sally a little later, "I think it would always be to die in the calling one had chosen—the sailor on the sea, the farmer at the plough, the pilot riding the air he strove to master."

*   *   *   *   *

It was Tommy who dashed into town to get Dr. Bastable. Tommy returned in a dangerously short time, the tyres of his little red sports two-seater screeching as he drew up alongside the hangars.

"Bastable's out on a case. I've left a message," he said. "Perhaps I'd better get another fellow though? I could go over to Market Garringham for Murphy."

"No, we'd better wait for Bastable," answered Sally wearily. "He's a member of the club and a pal of Furnace's. I'd rather he did everything. Not that there's anything to be done, anyway."

Time passed, but the doctor did not appear. At last he sent a message saying that he was still waiting for a future citizen of Baston. Sally tacitly acknowledged that the claims of life were more important than those of death.

The Bishop, after an hour of this, thought Sally looked dreadfully tired and drawn. But she resolutely kept her vigil, and it was not until the afternoon that the Bishop could persuade her to give up her place and get something to eat.

Then the Bishop passed into the darkened room where lay the mortal remains of George Furnace. Sally rose as he came in, and a moment after the Bishop was left alone. He lifted the sheet which hid the face of the dead man and looked at it silently. In his twenty years of priesthood he had seen too many of the spent cases of human souls to be much perturbed by the sight of sudden death. But he felt that to gaze on what had once been the mirror of that soul, and still retained its impress, might bring him more closely in touch with the personality that was gone.

Death had been gentle with George Furnace. There was indeed a ghastly wound on the temple, but the scar whose contrast of colour had disfigured the living features now mingled with the livid hues of death. The Bishop bent closer. Was it a trick of the light? No. Death had frozen on the face of the dead man an expression not of horror, or fear, but of melancholy, despairful reproach.

"Strange," said the Bishop. He meditated for a while, not replacing the sheet. Uncontrollably his thoughts went straying from the inspiring phraseology that should have occupied his mind to more questionable matters. The Bishop was by calling a clergyman, but because of the variety of duties that had fallen to his lot as a clergyman in lonely parishes in Australia, he was by way of being also a physician. And something in the tension of the features, as well as their expression, instantly aroused his curiosity.

At last he leaned over, raised the dead man's hand vertically, and let it fall. It curled limply on to his chest and slid to his side again.

The Bishop felt a thin shadow of horror, as if for a moment the forces of evil had invaded the room. Reverently he replaced the sheet, covering the dead man's face. The deepening shadows of the room found a more than answering depth in the sombre reflection of the Bishop's countenance.

More hours passed. Evening fell. Outside the Bishop heard Bastable's hearty tones, modified by professional concern. "Dreadful, Miss Sackbut! George, of all people! Such a fine pilot. I am so sorry I could not get here before. But he was killed instantaneously I understand, poor fellow!"

Dr. Bastable glanced at the Bishop without speaking, and gave a perfunctory peer at the forehead of the dead man. "Tut-tut! Most certainly instantaneous! Well, well!"

The Bishop walked quietly out.

CHAPTER III

INQUEST ON AN AIRMAN

The Ground Engineer's Evidence.

"I am a ground engineer. My name is Andy Ness. I have been employed by the Baston Aero Club ever since it began ten years ago. I hold Ground Engineer's Licences A, B, C, and D. I passed out the aeroplane XT after its annual overhaul for a Certificate of Airworthiness five days before the accident. Of course I examined the control cables. They had been renewed during the overhaul, and were in perfect condition. The aeroplane had been flown for ten hours after the overhaul by various people without complaint.

"I knew Major Furnace well. No, I know nothing of his home life. I mean I saw a lot of him at the club. I hadn't noticed anything unusual in his manner lately. He seemed quite cheerful before he took XT up. He only took her up to amuse himself for a few minutes, I thought. He often did that first thing in the day. He said it cleared his head. He never allowed his pupils to do acrobatics low down, and I never saw him stunt low myself. I did not actually see him crash. I was working on the tender and had the engine running when Mr. Vane (who was due for a lesson, after the Bishop) rushed in and said Major Furnace had crashed the other side of the aerodrome. We both jumped in and tore straight across. I cannot say what happened. Major Furnace was a first-rate pilot, one of the best. I can't understand it. I don't know any pilot I'd rather fly with. I am sure the cables or the rudder-bar did not jam. I've never heard of such a thing with this type of machine. It's in use in about a hundred clubs and schools, and is considered the best of its kind for all-round safety."

Captain Randall's Evidence.

"My name is Arthur Randall. I am a pilot. Yes, I knew Furnace well. He was one of our best civil pilots; a better pilot than I am, although he is less known. He ought to have had a much better job, but competition for the good test pilots' jobs was keen after the war. He often said to me, 'Randall, I suppose my trouble is I can't shoot a good enough line about myself.' And that certainly was his trouble—modesty. No, his lack of success didn't seem to worry him much, but it was difficult for anyone else to guess what he was thinking at any time. He might have been a little depressed these last few weeks, but it may have been just a passing mood.

"I should describe him as a most careful pilot. I simply can't imagine why the machine did not recover from the spin. It was too far away to see if he was trying to correct it with the rudder, but a pilot of his calibre would do this instinctively at the slightest danger. The type he was flying has never shown any vice in the spin to my knowledge. I was sitting in the office of Gauntlett's Air Taxis when it occurred. Directly I saw him crash I ran out and got into a car. But I had to go back for the ignition key, and by the time I got there Ness and Vane had done all that could be done and had got him out. It was good work, because one of the longerons had to be sawn to free him, and Vane hurt himself doing it. Furnace must have been dead before they released him, however. His safety-belt had parted and he must have slumped forward against the dashboard. It had penetrated his forehead and killed him. The throttle was closed, but the engine was not switched off. Yes, that is what one would expect if a pilot span into the ground without realizing it. I can't understand Furnace making such an error. The visibility was quite good—about two miles I should say. His death is a great loss to aviation. Furnace isn't replaceable."

Miss Sackbut's Evidence.

"I am Sarah Sackbut, manager and secretary of the Baston Aero Club. I have managed it ever since it began, and Furnace has always been our instructor. It would be quite normal for him to go up for a short flight by himself. I had a pupil waiting for him on the ground. We have never had any trouble with XT before. The machine belongs to a type used everywhere for instructional and beginners' flights. Our ground engineer has the highest possible qualifications. It is all nonsense to say Furnace was depressed. That was only his manner. He was always perfectly contented and happy. He was a very popular instructor and a most cautious pilot. He would never allow any pupil to spin to within a thousand feet of the ground, and he would never do it himself except at a flying display. I can't understand how the accident happened. He span into the ground, that was plain enough. XT would come out of a spin after opposite rudder and forward stick in a couple of turns. Could he have lost consciousness? I can't understand it at all."

Mr. Vane's Evidence.

"I am a pupil at the Baston Aero Club. My name is Thomas Vane. I have had only two hours' instruction. Furnace quite rightly considered me a slow pupil. He seemed to me to be rather irritable these last few days, but perhaps I should make any instructor irritable. Oddly enough, he span me in my last lesson. It frightened me. I don't think it's usual to do it to a beginner. Of course one has to learn it sooner or later before one goes solo. He made no attempt to correct the spin, and I honestly thought for a moment, when nothing happened, that he had lost consciousness. I got frightened and shoved the stick forward and pushed the rudder-bar over the opposite way, which I understood was the correct thing. Furnace didn't say anything except that what I'd done was correct. Of course he may have been just testing my reaction in an emergency. He was a fine instructor and I'm told he always studied a pupil's psychology. I haven't the remotest idea why the machine crashed. I helped to free him from the fuselage. He was quite dead then, just as Captain Randall said. He must have died instantly, I think."

The Bishop's Evidence.

"I am the Bishop of Cootamundra. I am in England on leave. I have just joined the Baston Aero Club and have never flown. As I only saw Major Furnace once I cannot say whether he was his normal self or not. The machine fell behind a bank of trees, apparently out of control—but I know so little of these matters. I arrived a little time after the crash tender. Then he was quite dead."

Lady Laura Vanguard's Evidence.

"I saw the spin as I was looking up from a map in the lounge. I did not fully realize the machine had crashed until it did not come up again from behind the trees. Then I ran out and found Miss Sackbut and the Bishop about to drive over there and I joined them. As they said, Major Furnace, who was my instructor, was a wonderful pilot, and I can't imagine such a thing happening unless there was something wrong with the machine."

The Technical Expert's Evidence.

"My name is Felix Sandwich, Flying Officer in the Reserve of Air Force Officers. I am in the Department of the Inspector of Accidents in the Air Ministry. Under powers vested in the Secretary of State for Air I inspected the crash and took notes from various witnesses. There was nothing in the machine's condition to account for the accident. The controls showed no trace of having jammed and there had been no structural failure before the impact. The impact was not severe—it rarely is in a spin. It is possible that the pilot tried to regain control at the last moment, for the machine took the main force of impact on the starboard wing, instead of the nose. As a result the shock was not severe, and if Major Furnace had been thrown clear he would probably have escaped with a shaking. It is hardly surprising that the safety-belt parted. It is meant to take only normal flying strains. No, Mr. Foreman, I do not agree that it would be a good plan to make it stronger, as it would do the pilot serious internal injury if he were thrown violently against its restraint. It was pure bad luck that Furnace was thrown against the edge of the dashboard so that his forehead struck it. He might have been thrown clear. He was evidently trapped by the telescoping of the longerons of the fuselage. Many pilots believe in loosening their safety-belts if they see a crash is inevitable, but Furnace (if he saw the danger at all) could only have realized it when a few feet above the ground, otherwise he could have regained control. This type of machine has never shown any vice and recovers easily from a spin. I can only attribute the accident to an error of judgment on the part of the pilot in delaying recovery from the spin. It is impossible to eliminate the human element. Most accidents of this sort are due to it."

The Doctor's Evidence.

"My name is Bernard Bastable. I am a Bachelor of Medicine of the University of London. I was called to inspect the body after the crash. I arrived rather late in the day, I'm afraid. Life was then extinct. Death had been caused by (in non-technical language) the violent blow of the forehead against the metal dash, which had penetrated to the brain. Death would have been instantaneous. The deceased was an exceptionally healthy person. He was nominally my patient, and I met him often socially, but my only professional attendance upon him was for a severe burn from an exhaust pipe on which he had inadvertently leant. This was his only illness in all the years I knew him. I should say it was quite impossible for him to have fainted in the air under normal circumstances."

The Medical Officer's Evidence.

"My name is Francis Goring. I am a Doctor of Medicine and a Medical Officer in the Royal Air Force with the rank of Flight-Lieutenant. As the holder of a licence, permitting him to fly for 'hire or reward', Furnace appeared before the R.A.F. Central Medical Board at least twice a year. His last appearance was a week ago. He was in perfect health, and I should at once discount the likelihood of his having fainted in the air, providing no change had occurred in his physical condition in the interval."

The Coroner's Charge to the Jury.

"Gentlemen of the Jury, you have heard the very clear evidence of the people on the flying ground at the time of the disaster, the medical evidence, and the technical evidence of Flying Officer Sandwich. You will, I am sure, agree with me that everything that could be done was done, and that Messrs. Ness and Vane deserve commendation for their prompt action in the emergency. I think there can be little doubt of your verdict. We all know of the tremendous advances that flying has made in the last few years, but it is still a perilous occupation, inasmuch as a terrible penalty is exacted for an error of judgment. Yet to err is human, and it seems, after what Flying Officer Sandwich said, that Major Furnace undoubtedly made that excusable error. You will, I am sure, ignore the evidence that has been given that Major Furnace may have been a little depressed the last few days before the event. None of us always remains bright and cheerful. Major Furnace had a fine war record, winning many decorations by his gallantry, and his reputation stood high in the world of aviation. Perhaps this is the first slip he ever made in a long and distinguished flying career, and it is lamentable that it should have been fatal, particularly as it seems he might have escaped uninjured had he been thrown clear. But accidents will happen, and so we are sitting here to-day considering our verdict on the sad end of this gallant officer and popular citizen of Baston. . . ."

The Verdict of the Jury.
  "Death by Misadventure."

CHAPTER IV

PERCEPTION OF A PRELATE

FURNACE's funeral took place in heavy rain. The Bishop had been pressed by Sally to attend it with her. Already, after his fourth flying lesson, he had been infected with the insidious disease of flight. As an enthusiastic member of the Aero Club, Sally told him he had a duty towards its dead instructor.

Furnace had evidently been popular. There was a large contingent from the Aero Club, a dozen Baston worthies, and a selection of bronzed-faced, quiet strangers who, the Bishop discovered, were Furnace's old comrades-in-arms.

As a matter of fact the Bishop had not needed much pressing, for he had an interest in the dead man which he had not so far disclosed to any other party. He had not mentioned it even at the inquest. The Bishop was a law-abiding citizen, but he was also (he told himself) a clergyman, and not primarily interested in the doings of the secular arm. He did not even disapprove of the practice of merciful suppression so often followed by friends of the deceased at inquests. Consequently, while his evidence had been, of course, the whole truth and nothing but the truth, he had not mentioned certain suspicions he had entertained. After all, they were not evidence, he told himself. It was Dr. Bastable's business to notice a point like that. But Dr. Bastable had not noticed it.

What, then, was the Bishop to do? Furnace had certainly seemed worried that day when he had flared up at Mrs. Angevin, but then we all have our moments of worry. Could it have been merely coincidence that the accident had occurred the very next day? Admittedly the accident was inexplicable except as an accident. But wasn't there an element of the inexplicable in all fatalities?

The Bishop groaned in spirit and composed his mind to the solemn English of the graveside rites. Obstinately, the words flickered out of his mind as out of a fog. "Why didn't the doctor notice it?"

Towards the end of the service the words stopped flickering and burned steadily. For the Bishop's eyes fell on the unexpressive face of Dr. Bastable.

The Bishop was only human after all. He decided to speak to the doctor. It was not morbid curiosity, he told himself, but a desire to pacify his conscience for not having mentioned the suspicion at the inquest.

The Bishop did not have to introduce himself. They had met on the evening of the accident. It was therefore natural for the Bishop to drift alongside Bastable and get into conversation with him.

"I suppose it will never be satisfactorily explained," sighed the Bishop. "A fine pilot, an aeroplane in perfect condition, and yet this accident."

"There is always the human element," answered Dr. Bastable conventionally.

"I suppose so." The Bishop hesitated. "I take it that it was quite impossible for him to have fainted in the air?"

"Certainly," answered Dr. Bastable brusquely. He plainly thought the clergyman's interest a little ghoulish. "Quite impossible. That was all cleared up at the inquest. I saw you there, I think. The man was as fit as a fiddle."

"There was no autopsy?" suggested the Bishop.

"Of course not. It was obvious what had killed the poor fellow. It didn't need a second glance. The police would only call for an autopsy if there was any doubt. In this case it was all plain sailing."

"I suppose it was," agreed the Bishop, in a tone that made Dr. Bastable look at him sharply. In spite of his wooden expression, Dr. Bastable was a man of occasional intuitions. He looked round, and then seeing there was no one near, stared at the Bishop inquisitively.

"Something struck you, eh?"

The Bishop did not at once answer. He asked a question instead. "When did the *rigor mortis* pass off?"

The doctor seemed a little startled. "It had already passed off when the body came under my supervision."

Dr. Marriott looked at him with an air of gentle surprise. "A little early for that to happen, surely?"

"No," said the doctor, with all the firmness of an expert to a layman.

"I know so little of these matters," murmured the Bishop. "But when I underwent one of those three-year medical courses at our local university—you know, for missionaries who may have to do a good deal of amateur healing in their lonely cures——"

"Oh, you've had some medical training, have you?" interrupted the doctor, a little disconcerted, as the expert always is when he finds he has pontificated to a hearer who has more knowledge of the expert's subject than he had realized.

"A smattering," answered the other modestly. "Well, from that course I have a faint memory that after ten hours the *rigor* should have been still fairly well developed even if it was beginning to pass off. And I calculate it was about ten hours after the accident that you saw poor Furnace."

"Yes, that is so," said the doctor stiffly. "But it varies tremendously. It was a cold and draughty hangar he was lying in, and nothing carries away bodily warmth so quickly as a draught. So it probably came on quickly, and, as you know, a quick onset means quick to go, and, of course, so many dubious constitutional factors come into play. It seemed to me perfectly possible that the *rigor* had come and gone before I saw him, allowing for the usual margin of error in these calculations."

The Bishop was silent for a moment.

"You don't think there's anything fishy?" asked the doctor, a little alarmed by the other's silence.

"Seven hours before you saw the body I was sitting beside it. There was no sign of *rigor* then."

"Good heavens!" exclaimed the doctor, his professional calm momentarily shattered. "None? No trace? Are you sure?"

"Quite," answered the other quietly.

Dr. Bastable began to fuss. "But this is serious. Furnace cannot have been dead when he was taken out of the 'plane. Concussion, I suppose, followed by a hæmorrhage in the brain. He might even have been saved! Dear, dear, dear!"

"We mustn't jump to conclusions," commented the Bishop quietly.

"The police should be informed."

"I think that would be a great mistake," Dr. Marriott said with quiet firmness. "After all, I may have been wrong."

"But you said you were sure."

"*Errare est humanum*. The man is dead, anyway. If you will be guided by me, Doctor Bastable, you will say nothing more for the moment. You saw the man's wound. Whether it killed him instantaneously or a short time after is really a formality. Is it worth stirring up all sorts of unpleasantness? My dear Doctor, as a professional man, you must appreciate that. I see Miss Sackbut is looking round—waiting for me, evidently. I must leave you." He gave the bewildered doctor a friendly pat on the arm. "Leave the matter in my hands. Good-bye."

* * * * *

"How terribly depressed you're looking, Bishop!" remarked Lady Laura. He was sitting in a deck-chair mournfully studying the sky, out of which Lady Laura, a little earlier, had side-slipped in one of her usual masterful landings, to alight almost on the terrace of the hangar, whose roof she had skimmed with her wheels.

"I believe," said the Bishop very solemnly, "that in this life at least I shall never learn to land an aeroplane."

"Why? What's wrong?"

"Several things appear to be wrong," answered the Bishop sadly. "Miss Sackbut, who is attempting to instruct me, has explained them in great detail. She tells me I 'glide in like a bat out of hell', 'check too late and too hard, so that I balloon up and then attempt to give an imitation of an episcopal pancake'. I only grasp dimly what she means, but it has already dawned on me that the difficulty in flying is not the flying but the not-flying, so to speak. In other words, the landing."

"Cheer up. We all go through that stage. I doubt if Sally is the best instructor, all the same, although she was the first woman to get an instructor's endorsement," admitted Lady Laura, proving to be an unusual woman herself by dropping into a deck-chair with grace.

"Really?" said the Bishop in surprise. "I thought she was a splendid pilot."

"She is. Probably our best woman pilot. But the best pilots are often the worst instructors. Too impatient, you know, and too much temperament. That was where Furnace was exceptional."

"Yes," said the Bishop. "I've been thinking a good deal about Furnace lately."

"I have been trying to forget it!" remarked Lady Laura with a curious air of desperation. The Bishop remembered Sally Sackbut's words to him, that Furnace was supposed to have nourished a disappointed passion for Lady Laura. The hopeless train of that lady's admirers was a social commonplace known even to the Bishop. But Lady Laura seemed to have been peculiarly affected by Furnace's death. He had noticed it repeatedly since the day of the accident. Had there been more in the affair on Lady Laura's side than anyone had supposed?

They were both silent for a minute. Sally Sackbut, in the new club machine, was practising inverted flying for a forthcoming inter-club competition. Its wheels splayed in the air, the little red and silver machine banked and rolled and span in the clear blue sky.

"Do you think it really was an accident—that crash of Furnace's, I mean?" said Lady Laura, without taking her eyes off the dancing 'plane.

The Bishop studied her delicate but impassive profile.

"What has the woman got on her mind?" he thought uneasily. Aloud he said: "There is no reason to suppose anything else, is there, Lady Laura?"

"Yes," answered the girl in a quiet little voice.

"Oh!" The Bishop was too wise to attempt to force a confidence.

Now she looked at him. "I suppose you think if I know anything I ought to tell it to the police?"

"Not necessarily. It is a common error that a clergyman is more concerned with keeping the laws of the land than other people. He is concerned with keeping the moral law, but the two don't always coincide. Render unto Cæsar the things that are Cæsar's, you know. In fact, I already know something about Major Furnace's death which I haven't told the police."

She looked at him, startled. "Oh, you know something, do you?" she said uncertainly. "So do I. But I'm not so positive about it as you are. It's so comforting to be a clergyman. One always knows exactly what is right and wrong. I muddle them so easily."

The Bishop bowed his head.

Lady Laura was turning over the miscellaneous contents of her bag. She now held a letter toward him.

"Read it. It's been worrying me ever since I received it. I do wish you'd tell me what I ought to do about it—if I ought to do anything, that is."

The letter, the Bishop noted, looking at once at the signature, was from Furnace.

He glanced at the date. It must have been sent some weeks before the crash, as far as he could remember. Then he read the letter.

Laura,

I don't know whether you meant to give me hope on the day we flew to Marazion, and I was happier than I ever was before or ever have been since. I never tried to find out afterwards, but I tell myself it was so, that I had hope.

Laura, I've never tried to find out since then, not because I'm afraid to try my luck, but because I've been getting into an awful mess, one of those messes one drifts into like a damned helpless fool. Suddenly, two days ago, I realized what a damned awful hole I was in, and how much worse it would be if I didn't end the whole business. You won't know why I'm telling you this. In a few days' time you may know. But I promise you this: I'm going to end it decently.

George.

The girl took the letter back from the Bishop and stuffed it roughly into her handbag. There was a sulky, angry expression on her face which might have repelled the Bishop had he been less understanding of human nature.

"Why did he do such a silly thing? I am sure I never had the least idea he was really in love with me. Goodness, what did I say to him at Marazion? I forget. We were just playing the fool all that day. Of course, I wrote a note back, telling him that I wasn't worth taking seriously, that he mustn't take me seriously. And then there was the crash."

"Yes," said the Bishop; "the crash, and the inquest."

Lady Laura continued to look sulky. "Oh, I expect you think that the reason I kept this letter back was to prevent myself being involved in the inquest and all the publicity. Naturally, I thought of that, but I really was more concerned with preventing their returning a verdict of Suicide against George. Very wrong of me, I suppose, but I think the attitude of the law towards suicide is barbaric."

"I have always understood that suicide is considered noble by barbarians and that it is civilization which has condemned it," remarked the Bishop silkily. "However, you showed me this letter to get my advice as to what to do. For the moment I should do nothing."

"Nothing?" asked Lady Laura in surprise. "Do you really advise that?"

"Yes," said the Bishop thoughtfully, "indeed I do. For the moment. Do not lose the letter, of course. In fact, better give it to me. Then I can show it to the police when and if necessary."

Lady Laura opened her bag again.

"I suppose you think I'm a callous brute, not trying to stop George?"

"In the circumstances," said the Bishop carefully, "I doubt if your interposition would have made any difference. It is a very strange business."

On his part he apparently dismissed the matter and resumed his contemplation of the evoluting aeroplane.

"Can you tell me," he asked after a time, "why Miss Sackbut's blood does not run into her head when she remains upside-down for such a prolonged period?"

"It does run," answered Lady Laura, "horribly. She'll look like a beetroot when she comes down."

*   *   *   *   *

"I am a patient man," said the Bishop, breathing heavily, "but if you scream 'BACK! BACK! BACK!' at me again I shall say or do something which I shall subsequently repent."

The Bishop was sitting in the rear cockpit of the club Moth, which itself was sitting in the middle of the aerodrome. Miss Sackbut was in the front cockpit.

"If I didn't say it, you would fly straight into the ground," she answered reasonably.

"I think even that would be preferable to your wild scream, which is profoundly unsettling."

"I scream in order to make you realize that your movements of the control column *must* be coarse as the machine loses flying speed. Your elevators are losing their grip on the air."

"No doubt all that is true," answered the Bishop with dignity. "It means very little to me. I am afraid I must be constitutionally incapable of flying."

Sally laughed. "Now then, don't despair. Everybody makes the same mistakes. Remember, the first check is *just* a check. Then wait. Then back, back, BACK!"

"There you go again!" said the Bishop sharply.

"Put your finger and thumb lightly round the control column."

"They are."

"Now—back, back, BACK! Do you get the idea?"

"The control column hit me in the tummy!"

"Exactly. It *should* do. Now, if you want to avoid my scream, bring it back in time, just as the machine is about to sink on the ground."

The Bishop's pleasant and ruddy face took on the expression of a sulky child. "I really think I would much rather do no more flying at all to-day. I get worse and worse instead of better and better."

Sally recognized the expression. "Well, you've done about twenty minutes, so perhaps you are getting tired. Taxi her back to the hangars."

"I don't like taxying," said Dr. Marriott stubbornly. "I appear to have no control whatever over the machine."

"One hasn't in taxying, in aircraft like this," answered his instructor airily, "without wheel brakes."

"Then how do I get to the hangar?" asked the Bishop querulously.

"Just ooze over in the general direction of the hangar," said Sally with a gesture. "*Coarse* movements of the rudder. Use the stick against the turn."

The Bishop succeeded in oozing in the general direction of the hangar, and accepted Miss Sackbut's suggestion of a coffee. They drank it in the lounge. This was deserted except for a novice, a youth who was, it seemed, laboriously, and a little palely, preparing for his first cross-country flight as he bent over a table map in the corner.

"He is flying to Marsham, ten miles away," explained Miss Sackbut.

"Why is he moving that piece of string round the map?" asked the Bishop curiously.

"He is finding at what point of the compass Marsham is in relation to here."

"Really! And then he merely has to fly by his compass on that course and he arrives there?"

"No," said Miss Sackbut; "he must allow for deviation, according to a table placed on his compass."

"Oh!" answered the Bishop.

"He has also to find out the wind strength and direction and work out a small vector triangle or use a little instrument which solves the problem automatically. The result will tell him the course he must steer."

Dr. Marriott pressed his brow. "How much more reasonable theology is! It sounds absurdly complicated. And does that bring him over Marsham aerodrome?"

Sally shook her head. "No; because while he is up the wind will change and he will get hopelessly lost."

"Dear me! However will he reach Marsham?"

"The chances are that he will not," answered Miss Sackbut. "If he is unscrupulous, he will fly to the railway line as soon as he is out of sight and follow it to Marsham, forgetting all about his compass. However, he is young and probably scrupulous, so he will wander all over England and finally land in a ploughed field to ask the inhabitants where he is. In getting off the ploughed field again he will hit a tree, and some time later we will send out a crash tender to bring the 'plane in, if repairable, and himself, if conscious."

"Really!" said the Bishop. "I don't think I shall like cross-country flying."

"Don't worry," answered the girl reassuringly. "You'll be flying in a club machine, so I shall escort you. We take care never to damage a club machine. This bloke is flying in his own bus, so, of course, it's all to the good if we get the job of repairing it."

The Bishop shook a playful forefinger. "Either you are very heartless, Miss Sackbut, or else you are a little given to exaggeration."

After sighing audibly and going out twice to look at the wind-sock, the youth left. Then Sally turned firmly to the Bishop. "I'm glad we are alone. I've wanted to talk to you seriously. I believe you have something on your mind. You were getting on quite nicely with your training until the last day or two, but now your mind doesn't seem on the job."

Dr. Marriott felt a little defenceless before Sally's very direct methods of approach. Even his episcopacy seemed no barrier against it.

"There is something on my mind," admitted the Bishop at last. "Some very fishy things have turned up about Furnace's death, and I'm reluctantly coming to the conclusion that I shall have to speak to the police about it. That's not a thing I like doing."

"Good lord!" exclaimed Sally, genuinely shocked. "You, of all people! What on earth could *you* have heard? I am sure there is some mistake."

"I do not think so," he answered quietly. "Lady Laura apparently had a letter from Furnace in which he told her he was going to put an end to things."

Sally flushed. "It's abominable! Laura is always saying that sort of thing. I don't believe it. Why didn't she mention it at the inquest? It's sheer publicity lust! I'm sure she wrote the letter herself." Sally panted with fury.

"I understand she kept quiet about it out of regard to Furnace's reputation," explained the Bishop, looking at her closely.

"A hell of a lot she cares for anyone's reputation! She nearly drove the poor fellow crazy and then dropped him like a hot cake. Bah!"

"All the same, she appears to have had the letter. Here it is."

Sally seized it and read it through with a puzzled expression. It changed to one of concern. "The letter's genuine enough. Poor George! I could murder Laura. I don't believe she has a vestige of a heart. Is it really necessary to drag all this up?"

The Bishop did not answer immediately. "No," he said at last, "I don't think it is—not as it stands. It is not necessarily evidence that the crash was deliberate. Indeed, a suicide would be a slight matter compared with what I have discovered. The truth is, Miss Sackbut, Furnace was not dead when he was taken out of the aeroplane. He died subsequently. What that may mean, I hardly dare to think. In fact, for the moment I refuse, deliberately refuse, even to speculate."

CHAPTER V

DISCOVERY OF A DOCTOR

INSPECTOR CREIGHTON put his pince-nez carefully on the desk in front of him and regarded them thoughtfully for a moment. Then he picked them up and polished them with an air of fury. He was silent throughout this operation, and the Bishop watched him in equal silence. An odd policeman, reflected the Bishop. He looked just like a shopwalker. He had the same precise clothing, vaguely soothing gesture, and imitation genteel voice.

"Really, my lord," said the Inspector, "this is a very remarkable suggestion you make."

"I make no suggestion," replied the Bishop patiently. "I am merely presenting you with two facts. As far as I can see, they can have nothing to do with each other. Or, rather, if you believe one, the other is of little importance."

The Inspector picked up Furnace's letter to Lady Laura and dropped it again helplessly. "Well, look at this. As I suspected all the time, it *was* a case of suicide. But now, what about the *rigor* business? Why didn't you tell me of it before, my lord?" he asked plaintively.

"My observation became of no importance until I heard Bastable's story," explained the Bishop disingenuously. "Then it became plain that Furnace must have died very shortly before I was left alone with him. Until then, it seemed to be on the surface merely a case of *rigor* delayed, abnormally, but not *more* than might be possible. Bastable's story gave an entirely different interpretation to it."

Inspector Creighton looked the Bishop straight in the eye. "You don't put a sinister interpretation to it, do you?"

"Of course not!" Dr. Marriott hastened to answer. "The letter makes it plain that Furnace intended to commit suicide. *My* discovery at present only shows that he did not make a perfect job of it. He died as a result of injuries received in the accident, but death did not take place immediately."

"I am glad you agree with me there. One has to go carefully, you understand. I mean Lady Laura is a person of influence. Naturally, that does not weigh with us directly, but it does remind us that if we do make a mistake, it will be all the more prominent."

The Bishop felt it was time to cease fencing. "Are you having an exhumation?" he asked bluntly.

"H'm, yes," admitted the Inspector. "We *are* having one. As a matter of form. Please remember that, my lord—a matter of form. We are applying for the order to-day."

"You might keep me posted," said the Bishop, "for various reasons."

"We shall, of course, tell you in the unexpected event of anything coming to light at all out of the way, if you understand me. Most certainly we should. Let me show you to the door. This way, my lord." Dignified and impassive, the policeman rose to his feet and gravely escorted his visitor to the street entrance.

The Bishop of Cootamundra left Baston police station with a certain amount of satisfaction. He liked Inspector Creighton and felt he could get on with him. They had understood each other. The Bishop, however, anticipated a modicum of difficulty if anything unexpected did turn up, and he still felt it his duty to try to guide matters so as to cause the minimum of unpleasantness all round. But the shopwalker was not to be bluffed, as the Bishop gathered from a certain shrewd sharpness in his eyes.

Now, the question was, would anything unexpected turn up?

*   *   *   *   *

Two days later, as the Bishop was walking quietly through Baston, a car stopped suddenly beside him. The screech of its braked tyres on the road made him look up. Dr. Bastable's face was poked out of the window.

"Good afternoon, Doctor Marriott."

"Good afternoon, Doctor."

"Your guess has proved right."

"My guess? I don't quite follow?"

"We completed the autopsy to-day. Major Furnace was killed by a bullet in his brain."

"A bullet!" The Bishop was genuinely startled. "This is dreadful!"

Dr. Bastable's wooden face wrestled with a knowing expression. "Come, come, you guessed something of the sort from the moment you discovered about the *rigor*!"

"I assure you, most positively no," answered the Bishop in distress. "All I guessed then was that Furnace had died after the crash. But a bullet! It is really too dreadful."

"Well, naturally, if you say you didn't guess it, you didn't." Dr. Bastable seemed a little downcast. "It'll be a great disappointment for the Inspector. He thinks you knew all along, and that you'll be able to give him some valuable information. I promised that if I saw you I'd let you know he wanted to see you."

"I will call in on him to-morrow," promised Dr. Marriott.

*   *   *   *   *

Early next morning the Bishop was back again in Baston police station. Dr. Bastable and Inspector Creighton were treating him with flattering deference, referring repeatedly to his foresight. The Bishop continued to insist that he had foreseen nothing, but when he came to look back on it, he knew that deep down in his heart he had suspected something quite as bad all the time. The sensation of evil, for instance, when he had watched beside the body—aroused by the abnormality of the physical condition of the body certainly—but wasn't it perhaps also inspired by some aftermath of violence in the atmosphere?

The murderer must have left the hangar shortly before the Bishop went in. ...

"Well, my lord, this is the position, isn't it, Bastable? The revolver-shot *must* have been fatal. The crash injuries were of a character which *might* have been fatal or might not. Actually a good deal of the injury which, from superficial examination, had been attributed to the crash was really caused by the bullet. So when Furnace was dragged from the aeroplane he must have been still living, although undoubtedly unconscious. Perhaps he was just on the borderline of death. But for some reason, it was so much to somebody's interest to have Furnace dead, that they took the risk of making certain. They relied on the head wound masking the revolver bullet, I suppose. A risky business, it seems to me."

"Very risky," said Dr. Bastable. "It amazes me that the bullet did not pass right through the head and out again, in which case the point of exit would have given it away. But these things happen. I shouldn't like to depend on it if I were a murderer."

"Well, now what does all this suggest to you, my lord?" asked Inspector Creighton in a tone of deferential enquiry.

The Bishop answered hesitantly. "I must say it makes me think, very reluctantly, that whoever shot Furnace must have had some hand in causing the crash, and so the crash couldn't have been accidental, after all. We might even assume that the circumstances which caused the crash were such that if Furnace had been able to regain consciousness he would have been able to guess the murderer. That is what occurs to me."

"Bravo, you have the mind of a detective!" exclaimed the Inspector.

Dr. Marriott smiled deprecatingly. "Or a criminal. I see one difficulty, however. How can one account for the letter to Lady Laura, written, I am afraid, in the definite contemplation of suicide?"

"That is a difficulty," answered the policeman, sadly shaking his head. "It's the one thing that doesn't make sense."

The Bishop placed the tips of his fingers together. "A further reflection suggests itself to me. Could there, do you think, be a doubt as to the authenticity of the letter? If I were a criminal and my victim was known to be in love with a certain lady, I might arrange for a letter threatening suicide to be sent to the lady."

The Inspector permitted himself the familiarity of a wink. "Bless you, my lord, I thought of that. No doubt about the authenticity at all, unfortunately. I spent the morning comparing it with other specimens of the deceased's handwriting. Not a doubt of it; it's genuine."

"Then our chain of deduction appears to have reached an *impasse*."

"We are stuck," agreed the Inspector, "for the moment."

"The whole thing seems to be very extraordinary," interrupted Dr. Bastable fretfully. "It was all so unnecessary. The man would have died from that head wound, anyway, and it was quite unnecessary to kill him. If only they had not done that it would merely have been a clear case of suicide. Very foolish. Meanwhile, gentlemen, my patients are waiting for me. Do you want me any more? Or can I leave you in your *impasse*?"

"Just before you go, Doctor Bastable, tell us this," said Creighton. "Bearing in mind the nature of the head wound and the circumstances of the crash, what appearance would the deceased present when dragged out of the—er—flying machine?" The policeman spoke very carefully, as if threading his way among obstacles.

"What the devil do you mean, Inspector?" asked Dr. Bastable peevishly.

"I mean—well, I don't want to make this a leading question, you see—but, tell me, would it have been a reasonable mistake for a layman to think him dead?"

"Laymen are never reasonable," snapped the doctor. "I believe them capable of anything. They might think a dead man unconscious or a senseless man dead. You'd better," added Bastable a trifle maliciously, "ask the Bishop, who is a medical expert and saw the fellow when he was pulled out of the aeroplane. I really must rush off now. Good-bye."

"Bastable's rebuke is called for," admitted the Bishop. "I ought to have ascertained at the time whether life was extinct."

"Well, well, I'm sure you're not to be blamed. He would not have lived, anyway. But you understand what I am getting at?" commented the Inspector meaningly.

"I do. And I can only say that Furnace was quite motionless when he was lying on the grass and that the aspect of the head wound was such that anyone might have been pardoned for supposing him dead. At the same time, I find it difficult to forgive myself for not attempting to make sure. I can only plead the rush, the circumstances, the strangeness of it all."

"No one is blaming you for a moment, my lord. The point is, are we to blame the three gentlemen who got Furnace out? I mean Captain Randall, this young fellow Vane, and the ground engineer, Ness?"

The Bishop shook his head. "I don't see how you can blame them for a moment. It was a mistake shared by all of us."

"Very well. We will acquit them of negligence. But note this well, my lord. We don't cease to suspect them. On the contrary. They may have been guilty of much worse than negligence. The very contrary, in fact."

"Come, come, Inspector," said the Bishop blandly, "aren't you trying to make my flesh creep? You surely don't consider, even for a moment, that those three men murdered Furnace after taking him out of the wrecked 'plane?"

The Inspector became vague. "I suggest nothing, my lord. I merely offer the point. The murderer must have found out, some time that morning, that Furnace was not in fact dead but still living. Now who was in a better position to do that than one—I say one, mark you; it might be any one—of the three who got him out of the wreck?"

The Bishop nodded.

"Now, of course, this is only one suspicion. Another line to follow is, who else came into contact with Furnace between the time of his supposed and real death? Not many, surely; nor should they be difficult to find. One of those must be the murderer. Here is a third line of approach. How was the aeroplane caused to crash if, as we think, there was an earlier murder plan to get rid of Furnace, and the fact that it miscarried was the motive of the second murder? Without some such supposition the murder is pointless—the act of a madman. And even a madman would have waited to see whether Furnace would recover or not. Now here we come up against two difficulties. The Air Ministry expert suggested that the machine was in perfect trim. Then, as a second obstacle, Furnace had previously recorded his intention to commit suicide. A very tangled business here, my lord."

"It is indeed," admitted Dr. Marriott. "It seems to me that you might find it a little less tangled were you able to ascertain why any person should want to murder Furnace. I can't conceive why, myself."

"You took the words from my mouth, my lord," said the Inspector reproachfully. "Yes, the motive is the important thing. Now

I have told you the general plan of campaign and, of course, it will be my duty the next few days to work on it. I cannot disguise from you, my lord," went on the policeman insinuatingly, "that I am relying a great deal upon your help."

"And how, precisely, can I help you?" replied the Bishop with a warning coolness.

"You are inside the club. You are meeting the people. You can give me invaluable inside information which," added the Inspector with a touch of pathos, "would result in apprehending the perpetrator of this dastardly crime."

"I cannot consent, I am afraid," replied Dr. Marriott with hauteur. "You must see that I cannot figure in the life of this excellent club as a mere spy."

"But, my lord, I am appealing to you as a citizen!"

"I am certainly aware of my duties as a citizen," answered the Bishop, capable, even in flannels, of an episcopality which over-awed the Inspector. "I do not think you will find me lacking in them. At the same time, I am no policeman, but a clergyman."

"Of course, my lord," agreed the Inspector humbly.

"My clerical duties are primary, and, if anything, they encourage discretion rather than the reverse.

"Naturally, my lord."

"At the same time," added the Bishop, whose studies in casuistry had given him an unconscious facility in finding good reasons for indifferent actions, "there is some evil canker at Baston Aero Club which may well spread. It is certainly my duty to fight its spread, mainly by spiritual means, I hope, but I shall co-operate with the civil arm where necessary. In any case," added the Bishop, "I think you should keep me informed of the progress of the case."

"Certainly," agreed the policeman with alacrity. "It's a do, my lord."

CHAPTER VI

SHORTAGE OF SUSPECTS

INSPECTOR CREIGHTON waited until the Bishop was safely down the stairs and out of the police station. Then he went quickly out of the back door, got into a police car, and drove to Baston Aerodrome. His purpose was the not very trustful one of getting to the aerodrome before the Bishop had time to tell anyone of the new development in the aerodrome accident.

It may be wondered why the Inspector did not request the Bishop himself not to reveal the information until asked to do so. It is unfortunately necessary to record that Inspector Creighton was deeply distrustful of everyone, even of clergymen, when engaged in the prosecution of an investigation. In excuse it must be admitted that the Inspector had had some experience of requesting persons to keep a confidence strictly, such persons invariably supposing that it is in their discretion to communicate the information in strict confidence to other persons, those other persons thinking the same.

His first call was on Miss Sackbut, who winced when she saw his familiar figure appear on the aerodrome.

"Who's been low-flying now?" she asked wearily. "I suppose it's Miss Miffin complaining that club members keep on banging against her roof and knocking her tiles down so that she has to take refuge under the drawing-room table."

The Inspector gave a sickly grin at the recollection.

"I'm afraid it is more serious than that, Miss Sackbut. Certain facts have come to light," he said formally, "that make it necessary for me to institute further enquiries into the case of George Furnace's decease."

"Damn that Bishop!" exclaimed Sally warmly. "And I thought he was such a nice, kindly man! Damn Lady Laura too! I believe she forged that letter, Inspector."

"Indeed, miss. Well, we might go into that later. First of all, I should like to interview the three gentlemen who got Furnace's body out of the aeroplane."

"Let me see. Ness is giving a top overhaul to BT's engine. He'll be in the engine shop. That's the little lean-to behind the main hangar. Tommy Vane's up with our new instructor, Flight-Lieutenant Winters. He'll be down soon. I'm afraid Randall's not about. Wait a minute, though. He went out on a charter job for Gauntlett's Air Taxis. He'll be popping back this afternoon. It was only over to Paris, and he left early this morning, just after dawn."

"Thank you, miss. Well, then, I'll go round and find them."

"Right; I'll go with you," said Sally, getting up.

"I needn't trouble you, thank you. No doubt you'll be very busy."

"It doesn't matter," she said.

"Very well." The Inspector, purposely misunderstanding her, walked rapidly away before Sally could put on her hat.

Sally stared after him. "What the devil is he up to?" she muttered. "Wait till I see that Bishop!"

The Inspector came upon Mr. Ness grinding-in a valve to the mournful strains of some unrecognizable melody. He looked surprised when Inspector Creighton peered in with a murmured apology.

"May I have a word with you, Mr. Ness?" remarked the Inspector formally.

"Uh-huh," agreed Mr. Ness.

The Inspector explained that he had decided to make further investigations into the death of George Furnace. It now appeared that it may not have been an accident.

The red-headed man grunted.

"Something has come to light which suggests that the cause of death might have been …" The Inspector hesitated and Mr. Ness looked up.

"Suicide," finished Creighton. Under his scrutiny the ground engineer's face showed no sign of relief, or, in fact, of any emotion.

"Naturally, such a suggestion means we have to turn over everything from top to bottom once more. Now, Mr. Ness, you came on the scene after everything had happened; but even so, as a matter of formality, perhaps you will tell me what you remember?"

"I dunno I can say more than I said at the inquest," said Ness, gloomily regarding the shining rim of the valve head.

"Afterwards you helped to transfer the body from the ambulance to the hangar, where it lay till the evening?"

"Yes," the ground engineer admitted.

"Did you drive the van back after putting Furnace on it?"

He nodded.

"Did you watch beside the body at all?"

"No. Miss Sackbut did that. I went back to stand by the wreckage."

"Did you go into the hangar again that evening?"

"No," he said positively. "I was busy going over the bits with Mr. Sandwich and the insurance man."

The Inspector closed his notebook regretfully and left. As he closed the door, Mr. Ness again burst into mournful melody.

"I reckon he knows less about it than I do," thought the Inspector, "if that is possible."

For ten minutes the Inspector sat bolt upright in a chair outside the club-house, waiting for Tommy Vane to descend. Eventually the scarlet-and-white Moth glided over the hangar. Before the wheels touched the ground, however, it shot upwards with a wild bound which made the Inspector clutch the sides of his seat. "Ride her, cowboy!" yelled a youth next to him cheerily.

"Whoopee! That was a good landing for Tommy," he said communicatively to the Inspector.

The machine dropped towards the ground a second time. But on this occasion there was a roar from the engine and the 'plane ascended again.

"Very odd," commented the Inspector.

At the next attempt the machine landed successfully, and Flight-Lieutenant Winters and Tommy Vane got out.

Winters was a lean man, with hair greying round the temples, and an air of gentle melancholy easily explicable by the fact that he had been a club instructor for ten years. Tommy Vane was now wearing large flannel trousers which trailed on the ground and an offensive canary-yellow pullover with a bright green scarf.

"I'm pretty ghastly, aren't I, boss?" he said cheerfully to Winters as they came up.

"As a matter of fact, Tommy," answered the other seriously, "you'd be quite good if only you'd get over this casual manner of yours. You don't seem to have your mind on the job. You've got good hands and quick reaction. But there's something lacking here." He touched his head.

"The truth is," said Tommy confidingly, "I'm so scared all the time I'm up in the air that my mind just goes round and round!"

Flight-Lieutenant Winters smiled at Vane. "I should say you're singularly free from nerves."

Creighton buttonholed Vane and managed to lead him aside. He gave the same explanation for his enquiries that he had given to the ground engineer.

"Can't you let poor old Furnace rest in his grave?" protested Vane. "Well, if you want to give me a once-over, let's do it elsewhere."

In spite of the Inspector's protests, Vane insisted on going into the bar lounge. They sat at a table. The Inspector consented to accept a bitter, and Vane brought back a stiff-looking double Scotch for himself. Creighton was a little staggered to see the youth swallow it neat, almost at a gulp, and follow it with a mouthful of soda-water. In fact, he began to look at Vane more closely. At least he was a more promising suspect than the ground engineer, that quiet, peaceable body. Though the Inspector was a shrewd judge of character, Vane puzzled him.

He had one of those pale, noncommittal faces, with frank blue eyes and rather babyish red lips which show little trace of age, so that the Inspector found it genuinely difficult to decide whether he was twenty or twenty-seven. He spoke in an accent the Inspector found it equally difficult to locate. It was well-bred English basically, but overlaid with something else. Was it a trace of dialect? Behind his ingenuous bearing and boyish face there were occasional hard streaks that made the Inspector thoughtful. He had come across this type among young men who drove cars with such consistent and unreasonable recklessness that the Inspector's efforts had generally resulted either in a trial for manslaughter or a permanently suspended driving licence.

On the face of it, however, Vane got off as scot free as Ness. He had helped get the body out and had never been near it again.

"So he says. We'll see," was the Inspector's mental comment.

He had lunch at the club, parrying with the skill of years Miss Sackbut's pressing enquiries. After lunch he went out with her on to the club lawn, and she pointed to the horizon, where a tiny speck could just be made out.

"That's a Gull," she said. "Gauntlett is the only bloke with a Gull round here, so it's probably Randall."

"You said he was on a taxi job," remarked the Inspector. "What exactly does that mean?"

"An air-taxi flight," answered Miss Sackbut. "Sixpence a mile or what-have-you. Valentine Gauntlett runs our air-taxi show and does very well. I'm damned if I know how he gets so much business from this one-eyed place. Of course, newspaper deliveries between Paris and London help a bit. Randall's doing a newspaper delivery job now."

"I'm surprised an airman as well known as Captain Randall needs to do that sort of thing."

"Good lord, there's not so much money in that kind of transatlantic business as people think. It's like getting blood from a stone to screw the bonuses out of the aircraft and petrol people now. Still, Randall needn't do it. It's only because he's got a half-share in Gauntlett's air-taxi business, so if he's down here and they're short of pilots he sometimes goes off on a job. It keeps his hand in, you see, and it isn't like regular work. That really would be fatal for Randall."

By this time the Gull had arrived. Randall taxied it into the hangar, and then Creighton, deftly shaking off Miss Sackbut, intercepted him as he walked back to the Gauntlett Air Taxi's scarlet-and-yellow hut.

Randall, the Inspector felt, was the least likely candidate of the three. Whether the Inspector had been prejudiced by a long-standing admiration for the airman was another matter. Randall had, apart from his blond impressiveness, a certain direct manner, deprecating his own achievements, and resolutely insisting that commercial motives alone inspired him. This was refreshing, and the Inspector had liked him for it.

Randall continued to be frank and also disconcertingly penetrating. "Look here, Inspector," he said, when he had heard the Inspector's story, "the suicide business doesn't wash. I'm sure you wouldn't come round here in full cry just because of a suspicion it was suicide. There's something more behind it, eh? Do you suspect someone of monkeying with the machine?"

"That's as may be," answered the Inspector.

"I don't want to pump you, but look here, what the devil difference does it make what happened after the crash?"

"Everything counts," said the Inspector with an air of innocence.

"Have it your way. Anyway, there's nothing much to tell. By the time I got there poor Furnace was laid out cold. I helped get him into the crash tender and drove back with him. We put out trestles in the hangar office—the room that's boarded off—and laid the poor bloke on it, with something over him, of course. Then Sally shooed us away and she was there all the morning, and like the dear he is, the Bishop was there in the afternoon."

The Inspector groaned. The case seemed infernally free from any loophole for suspicion. He walked thoughtfully away.

The interview with Miss Sackbut was a little wearing. She returned with insistence to the point that the enquiries he was making were entirely irrelevant. The Inspector possessed himself in patience and extracted from her a confirmation of the stories of the other three. Furnace's body had been put in the hangar. She had never left it until the Bishop relieved her.

It was only then that the Inspector told her, as if incidentally, of their discovery.

"You see, it's all very difficult, miss. Major Furnace wasn't killed by the crash. He was shot afterwards."

"Shot!" exclaimed Sally, turning white. "Do you mean murdered?"

The Inspector nodded. "I'm afraid so."

"Then he wasn't dead when he was pulled out?"

"It seems so."

"Poor George. We might have saved him. Oh, why didn't we try——"

The Inspector interrupted. "No; from what the doctor says, he wouldn't have lived anyway. That makes it all the more extraordinary, miss."

"Oh, something is wrong!" exclaimed Sally. "For there were several of us with him up to the time he was put in the hangar. And then I was with him until the Bishop relieved me."

"Exactly, miss," said the Inspector. Their eyes met, Sally's sad, distracted, surprised; the Inspector's sharp and inscrutable. Then the Inspector made his exit.

Early next morning he left Baston for London and walked from Victoria to Gwydyr House. He climbed the stairs to the Department of the Inspector of Accidents thoughtfully. A lot depended on the clues he could pick up here, but after Flying Officer Felix Sandwich had listened carefully to his story his hopes were dashed.

"I'm sorry, Inspector," said the expert, "but I can't hold out any hope at all. This was one of the few cases where we could be extremely sure about what happened. The machine was not much damaged by the spin and, in addition, it was watched by several people who were themselves pilots. The aircraft spun into the ground in an absolutely normal way. The engine had been deliberately throttled down and was in perfect condition. The control cables were unbroken and there was no sign of jamming. All the main members were structurally intact except for damage which could only have been caused by the accident. Quite frankly, I shouldn't waste any more time over any theory that includes the idea of sabotage. Either there was an error of judgment or a deliberate act. But the machine was in no way to blame."

More thoughtful than ever, the Inspector returned to Baston.

He explained his doubts and difficulties to the Bishop with almost complete candour. The Bishop was recovering from a painful argument with Miss Sackbut, who, for some reason known only to herself, had decided that the Bishop was to blame for the whole deplorable affair. His episcopal blandness had been nearly shattered by her recriminations, and he had preserved his even temper with difficulty. While reproaching Miss Sackbut for her unreasonableness, he appeared to show a trace of the same failing by passing the blame on to the Inspector.

"I intended to go down and break the news gently to her," he said to Creighton. "It must have come as a shock to her when you blurted it out. What on earth did you want to rush down like that for?"

"Pure thoughtlessness, I'm afraid, my lord," said Creighton innocently.

"Well, it's done now. What is the present position, if I may ask, Inspector?"

"Undoubtedly the three men, Ness, Vane, and Randall, were together until the body passed into Miss Sackbut's care. No one, I understand, approached it during that time, and she was subsequently relieved by you. I take it you noticed nothing suspicious before then yourself?"

"No; and he was certainly dead when I saw him, for I looked at him fairly closely."

"Quite. Now here is the position," said Creighton frankly. "We are faced with two very difficult problems. First, I am assured by the Air Ministry that either the crash was accidental or it was suicide. We must rule out the question of foul play. Since we have the letter to Lady Laura, we must, I think, incline to the suicide explanation."

"Yes, that would be only logical. But it only makes the subsequent murder more unreasonable and more unpremeditated."

"Exactly. Now we come to the murder. As far as my inquiries go, none of the three men was left alone with the body even for an instant. So that rules them out. But the whole of the intervening period until you came on the scene, my lord—and Furnace was then dead—is accounted for by Miss Sackbut having been with the body."

"Look here," said the Bishop, "you aren't surely suspecting that child of having anything to do with this dastardly business?"

"Of course not. Had I suspected her, I should naturally have warned her before questioning her, as required by regulations." The Inspector looked indignant. "I am merely recounting the position. It is difficult, very difficult." He sighed. "We must find a motive."

CHAPTER VII

ADMISSION OF AN ANALYST

THEREUPON the Inspector began his fruitful search for the motive which had caused some person or persons unknown to slay George Furnace with so little apparent provocation or necessity. Had the Inspector been a member of a French police organization, no doubt he would have started by making discreet enquiries about Furnace's lady friends and the friends of the lady friends. This did not occur to him as the first line of attack. Instead, he paid a visit to Furnace's bank manager, and took the dead man's ledger record home with him to study. This gave him ample material for reflection. He made a few notes on the back of an envelope and called in on Sally Sackbut.

"What was Furnace getting from the club as an instructor?" he asked her.

"Four hundred pounds a year and flying pay," answered Sally, a trifle defiantly. "It's not much, I know, but since the subsidy was cut down it's been no easy job making the club pay. Though goodness knows I suppose we're lucky to get anything. In fact, if it weren't for that sweet old dear, Lord Anchorage, who gave us a Moth——"

The Inspector interrupted. "What would that amount to in all with flying pay?"

"About six hundred pounds on an average year."

"Would he have earned anything from any other source?"

"Well, he used to do taxi-flying for Gauntlett when it didn't interfere with club flying. That was part of the arrangement. In fact, I used to help him out by doing the instructing myself when he'd had a fat taxi job offered him. It was the main reason why I got an instructor's endorsement on my B licence."

"I see. Could you tell me how much his earnings there would amount to, in round figures, over a year?"

"Damned if I know. Might be anything. You'll have to pop across and ask Gauntlett." She peered out of the window. "We'll go along now and see him. His car's outside, so he must be in the office. What do you want to know for?"

"A matter of form, miss," answered the Inspector woodenly. "We have to ask these questions."

They went across to a small tin shed painted in bright yellow. On it was written in scarlet lettering, "Gauntlett's Air Taxis".

Miss Sackbut banged on the door and called imperiously, "Hi, Val!"

Valentine Gauntlett emerged. An impassive young man. He was slim but wiry, dressed in white overalls and carrying a white helmet of rather a foppish cut. He had bright expressionless blue eyes and an extremely decisive chin. He lived up to the Inspector's expectations of an airman, which were somewhat romantic, and, in fact, Gauntlett was a good pilot of the dashing amateur class, racing a good deal in machines that started from scratch and either won or blew their engines up. It was said that he was very rich and only went in for commercial aviation as a hobby. It was therefore all the more surprising that his taxi business had apparently been a financial success, for the fleet grew and the scarlet-and-yellow machines were seen at some time or other at every aerodrome.

"This is Inspector Creighton, the brightest jewel in our local constabulary," said Miss Sackbut. "He's trying to stir up mud over George Furnace's death. He's asked me a question that you can answer best, I think. I'll leave you both, because I can see that rat Sammy trying to sneak off without clocking in on his flying time. So long, Inspector."

Sally hurried off, and Gauntlett showed the Inspector into his private office, which was half of the hut, furnished with a luxury contrasting a little oddly with the ramshackle building.

"Have a cigarette?" asked Gauntlett, looking at him narrowly. "I'm curious to know how I could possibly tell you anything useful about George Furnace's death."

"It's a small matter," said the Inspector, "but you know we deal in small matters. How much did Furnace get from you in the way of remuneration in the course of a year?"

Gauntlett looked surprised. "Good lord, is that all you want to know? I thought at least you would ask me when I last saw the victim." He pressed a bell. "Saunders," he said to a clerk who answered it, "look up the outside pilots' salary list and see what we paid Furnace in flying pay and retainer during the last twelve months."

Saunders returned with a pencilled slip and Gauntlett pushed it over to the Inspector. "There you are. Hardly worth murdering him for it, what? Anything else, Inspector?"

On the slip was written, "Retaining fee £50. Fees £189 15s." The Inspector made a note of it.

"That's all I wanted from you at the moment. Glad to have met you, Mr. Gauntlett."

On his way home the Inspector did a small sum on paper. £400 *plus* £200 *plus* £50 *plus* £189 15s. made a total of £839 15s. Perhaps not a generous salary for a man of Furnace's age and skill, but less than that earned by most other pilots. The Inspector did not consider that. He was more struck by the fact that Furnace had banked during that year over £2000. Nearly £850 of this had been cheques from Baston Aero Proprietary or Gauntlett's Air Taxis. The remainder had been banked in the form of large, irregular amounts of cash. Policemen are by nature suspicious of large cash bankings.

The Inspector remembered that no near relatives had come forward at the inquest, and the administrator finally appointed to wind up the intestate estate had been an old fellow officer of Furnace's who had not seen him for two years. That suggested that Furnace was a lonely man, with no one bound to him by close ties. If not from relatives or friends, from whom then was this extra money coming? Not from investments, for then it would not have been in cash. It might have been a continuous realization of assets such as cars, furniture, and so forth, over a period, but in view of Furnace's previous history of poverty this seemed unlikely. But the £1150 not accounted for by salary must come from somewhere.

It was equally interesting to notice where the money was going to. Furnace had apparently had some difficulty in living on £850 a year, for red entries indicating an overdraft were frequent until the mysterious increment of cash had begun. Then there had been money saved, about fifteen hundred pounds of it, until shortly before his death this had been paid out by two large cheques to a person of the name of Parker. He skimmed through the ledger account again, and he noticed with a rising excitement that during the five years covered by the record cheques to this same Parker had appeared at regular intervals on the debit side.

"He was being blackmailed!" exclaimed Creighton. "I might have guessed it!"

*   *   *   *   *

Inspector Creighton paid a formal visit to the administrator appointed by the Court.

Major Harries lived in London and he was singularly unhelpful as to Furnace's personal affairs. Creighton had no reason for supposing he was concealing anything. Harries explained that although they had been very friendly during the war, they had gradually drifted into different spheres. All that had remained was a kindly feeling and occasional meetings devoted to reminiscences of their war-time days. There had been a few debts to pay and matters to clear up, and Harries had offered to take charge of them for old time's sake, mainly because Furnace had once mentioned that if he made a will he would appoint Harries executor. Harries had never heard of the name of Parker. However, he had all Furnace's private papers done up in parcels, and if the Inspector liked to take them away he might be able to turn up something himself.

Creighton did so. He was favourably impressed by Harries, who was a quiet, solid sort of man with likeable eyes. The

Inspector did not think he was the kind to hush things up under a mistaken idea he was being loyal to his friend. It was obvious that Furnace had not confided in him to any extent.

The Inspector went through the papers, and to his pleasure he found a fairly recent bundle of Furnace's cheques and among them several made out to "L. S. Parker". The Inspector looked at the endorsement.

"H'm, a woman's handwriting!"

He made a note of the bank whose stamp was on the cheques as bank of paying-in. It was the Bognor Regis branch of one of the big joint-stock banks. Evidently L. S. Parker had an account there, for all the cheques were stamped in the same way. If it was blackmail, not much attempt had been made to cover up the tracks. He dictated a letter to the bank and continued his search for evidence.

He came on nothing else which was of immediate value, but one thing intrigued him so much that he decided to follow it up. It was a letter in a large envelope, marked "Private", whose contents consisted almost entirely of family papers—Furnace's birth certificate, death certificates of his father and mother, his R.F.C. commission, and the like. Its presence in this collection gave it its main interest, for the letter itself was ordinary enough. It was from a firm of analytical chemists at Market Garringham, Baston's larger neighbour, and it read as follows:

Dear Sir,
  We have now completed our analysis of the substance you left with us on the fifteenth instant. In the circumstances, we think it better if

you would be so good as to call in and see our secretary when you are
next in Market Garringham. He will be able to give you the results
of the analysis, and there are certain points he wishes to raise which
can best be discussed verbally.

Yours faithfully,
Swinton and Jackson.

"Now what exactly lies behind this letter?" reflected the Inspector.

*   *   *   *   *

The manager of the bank readily gave him Mrs. Parker's address—3, The Way, Bognor Regis—and the Inspector found himself knocking at the door of a dismal grey-stuccoed house whose dejected air proclaimed "Apartments" even without the evidence of the card hung slightly askew in one of the windows.

The Inspector had prepared himself in his mind's eye for various possibilities, but when the authentic Mrs. Parker stood before him he was surprised. She was about thirty-five, with one of those perfectly vacant faces which generally only result from living in the country alone for years on end. She was dressed in a slovenly way, but had obviously been pretty once, with that blonde, ruddy-cheeked prettiness which tends to get a little blowsy with the passage of time, particularly if, as seemed to be the case here, the owner of it becomes bored with its upkeep. The only thing that confirmed the Inspector's suspicion was that the woman was obviously frightened of him.

She dropped into a chair. "What do you want, please?" she asked, nervously clasping her hands.

"I come from Baston, in Thameshire, and I want to question you about certain matters arising from the death of George Furnace."

"Oh dear!" said Mrs. Parker forlornly. "I knew it would come out!"

"Come out! What would?" asked the Inspector, a little surprised by her lack of caution.

"That I am—that is to say—that I was—his wife!" answered Mrs. Parker.

The Inspector performed a mental gymnastic. Perhaps it wasn't blackmail after all, then. In fact, if she was his wife it couldn't be, since it is legally impossible for a wife to blackmail a husband.

"You knew he was dead?" asked the Inspector.

Mrs. Parker nodded. "I saw it in the paper."

"Then why didn't you get in touch with someone? You were his nearest relative."

"Well, it's like this," said Mrs. Parker, with a suspicion of a whine in her voice. "We'd been separated so long. During the war he married me, when he was staying on my mother's farm to get over his wound. He was a bit above me, I suppose; I didn't hit it off with his friends, I admit. It might have been different if there'd been a child, but there wasn't, and we used to quarrel. I'm not a saint myself, and I reckon it was six of one and half a dozen of the other. Be that as it may, we agreed to separate seven years ago; and I'll say this, he sent me money as regular as clockwork. I settled down here and went back to my maiden name, except I put a Mrs. before it, in case it ever came out accidental that I had had a husband.

"Well, about six months ago my lord wrote to me begging me to fix up a divorce. I wrote back I was willing enough, for I guessed what was in the wind—another woman I suppose, and I don't blame him. But look here, I said, before you take on more responsibilities, you fix me up properly. He wrote back quite pleasantly, and the upshot of it was he sent me fifteen hundred to buy this boarding-house and furnish it, and so forth, and I promised that I shouldn't ask for anything from him when we were divorced, but I'd slip out of his life altogether. Well, almost before I could call on the solicitors here I read about his death. It gave me a turn, and I was thankful he'd sent me the money. Seeing that he'd asked me to slip out of his life I just kept quiet. Then when the maid said, 'Inspector Creighton', I knew it had all come out."

After a little cross-examination Inspector Creighton accepted her story. He made the mental reservation, however, that so far from her silence being due to fine feeling, it was due to a fear that she might have to restore the fifteen hundred pounds that had been sent to her. This emerged from her frequent hints, and the Inspector was able to reassure her that she had every right to retain the money. After this she became cordial, and recollected that she had some drink in the house.

The Inspector went back to Baston sorrowing. Undoubtedly he'd been barking up the wrong tree.

It was therefore in a melancholy frame of mind that he called on Messrs. Swinton and Jackson. The secretary was a fussy little person in whom the sight of the Inspector's card and the mention of Furnace's name produced a nervous spasm. He stared at the Inspector like a frightened rabbit.

"Dear, dear!" he panicked. "I told the chairman that we ought to have mentioned that business to the police."

"Indeed!" The Inspector removed his pince-nez and methodically polished them, the while he fixed the secretary with a cold eye. "Indeed, Mr. Thompson. Then perhaps you will now explain this letter, which I imagine has something to do with the business you mention, whatever that may be."

Mr. Thompson looked at the letter without reading it. Evidently he was only too familiar with its contents, and later the Inspector noticed its carbon duplicate on top of a bundle of correspondence on his desk.

"I had better tell the story from the beginning. Major Furnace came in—let me see—well, it would have been about a month before his death. He brought a screw of white powder in an envelope and he asked us to analyse it. Naturally we asked him to give us some indication of what he expected it to contain. He could not help us at all, however. Our analysts got to work, and you can imagine our surprise, Inspector, when we discovered the powder to be cocaine."

The Inspector looked almost equally surprised.

"As you may imagine, that put us in a very difficult position. On the one hand, we had been consulted professionally and in confidence; on the other hand, here was a layman in possession of a drug and, presumably, in illegal possession. I was very worried, but after talking it over with the chairman we wrote the letter you have in your hand. The chairman and myself both saw the Major. I must confess that he seemed astonished when we told him the result of our analysis. Naturally we pointed out our position, and told him that it was essential we should have some satisfactory explanation of how he came into possession of the drug if we were to let the matter rest there. He told us a very circumstantial story of how a total stranger had pressed a matchbox into his hand and how he had found this inside. We told him that he must, of course, tell the police, and he agreed at once. In view of his assurance we left it at that."

"He certainly never told us," retorted the Inspector.

"Dear me!" said the secretary dismally. "And he seemed so straightforward about it. Well, as soon as I saw about his death, I said to the chairman, 'Don't you think, sir, we ought to tell the police?' But the chairman was positive. 'How can the two things possibly be connected, Thompson? We shall only stir up a lot of trouble.' Very positive he was." The secretary gave a placatory glance. "I can assure you if I'd guessed for a moment that Major Furnace hadn't told you about the incident we should never have kept quiet."

"Well, you've told me now," said the Inspector mildly. "Have you the paper and the cocaine?"

"I'm afraid not. We gave it back to the Major. But here is the analyst's report."

The Inspector was genial when he left, for undoubtedly he had at last come upon a clue of real importance.

Sitting in his office, he turned it over in his mind. Major Furnace had somehow or other come upon a drug trafficker or addict. It must have been in such circumstances that he had been suspicious of something without being certain. Had he been certain, he would not have taken the risk of going to near-by analysts and giving his own address. Directly Furnace heard that it was cocaine he had evidently decided upon some plan of action, otherwise he would have gone at once to the police in accordance with his promise to the secretary. The Inspector dismissed at once the story of the matchbox. Furnace had only told it after being pressed for some plausible explanation of his possession of the drug, and had it been true there would have been no reason for him to conceal his story from the police.

No, whatever the provenance of the drug, it had been such that it had given him a hold over some person. He had exploited that hold for blackmail, and thus the mysterious income was explained.

Now blackmail at once gave a motive for the murder. The blackmailed person was evidently someone of unusual spirit, for apparently towards the end Furnace himself had begun to be afraid. The Inspector read his letter to Lady Laura carefully. He noted that Furnace did not definitely say that he was going to commit suicide. All that he said was that he was in a nasty mess and that he was going to end it. Naturally, in view of his death, they had interpreted the end as being suicide. But need it be? Mightn't it be that he had begun to be afraid of the blackmailee—that that was the nasty mess—and that he proposed to end it by exposing the affair to the police? Then, assuming the blackmailee suspected this, wouldn't it be explicable for the blackmailee to plan the crash of the machine and afterwards finish him off, knowing that the survival of Furnace must be prevented at all costs?

As far as the Inspector could see this theory only left two loose ends. The Air Ministry man had insisted that the crash was either an accident or deliberate action on the part of the pilot. But, damn it, thought the Inspector testily, you can never trust these experts!

The other loose end, if indeed it was a loose end, was that the only person who seemed to have been in a position to shoot Furnace was Sally Sackbut, and was it really possible that she was the ruthless criminal of his theory? He doubted it, and yet there was the undeniable fact that as manager of the club, and herself a pilot, she was in an exceptional position to plan the crash.

However, the Inspector felt pleased, for he had cleared up so many conflicting features that a loose end or two might safely be left out for a moment.

The next question that troubled the Inspector was—setting aside for the moment the possibility that Sally Sackbut was the mysterious unknown—how far was this cocaine business connected with flying? Had Furnace merely stumbled on it in his private capacity as a resident at Baston? The Inspector found difficulty in believing this. Whatever the vices of Baston, and the little town had its share of them, they were mostly bucolic, and drug-taking was not among them. In fact, the Inspector knew singularly little about this form of wrong-doing.

Well then, was it a vice endemic to aviation? The Inspector imagined that a pilot would necessarily require to be physically fit, which *ipso facto* excluded drug-taking. But he was not sure, and for all he knew drug-taking might be a recognized aviation cult. He realized that here he would have to get advice. But from whom?

His train of thought was momentarily interrupted by the tinkle of his office 'phone. He lifted the receiver.

"Gauntlett here. You know you called in to see me about poor Furnace the other day? Look here, Inspector, can you come round and see me—at once? I've discovered something that I think will interest you. Yes, genuinely. No, I can't very well explain on the 'phone. In half an hour? Right ho, come straight to my office."

Val Gauntlett was as delighted as a terrier with a rat as he led the Inspector to a portion of the aerodrome where lay a small block of wood. Over it a ground engineer in the scarlet-and-yellow overalls of Gauntlett's Air Taxis was mounting guard.

The ground engineer removed the block of wood, and the Inspector saw that it concealed a hole in the ground. He knelt down to inspect it. From the bottom of the depression projected a thin cylinder. The Inspector looked at it more closely and then gave a whistle of amazement.

It was the muzzle of a revolver, and its position could be most readily explained by the fact that it had fallen from a great height, embedding itself in the soil of the aerodrome like a bomb.

Very gently the Inspector loosened it. The firearm was rusty, as if it had been in the soil for some time. He examined it carefully, and measured the bore with his pocket callipers. Unless it was a remarkable coincidence, this was the revolver that had killed Furnace.

"Well, anything important?" asked Gauntlett eagerly.

The Inspector nodded. "It is. Extremely important, I fancy. Very good of you to have got in touch with me so promptly. Could this have been here long without being overlooked?"

"Good lord, yes! See for yourself the size of the aerodrome! If my 'plane hadn't happened to have been parked just here, Lumb would never have noticed it, and I know I shouldn't have."

Creighton nodded, and walked slowly back to his car. Assuming that on further examination this proved to be the revolver which shot Furnace, did it alter his reconstruction? Not necessarily. After all, it wasn't a bad way of getting rid of an incriminating weapon to take it up in an aeroplane and drop it.

This, however, suggested still more strongly a link between flying, the murder, and the drug-taker. Not only did the murderer have something to do with flying, but almost certainly he was a pilot, for it would have been too risky for a passenger to throw it overboard. Ignorant as the Inspector was about aviation, he did know, from his solitary joy-ride, that in a two-seater aeroplane, such as the club used, the passenger sat in front of the pilot.

A pilot. ... Sally Sackbut's image flitted again before the mind's eye of the Inspector. ...

CHAPTER VIII

AUTOROTATION OF AN ECCLESIASTIC

MEANWHILE, Baston Aero Club had become the scene of activities which for a time obliterated the loose ends of the Furnace tragedy. The efficient cause was a remark made at breakfast by the Lord-Lieutenant of Thameshire, Lord Grunnage, to his sister, the Countess of Crumbles, to the effect that he hoped "that accident hasn't affected the Aero Club I'm president of. Sally Sackbut's a game little woman, and I should be sorry if she got into difficulties. Of course, the club's always on the verge of bankruptcy in this one-eyed town."

Now Lady Crumbles lived in a passionate whirl of organization. Charity matinée succeeded to hospital ball with the inevitability of the seasons, and people instinctively (but vainly) put protecting hands over their cheque-books when she approached. Vainly, because Lady Crumbles' masterful and obtuse personality had the effect of a tank, and to be perfectly candid, her figure was planned on similar lines, which made the joint effect the more overpowering. Although Lady Crumbles was never in want of charitable objects for which to organize, or time in which to organize for them, she did sometimes find it difficult to originate new devices by which to abstract money from people under the show of giving them pleasure. Consequently she leapt at the remark thrown out, in all casualness, by Lord Grunnage.

"Gillie, you've given me an idea!"

"No, surely not," said her brother nervously.

"Positively! Baston Aero Club must have an air display."

"I don't think they'll like that at all."

"Of course they won't. That's not the point. It's for a cause. For my Air Fairies!"

"Your what?" asked Lord Grunnage incredulously.

"My Air Fairies. You've heard of Brownies, I suppose?"

"A particularly repellent breed of Girl Guide, aren't they? Whenever I review a public function they seem to creep in on it somehow toward the end. They must be the most accomplished gate-crashers in this county."

"Gilbert," said Lady Crumbles sternly, "*I* am the patron of the Brownies in this county!"

"That, of course, explains it!"

"The Air Fairies are the aerial equivalent of the Brownies," went on Lady Crumbles. "In time of war they will do their duty for King and Country by assisting our gallant airmen."

"I don't think the name is very happy," he suggested.

"And pray why not?"

Lord Grunnage coughed. "It might give rise to misconception."

"I don't follow you," answered Lady Crumbles brusquely. "However, as you seem to have taken some absurd prejudice against the name—what about the Airies?"

"That is better," admitted her brother.

"Very well. Now we must have some money to get the Airies started. And what could be more suitable than an air display?"

"Why don't you put up the money yourself?" said Lord Grunnage, without thinking.

Lady Crumbles stared at him in horror. She had been organizing for charities for twenty years, and it was the first time that anyone had ever asked her to provide money for them herself. And her own brother to be so tactless!

"My dear Gilbert," she said gently, "I have my duties to my family!"

"Your family? Do you mean old Frankie? I should have thought he'd got more than he knew what to do with. I see his tinned meat wherever I go!"

"Please remember he is my husband," said Lady Crumbles. "You may be sure that if I could merely sign a cheque for these charities instead of working my fingers to the bone it would be a tremendous relief." She sighed and then brightened. "You must be president of the display, of course."

Lord Grunnage bowed his head meekly. "As long as I don't have to do anything."

"Of course not. You know you never do. I shall look after everything. All I ask of you is to open the show and stay for a little. I must start forming the Executive Committee at once. While I remember, here are two tickets for the Midnight Matinée for Market Garringham Cottage Hospital. We should so love to see you and Lucy there."

"Very kind of you to ask us," mumbled Lord Grunnage.

"They are a guinea each. Send us the cheque along any day. Dear me, look at the time. I must fly."

Next day Lady Crumbles appeared at Baston Aero Club with the nucleus of her Executive Committee—a formidable trio. Lady Crumbles was, of course, herself chairman, and her vice-chairman was Sir Herbert Hallam, one of the few pilots who had been able to make a commercial success of long-distance flying in the early days. He had been knighted for his exploits, and now functioned as the director of several aviation companies, while avoiding, as far as lay in his power, any more flying. He was an energetic man, with a loud voice which had not lost the somewhat Cockney accent of Sir Herbert's nurture. The third member of the Executive Committee was Dighton Walsyngham, a large, genial fellow, who was almost if not quite as successful in devising various pretexts for raising money as Lady Crumbles. The only difference was that in her case the ultimate object of the funds secured was charity, in his case it was himself. Walsyngham was a company promoter.

At the moment he was engaged in organizing a gigantic internal air line project. He had recently swum into Lady Crumbles' ken, and she had at once decided that he was a useful person, and had invited him on to the Executive Committee, to which he had blandly agreed. Walsyngham was built on the same imposing physical scale as Lady Crumbles, but he possessed an oily suavity which she lacked, and this supplied, as it were, a soft unguent which soothed his victims even as he advanced remorselessly over them quite in Lady Crumbles' tank-like style.

Miss Sackbut gazed at this trio with a kind of incredulous horror when they walked into her office. Lady Crumbles she knew, having seen her with the Lord-Lieutenant on the occasion when he had presented the club with a 'plane. Sir Herbert's physiognomy was, of course, known to her and to everyone in aviation, owing to his unequalled pervasiveness, but Walsyngham's was a new face.

She feebly motioned them into chairs.

"We are the Executive Committee of the Baston Air Display," explained Lady Crumbles briefly and directly.

"Air display, did you say?" asked Sally incredulously.

"Certainly. We have decided to organize a flying meeting at Baston in aid of the Airies."

"Did you say *Airies*?"

"Please don't keep repeating my words, Miss Sackbut," said Lady Crumbles irritably. "Yes, I did say Airies. They are the air corps of my Brownies. Now all we want from the club are the club machines, and the aerodrome, the services of your pilots, and, of course, the co-operation of the members."

"Is that all?" asked Sally.

"For the moment, yes," answered Lady Crumbles, whose obliviousness to sarcasm was her greatest strength. "As further needs crop up, we shall, of course, get in touch with you. Now, my dear, as manager of the club you must, of course, serve on the Committee; in fact, you ought to be aviation manager of the display."

"But I don't think," said Sally, who felt the situation rapidly sliding out of her control, "that I'm very keen on the display idea. I don't think the members will be very keen on it either."

"My dear child," said the Countess winningly, "don't you realize that the whole idea of it is to *help* the club? The Airies are only a side issue. As soon as Gilbert said to me that he hoped the club was doing all right, I said to myself, 'I must help them, the gallant things, and all they are doing for the country.' And so the idea of the display came to me."

"It's awfully good of you, of course——"

"Not at all."

"It really is, but——"

"Lady Crumbles spends her time doing good. How she has the time to fit it in I don't know," interrupted Walsyngham.

"Wot amazes me is 'ow young she looks on it," said Sir Herbert Hallam. "Work agrees with you, Lady Crumbles."

"It really is most awfully good of her," insisted Sally with a quiet desperation, "but I am sure club members would resent the time taken up in practising and so forth."

"My dear Miss Sackbut, I am used to dealing with resentful people," laughed Lady Crumbles. "If you get any complaints from a club member, I will have a little chat with him and point out that it is for the good of the club. Don't you worry on that score."

"I hope it's not going to cost anything," said Sally, unwilling to give in without a struggle. "We really can't afford a penny of capital expenditure."

"Leave that to the Executive Committee! We'll raise the money. My dear, you seem to have so many odd objections … you don't resent my coming in, do you? I mean, if you would prefer to be chairman of the Executive Committee yourself, I should gladly serve under you. I always say that we women shouldn't let our feelings stand in the way of charity."

"Good Lord, no! I am delighted you should run the show," said Sally, now fairly cornered. "I'll co-operate with you all I can. I don't want to have to do anything but the flying side."

As Sally thus succumbed to Lady Crumbles' powers, there was the sound of a song outside, and Tommy Vane threw open the door. He was carrying a glass of beer, was dressed in a cherry-coloured, open-necked shirt, and wore dark-green flannel trousers with an orange belt.

"Hi, Sally!" he shouted, holding up something in his fingers. "Look what I've found in the beer!" Then, seeing the formidable bulks of Lady Crumbles and Mr. Walsyngham and the familiar figure of Sir Herbert Hallam, he started to retreat with a muttered apology.

Lady Crumbles, who had scrutinized him closely, suddenly gave an exclamation. "My dear Mr. Spider!" she exclaimed effusively. "Fancy seeing you here! Have you been in England long?"

Tommy Vane gave her a startled stare. "I think you have made some mistake!"

"I never forget faces," exclaimed Lady Crumbles positively. "Surely," she added, a little plaintively, "you haven't forgotten me, Mr. Spider? Don't you remember in Hollywood, showing me round, when they were filming Veronica Gubbage in 'Naughty but Nice'?"

"Merciful heavens? A maniac!" exclaimed Tommy Vane loudly. He backed out and closed the door rapidly behind him.

Lady Crumbles looked indignantly round. "How extremely impolite! Mr. Spider was introduced to me when I visited Hollywood two years ago. He was in the cast of 'Naughty but Nice' when I saw it being filmed, and as he was English they gave him the task of looking after me. He did it very sweetly too; and now he seems so abrupt. I really cannot understand it!"

"Surely there is some mistake," suggested Sally, concealing a smile. "His name is Vane—Thomas Vane—and I'm sure he's never been out of England; certainly not on the films. Are you *sure* the name was Spider?"

"Perhaps it isn't the same man," admitted Lady Crumbles, in a tone that indicated she was fairly certain it was. "As for his name being Spider, now you mention it, perhaps it wasn't. Everyone called him Spider at the studio, so naturally I called him Spider too, but it may have been only a nickname."

"I 'ad a monkey called Spider wot I brought 'ome from Singapore," said Sir Herbert. "The pore little beast pegged out though."

"What on earth has a monkey to do with it?" said Lady Crumbles. "Really, Sir Herbert, you do say the most extraordinary things!"

Walsyngham had meanwhile noticed Sally's growing impatience. "Perhaps we've done enough business for to-day," he said soothingly. "Shall we make our next meeting here at, say, noon to-morrow? Does that suit you, Miss Sackbut?"

"Perfectly." She nodded resignedly. How she wished Furnace was still alive. He would probably have been equal to Lady Crumbles. The new instructor, Winters, was too broken to the slings and arrows of outrageous committees at his previous clubs to offer much resistance. If only the woman hadn't been Grunnage's sister she would have told her to go to hell. She might yet. . . .

The Executive Committee walked out. Sir Herbert, the last to go, favoured Sally with a wink and an expressive thumb jerked in the direction of Lady Crumbles, which heartened her a little.

On her way to the car, Lady Crumbles halted as she saw a familiar figure hurrying by.

"Lady Laura!" she hailed it. "Fancy seeing you here! But, of course, you do fly yourself, don't you, you clever thing!"

"Hallo!" said Lady Laura in her loud clear voice. "I haven't seen you since we met at Hollywood."

"Well, so it was, at Hollywood. How very strange. Only just now I was reminded of that visit. Do you remember Mr. Spider, that man who showed us round?"

Lady Laura laughed. "You mean 'Spider' Hartigan? A rather amazing young Englishman?"

"That's the man. My dear, I met somebody just like him, a member of the club."

"Oh, that would be Tommy Vane," said Lady Laura. "They are rather alike; I've noticed it. He's younger though, I think. What are you doing here, by the way? The charity racket, I suppose? You aren't dragging Sir Herbert round for nothing!"

Hallam gave a deprecating grin.

Lady Crumbles became enthusiastic, a quality she could turn on like a tap. "Haven't you heard? I'm organizing a display for the club. Half the profits are going to the club and half to my Airies. What do you think of the idea?"

"Stinking!" retorted Lady Laura coldly. "It means having thousands of people tramping all over the aerodrome, and flying will be dislocated for the day, and there's always a dozen or so drunks left over in the bar one doesn't know what to do with. I know these shows."

"You're always so witty, dear!" said Lady Crumbles, who was not to be put off by a Lady Laura. "Of course you won't refuse to take part in the *concours d'elegance*?"

"No. I shan't. Not if there's a decent prize. The last prize I won at a *concours d'elegance* was in the Brighton Hospital Motor Rally. It was supposed to be a silver cup, but when I took it home I found it was only electro-plate."

"*I* presented the prizes at the Brighton Hospital Motor Rally," said Lady Crumbles icily. Hallam gave a gurgle which he changed into a cough as Lady Crumbles' eye fell upon him.

"I'm so sorry! Did you really? How frightfully tactless of me!" said Lady Laura indifferently. "Well, anyway, see that the Press are looked after at this show, whatever happens. So long!"

"I really cannot see what people find to admire in that girl," complained Lady Crumbles. "Look at her! As thin as a rake, and absolutely no distinction of manner at all. How she manages to run an aeroplane and a car I don't know, for the Vanguards always were as poor as church mice. However, perhaps it would be more charitable not to enquire."

Meanwhile, on the retirement of the Executive Committee, Miss Sackbut had walked sadly out on to the flying field to take the Bishop for his lesson. He ventured to comment on her abysmal gloom.

"I really begin to wonder whether I'm cut out for this kind of thing," said Sally, explaining it. "First of all poor Furnace, and then this Crumbles visitation. The club is getting out of hand, that's the truth. I can't control it."

"Come, come, now. You can't be blamed for poor Furnace's death."

Sally transfixed him with a perceptive stare.

"Can't I? I don't put it beyond Inspector Creighton. He's been drifting into my office asking me questions altogether too often for it to be accidental."

The Bishop, too well aware of the truth of this, became a little agitated. "Miss Sackbut, can't you help at all? I mean, you must see now that things have gone too far to stop them, even for Furnace's sake. There was a mystery in his death, and it has got to be solved by the police wherever the solution leads. You know the actors in the drama. Can't you possibly think of anything that will throw light on it? Anything in Furnace's previous life, for instance?"

Sally looked at him frankly. "The truth is, Bishop, I hardly dare. During the last two years I have had the sensation that something queer was going on in this aerodrome. It was the change in Furnace that made me notice it most. He was always secretive, certainly, but during the few months before his death it was something out of the ordinary even for him. Something was worrying him badly, I knew. That was bad enough, but it isn't only that. It's a silly feeling I used to have that there was something a little mysterious going on here. You know when you walk into a room and people stop talking suddenly, and you think they are talking about you? That sort of atmosphere. And queer little incidents which meant nothing separately, but were queer because they happened so often. There's never been anything one could take hold of, you understand, until Furnace's death. And even that looked a pure accident on the surface. But when you went into it, you see, we found it wasn't an accident, but something dreadful. And ever since I've been wondering if something dreadful has been going on below the surface with those other little things." Sally smiled painfully. "Oh, I suppose it all sounds a little hysterical. I don't know why I tell you all this. I'm a bit under the weather, that's all."

The Bishop became thoughtful. "Have you any definite suspicion—let us be frank—of any one person?"

Sally nodded miserably. "I don't trust Randall."

"Randall!" exclaimed the Bishop, startled. His mind jibbed at associating the gay and famous airman with these suspicions.

"What on earth makes you feel that? Surely he was a friend of Furnace's? He was very much distressed after the accident. And then, at the inquest, he spoke so generously about him."

"That's just it!" exclaimed Sally. "My suspicions do sound silly when I mention them."

"But you must have some reason," suggested the Bishop patiently.

"Well, I haven't. At least, it's not much more than a feeling. But I'm certain Furnace and Randall were in something together. They were always whispering in odd corners, and then they would shut up in an unobtrusive sort of way when I came near."

"Possibly—ah—they were exchanging anecdotes unsuitable to the female ear," remarked the Bishop jocosely.

"Not to my ear!" said Sally with withering scorn. "No, they had some scheme on, and yet I'm quite sure Furnace didn't like Randall. In fact, I overheard them definitely quarrelling twice. And sometimes Furnace's eyes used to follow Randall in a way that made me—oh, I don't know! I used to think it was a woman, but when George fell for Laura and it still went on, I knew it wasn't that, for Randall and Laura didn't like each other. Got in the way of each other's publicity, I suppose."

"Randall …" mused the Bishop. "I can't imagine what there could have been between them. And yet there is a streak in his character, I suppose, which might be capable of strange things. But murder … I think the whole thing is too vague even to tell Creighton yet."

"Oh, of course," said Sally, with a return to her former brightness. "It sounds rather silly when one says it, doesn't it? I see Andy is looking at us reproachfully. The engine's ticking over and we're wasting petrol. It's too bumpy for you to practise landings, so we'll take you up for a spin."

"Really," said Dr. Marriott nervously; "do you think I am sufficiently advanced for that?"

"Of course. I want something drastic to cheer me up." Sally dropped into her instructional tones as they climbed in and her voice came over the 'phones like that of a disembodied spirit. "Now the whole object of modern instruction is to ensure that you know how to get yourself out of any possible difficulty you may get into in your subsequent flying career. One possible difficulty is that if you stall with rudder on you'll spin, so I'm going to teach you how to get out of that spin. Technically a spin is known as autorotation. Are you ready? Tail slice two-thirds forward. Stick right forward. Full throttle. Now she's yours. Whoa! Keep her nose out of the ground. Don't climb yet. Now. Climb at fifty-five miles per hour. Now stick forward a little for the turn. Oh, Bishop, Bishop, where's your rudder! Come out of the turn altogether. Splendid. Very neat that. Climb again."

Steadily and grimly the Bishop mounted up, up, through the fleecy puffs of cloud. Up, up, until the aerodrome below looked like a square in the pattern of some terrestrial counterpane half obliterated by a drifting haze of tobacco-smoke. Up, up. So, reflected the Bishop uneasily, must the earth have looked when Furnace span to his doom—knowingly, or prey to some superior ingenuity of destruction?

Sally was speaking, however. The voice coming so thinly through the 'phones was again admonishing him. "Remember that you spin with your rudder. You must stall first, but it is also necessary to misuse your rudder, particularly on a 'slotted' machine like this. Watch me. To make her spin I'm going to stall her, then put the rudder hard over. To stop her spinning I shall put the stick forward a little and then give her hard opposite rudder to stop the spin, then put the rudder in the neutral position again just as she comes out of the spin. All right. I've got her!"

The engine's roar ceased dramatically. He let go the controls. In the deadly silence that followed the nose of the machine aspired madly above the horizon. Up, up. The whispering of the wind died away. The silence was really ominous. It surely couldn't last.

Flick! With the vicious plunge of a mad horse the aeroplane dropped—dropped like a thing shot through the heart, and seemed, in doing so, to leave half the Bishop's internal functionings behind it. And as if horrified by that mad plunge, Creation began to spin dizzily round the front of the Bishop's nose—the fields, the vast terrestrial counterpane, shot round like a great wheel below them; the horizon was the felloe and the roads the spokes, and all whirled round fast and faster in a devil's Catherine wheel. The Bishop clutched the cockpit's edge. Though they were diving headlong, the wind was still only whispering through the wires as if they were floating earthward like a spinning sycamore seed, and this seemed to make it yet more sinister.

"The spin is now fully developed," came Sally's incredibly calm voice. "Notice that although we are in a diving position, the air speed is only forty-five miles per hour, and we're still stalled. Now I'm coming out of the spin. I bring the stick just forward of neutral, and apply opposite rudder."

The great wheel that was the earth hesitated, and then quite abruptly stopped whirling. The whispering in the wires rose to a whistle. The nose scooped up towards the horizon. They were flying level.

"You've got her," said Sally. "Now do the same."

The Bishop shuddered, but the voice was inexorable. "Back with the stick. Come on, don't be afraid—right back! Now kick the rudder! Harder! That's right."

Again the deadly flick. Again the round world spinning on a devilish wheel.

"Opposite rudder now. Decisive! Stick forward."

The great wheel stopped whirling. The wind in the wires rose to a scream.

"Hi, you're not a single-seater fighter!" yelled Sally. "You've put the stick too far forward. Wow, we're doing one hundred and thirty miles per hour! Back a bit. Gently. Ease her. Centralize your rudder. That's got her. Now again."

"Please not again!" murmured the Bishop into his speaking-tube.

"Again!" said Sally firmly. "And don't come out of it so fast this time."

Once again the wheel. This time the Bishop looked inside the cockpit. . . .

"Much better! Now *I'll* spin you! Off a sideslip. And you recover her."

Limply the Bishop obeyed. As they flew level again he picked up the speaking-tube. "That is the last spin," he stated firmly. "I shall certainly be extremely indisposed if we spin again!"

"Oh, all right," said Sally, in tones that seemed disappointed. "Now, you see the aerodrome over there, about two points to your right? If you glide straight in from this height you will overshoot it, so approach it in a series of gliding turns, always keeping it in sight. Remember your gliding speed is fifty-five miles per hour. Neither more nor less. You've got her!"

Still a little shaken, the Bishop glided earthwards raggedly, while his airspeed indicator flickered nervously between 50 m.p.h. and 70 m.p.h. Two or three hundred feet above the aerodrome Sally gave an exclamation.

"There's the Executive Committee just going out to Lady Crumbles' car. I'd recognize that woman's figure from ten thousand feet. I'll take over now. I'm going to beat the woman up. Are you game?"

"Certainly," agreed the Bishop, blissfully unaware of what the process of "beating-up" consisted.

He was soon to be enlightened. The nose of the aeroplane went down and the airspeed indicator needle quavered over to 140 m.p.h. They were diving straight at the trio, who for a moment were unaware of the approaching aeroplane. Then, as they got nearer, he saw the pink faces of the three turned up with startling awareness. Lady Crumbles began to run first, with a shaking waddle, and was followed by Walsyngham. The smaller figure of Sir Herbert Hallam, more used to the process of being beaten up, stood its ground, waving a hand.

The Bishop clutched the side of his seat. Surely they were going to hit the ground! His inner being oozed away as the machine stood on its tail, then flicked over on one wing tip, both wings vertical, and rotated round the tip in a turn that for the first time made the Bishop realize what a high-speed manœuvre on an aeroplane was like. Then the nose dropped again. But Lady Crumbles and her companion had disappeared.

The Bishop's subsequent landing was more than usually erratic, but, oddly enough, it was Sally who came in for reproof. Tommy Vane, who was on the tarmac, gave a reproachful look.

"Was that our worthy manager and the Bishop! Guilty of such shocking bad manners! I seem to remember a 'Notice to Pilots' in our club-house strictly cautioning them against low flying— signed by our manager too. Also various verbal reproofs given by her to budding aviators. I'm shocked. Really shocked."

Sally looked a little embarrassed. "Well, damn it," she said, "it was only Lady Crumbles! That's justifiable!"

"Is that the lunatic old fish who was in your office when I barged in?" asked Tommy anxiously.

"Yes, it was."

"Right. That does explain it! She suffers from suppressed sex, doesn't she? She made a most definite set at me."

"You flatter yourself, Tommy. You reminded her of someone she knew. A spider or something."

"I feel most extraordinary," interrupted the Bishop. "Although my body is certainly stationary, my interior appears to be still revolving, and the effect is profoundly unsettling."

"Brandy," prescribed Tommy Vane. "I know the feeling."

"I think I will," said the Bishop. "I do not often touch stimulants, but I certainly imagine I shall be the better for something of that sort."

CHAPTER IX

FRANCOPHILIA IN GLASGOW

AFTER consultation with General Sadler, Chief Constable of Thameshire, Inspector Creighton went to London and called on New Scotland Yard, with an introduction to Inspector Bernard Bray. Bray, according to the Chief Constable, was at the moment investigating the white-drug traffic in Britain for the Home Office, and it was possible he might be able to help Creighton as to the source of the cocaine presented by Furnace for analysis shortly before his death.

As a policeman, Bray was a contrast to Creighton. Creighton himself appreciated it when he met him. Bray had been intended for the law, and would in due course have been called to the Bar, and fought or failed to fight his way into one of the few profitable practices of the legal profession. As it happened, the post-war slump had made it impossible for him to support himself during the long probationary period of brieflessness which every barrister undergoes.

Instead, he had joined the C.I.D., which then, for the first time in its history, was endeavouring to get into its ranks men of the professional classes. Bray might have been a mediocre success in the legal profession—he certainly had a lucid and logical mind, even if he lacked other of the qualities of a great advocate—but he made a first-rate detective.

This was a new type to Creighton. The rough-and-tumble of Creighton's experience had taken off his edges and made him capable of being all things to all men, but he bore about him the social marks of his long apprenticeship in the ranks.

The two men—the young one with the clear-cut incisive features and an easy manner, the older with the shrewd eyes surprisingly set in his heavy ruddy face, and the ingratiating voice of a shopwalker—took each other's measure rapidly and, contrary to mutual expectation, liked each other.

"I didn't expect a drug case from Baston, and no one was more surprised than I was when the Superintendent mentioned your visit," said Bray. "I don't know more than the mere fact that some cocaine has turned up there unaccounted for. How did it come about?"

Creighton explained the circumstances.

"Murder!" remarked Bray, with a lift of his eyebrows. "We don't often get that mixed up with drugs. Have you brought the stuff you found?"

"Unfortunately we only know of it by hearsay. But as proof that it really existed, I've brought the chemist's note of his analysis."

"That's just as good," said Bray. He studied the slip of paper. "H'm, some of those ingredients are familiar to me."

He pulled a file out of his desk and ran rapidly through it. He explained his purpose as his strong fingers turned over the papers.

"Almost anything is used to adulterate 'snow', you know, from icing to boracic powder. Generally there is a mixture of several ingredients. If we get two samples which analyse similarly it suggests that they both come from the same source of distribution. Of course it's only presumption. Now in this case—ah, here we are?"

He pulled out a paper and studied it for a moment.

"This tallies exactly with your analyst's report," he said. "Two and a half parts cocaine, three and a half parts sugar, five parts bicarbonate of soda, four parts finely divided flour, a pinch of lime salts of some kind. Quite a decent percentage of cocaine compared with some we get. Evidently an honest drug dealer."

Bray smiled at Creighton. "Well, we have to establish a connection. Here is Exhibit A, found, you say, by a now dead flying instructor at Baston. Here is Exhibit B, which was found on the person of a pickpocket in Glasgow. Where's the link?"

Creighton shook his head: "Ay, it's not easy on the face of it. But it does look like there might be something ... How did your man get his drug?"

"Unfortunately we don't know," admitted Bray. "These dopeys are all as close as the devil about their source of supply—afraid it will get cut off if they give it away, you see."

"Well, here's another point you can help me on," said Creighton. "Would it be that this fellow Furnace got on the track of his drug in the course of his job? Or is it nothing to do with the flying club? I mean, have you ever come across aviation in connection with your drug investigations?"

"No," answered the Yard man decisively. "Of course the doping type will take up aviation or motor racing as a new sort of thrill, but they'd not get past their medical examination when it came to becoming a pilot. I can't imagine any profession where they're less likely to be found."

Creighton looked despondent. He was about to gather up his hat and go when Bray gave an exclamation.

"Fool that I am! Of course, aviation would fit in perfectly— on the distribution side! Distributing drugs by aeroplanes would certainly be a new problem for my department, and a damned difficult one. Now look here: how far would it be possible for Baston Aerodrome to be a centre for drug distribution?"

"It's a bit too frequented, I should have thought. And the club machines are busy all day. Wait a moment though! I saw a fellow named Gauntlett there, who runs an air taxi business. That sounds the sort of thing."

"It *is* the sort of thing," said Bray excitedly. "By Jove, Creighton, I've a hunch we're on to something. Know anything against this bloke Gauntlett?"

"I'm afraid not. He's supposed to be rich; his only convictions are for dangerous driving and low flying."

"Look here, come round with me to the Air Ministry. It's just ten steps from here. Arendsen in the D.C.A. is a pal of mine, and he'll give us the low-down on Gauntlett."

Creighton's second visit to Gwydyr House proved to be as unencouraging as his first. Arendsen obligingly worried everyone in the D.C.A. for scandal and came back shaking his head.

"Gauntlett has never been blown on here, Bernard," he said. "All his business is perfectly aboveboard. Our A.I.D. people say his maintenance is O.K. He sends us detailed traffic and passenger returns, for which we bless him, as these are only voluntary for air taxi operators. He's got a fleet of thoroughly modern machines and seems in every way what we've always thought him, a successful private charter operator. I think you're on the wrong trail, old chap!"

"I don't see that he mightn't use a perfectly legitimate business to cloak his dope-distribution," argued Bray. "Can I have a look at the traffic returns you mentioned?"

"Certainly. Here you are. Take a dekko. They seem to be copied from his journey log-books."

"They seem extremely comprehensive," said Bray, looking up. "Is it usual to include dates of flights, time, and so forth?"

"No, it isn't," answered Arendsen. "Sometimes all we get is '*Carried* 2000 *passengers approx. in* 1933', scrawled on a bit of old paper after we've applied for it ten times."

"Curious the detail he's gone into. Almost as if he's tried to account for every minute of his time!"

"You suspicious old devil! And I suppose if he'd sent nothing you'd have said it suggested he had something to hide!"

Bray laughed, but did not reply. He looked at the returns again.

"A lot of newspaper deliveries, I see. Is that usual?"

"Good lord, yes!" replied the Air Ministry official. "Most air taxi firms seem to live on it."

"What is the nearest aerodrome to Glasgow?"

"Renfrew, for civil 'planes," answered Arendsen.

"H'm. See that, Creighton—a regular daily delivery to Renfrew?"

"Look here," said Arendsen, "where do you expect this stuff to come from—the Continent?"

Bray nodded. "Marseilles probably."

"Well then, why don't you go to Sankport in Kent. That's the aerodrome where Gauntlett's machines probably clear Customs when they come from France. I'll give you a note to the people there, and you can sniff round to your heart's content."

"Yes, but if he were smuggling, he surely wouldn't go through a Customs airport?"

"I think so. It's not so easy as you might imagine to fly from France to England and *vice versa* without clearing Customs. An aeroplane is still a pretty noticeable object, you know, and there are few enough of them for us to keep a close tab on them. If I were to do a spot of aerial smuggling, I should rely on bluffing or bribing rather than dodging. In fact, I should take damn' good care to go through a Customs airport. One or two johnnies have tried to smuggle stuff by air the other way, but we soon rounded them up."

"This seems to be leading us the devil of a dance," commented Creighton as he sped down soon afterwards in an official car to Sankport Aerodrome.

"It's always the way in a dope distribution investigation," answered Bray. "We shall be lucky if we keep in this country. I'm still not sure that the drug end is the quickest end to tackle your murder from, you know."

"I'm content enough to follow it for a little," answered Creighton. They stopped before a pair of impressive concrete pillars. "Is this the place? It's an imposing sort of aerodrome to find in this out-of-the-way spot, isn't it? It makes Baston look quite small."

They had motored through the early hours of the morning in order to be in time for the arrival of the first aeroplane from Paris two hours after dawn. They got there with enough margin of time for the detectives to have a preliminary chat with Grierley, the Customs officer on duty.

Grierley was, naturally enough, sceptical. "Good lord, no! Gauntlett's O.K. I don't know the fellow himself, but I know his pilots, and some of them are as likely to smuggle as I am. It's an aboveboard business, Inspector, I'm certain. I remember the day Gauntlett's chief pilot, fellow named Downton, came back with the contract with *La Gazette Quotidienne*. Ever since then they've been distributing these papers as regularly as clockwork. They come in bundles straight from the publisher without being opened. I've seen the seal on them. Still, we're pretty careful here, and we go through them every so often just to make sure."

Bray looked disappointed. "Isn't it an awfully expensive business, this newspaper delivery by aeroplane?"

"Was that what made you suspicious?" laughed Grierley. "Oh, most papers do it, including the *Daily Mail, Daily Mirror*, and so forth. It's an advertising stunt. The idea is to have a few copies available in a foreign country early on the day of issue. It impresses readers travelling abroad with the circulation of the paper and its general up-to-dateness, and they talk about it when they get home. Of course, in the case of the *Gazette*, it's French visitors to England they want to impress, and so they distribute the papers to any towns where there are likely to be visitors—London, of course, Glasgow, Edinburgh, Birmingham, Liverpool, Manchester, Bristol, and Belfast I expect, and that's probably all."

"You don't think they could slip anything small past you, buried in the newspapers?" queried Bray.

"We know our job, Inspector! I've been through Gauntlett's bundles often myself. I'll give you a golden sovereign for every speck of dope (it is dope you're after again, I suppose?) that gets past me in them. Possibly you're thinking of bribery. Well, you know how good the Customs record in that respect is, but even if it weren't, there are so many of us here, and our rota changes so much from day to day, that you can count it out in this case."

"We've drawn blank here, I'm afraid, then," said Creighton. "It's really my fault for starting you off on this chase."

Grierley pointed to the sky. "Look, I think that's one of Gauntlett's new Dragons from Paris with the newspapers. I'll go over the papers thoroughly and you can watch me do it if you like. Only be quick. You see those four single-engined monoplanes parked on the tarmac there—the scarlet-and-yellow 'planes? Well, the bundles are transferred to those aeroplanes and each flies off in a different direction to complete the delivery. One goes to Birmingham, Manchester, Liverpool, Glasgow. Another goes to Cardiff and Dublin. You get the idea? So don't keep them waiting. I admire Gauntlett's organization, and it wouldn't be fair to interfere with it."

After its circuit, the incoming biplane side-slipped over the hangars and touched almost on the tarmac. Then it taxied up to the Customs entrance.

As the pilot climbed out of the cabin, Creighton gave a startled exclamation. "By Jove, that's Sally Sackbut! She's the manager of the flying club at Baston. You remember, I mentioned her, Bray? Don't let her see me!"

Creighton concealed himself in the inner office. He was surprised and yet elated. Here was a curious link between Furnace's murder and the clue they were following.

Meanwhile Grierley and Bray walked up to her. "Hello, Miss Sackbut; it's a long time since I've seen you?" said the Customs man.

"Yes, Mr. Grierley, I'm helping Gauntlett out of a fix. Somebody hit Downton on the head with a bottle in a café row in Paris and laid him out temporarily. Gauntlett was in a flat spin with nobody to take the machine back and all his pilots still out on charter jobs, so I slipped over on the night boat. I say, why are you mauling all those bundles about? Damn it, the paper delivery is regular enough, isn't it! Do I look like a smuggler?"

Grierley gave a significant wink at the Inspector, who was, of course, in plain clothes. "Someone from head office," he whispered. "I'll have to do the job thoroughly this time. I'll be as quick as I can." Miss Sackbut accepted the story without hesitation, and Bray did his best to look like a Customs official.

When Grierley and Bray had finished their search of the aeroplane and its contents the Inspector was prepared to agree with Grierley that even a smell couldn't have been smuggled in. Grierley gave his hieroglyphic approval, and the scarlet-and-yellow Gauntlett Air Taxis porter hustled the papers on to a trolley and loaded them into the waiting aeroplanes, whose engines were already turning over. Meanwhile, Sally turned the Dragon round and a minute later was heading for Baston.

The Inspectorate held another council of war.

"I can't help feeling I'd like to follow this thing through," said Creighton. "The girl turning up has made me suspicious even if you do give her cargo a clean bill of health. You know she's the only one who had the opportunity to put a bullet through Furnace's head, and if only I could pin some kind of motive on her it would make all the difference."

"Well, let's do it," said Bray. "I'm game. I say, Grierley, do you think we could get somebody here to follow one of those little taxi 'planes?"

He laughed. "My word, you sleuths do take some shaking off! I don't think you'll find it possible to follow them; it won't be easy to trail an aeroplane through this muck that's blowing up and those Leopard Moths are pretty fast. I tell you what—there's Thorndike over there, one of Gauntlett's pilots. He hasn't seen you nosing among the papers, Bray, so I'll introduce you both as people who're trying to get a charter flight to Glasgow. Then you can travel with the actual boodle. Do your best to look like rich young men in a hurry!"

Bray studied Thorndike closely. He seemed a likeable and perfectly honest young man. If Gauntlett's Air Taxis was a criminal organization, it certainly seemed to have been able to draw into its meshes some remarkably ingenuous-looking people.

Thorndike gave a casual glance at Bray and Creighton. "What do you weigh? About one hundred and fifty pounds each, I suppose! I can just carry you in my Leopard Moth with the papers if I take only enough petrol to get me to my first stop. You'll have to have a couple of piles of newspapers on your knee—do you mind? It'll cost you ninepence a mile each, by the way. Cash!"

Fortunately Bray and Creighton's combined resources survived the calculation, and presently they were seated, one behind the other, gazing past Thorndike's red head at a landscape with the delicate colouring of early morning, but obscured by fleecy masses of flying vapour that grew increasingly thick as they sped northward.

"The Super will raise a squeal when he sees this on my expenses!" was all the comment the airscape awakened in Inspector Creighton.

Wide stretches of blackened country beneath a pall of melancholy smoke. Birmingham, Manchester, Liverpool. ... Fleeting glimpses of the sea. ... Mountains ... Glasgow and the arm of the Clyde, and the little hill-locked aerodrome of Renfrew. ...

A small van came to meet them. Bray had an inspiration.

"I say, can we get a lift in this delivery van to Glasgow?"

Either Thorndike was very guileless or very sure of his organization. He agreed with alacrity, and put them in the van, explaining the position to the driver.

The Glasgow bundle of *La Gazette Quotidienne* consisted of several smaller parcels, each of which was sealed and bore a newsagent's name. At the fourth newsagent Bray got out of the van on the pretext that the place was sufficiently near their destination.

They looked round. It was a squalid neighbourhood. Dirty children played in the gutter, washing hung forlornly from windows, and the streets were filled with rubbish. "Funny place for French visitors to come to!" exclaimed Creighton.

They looked at the newsagent's shop at which the newspapers were delivered. It was a typical slum newsagent's and tobacconist's business, with a few weary sweets in the window, tipsters' posters, and various highly coloured weeklies in a rack.

Bray peered in. "The scholarship of Scotsmen is proverbial, but, even so, the demand for French newspapers in a shop of this kind does seem extraordinary."

They went inside. A sandy-haired, red-eyed fellow without a collar was behind the counter. Bray asked for an unusual brand of cigarettes, which he was pretty certain they would not stock; and this gave him an excuse to discuss indecisively the merits of other brands. It was a one-sided conversation, but took enough of the red-eyed man's attention to allow the detective's eyes to roam round the shop. There was no sign of *La Gazette Quotidienne*, delivered in bulk so recently.

Having at last settled on some cigarettes, Bray proclaimed that he had lost his way, and this opened up fresh conversational possibilities. It was as these were beginning to be exhausted that the first customer looked in.

He also seemed a little out of keeping with this part of Glasgow. He was a corpulent gentleman, with puffy fingers, puffy eyes, and too much jewellery, but very neatly dressed. He placed two pennies on the counter.

"A copy of the *Gazette*, please."

The red-eyed man leant below the counter, flung a copy of *La Gazette Quotidienne* on it, and resumed his conversation with Bray. The customer folded the paper up carefully, put it in his pocket and walked out.

"Fancy seeing *La Gazette* here!" exclaimed Bray. "By Jove, I'm going to France this evening; I'd like a copy."

"That's the last," answered the man shortly.

"But I saw some more under the counter."

"They're all ordered for regular customers."

Bray tried a different tack. "Look here, I know more than you think. I was recommended here by a regular customer."

"Come inside," said the red-eyed man without altering his expression. He held open the door to the parlour, then followed the detective in.

"Now, what's all this about your *Gazettes*?"

"Simply that I was told by a regular customer that I could deal here for my wants."

"His name?"

"I don't think I ought to tell you that. Why all this fuss? I've money."

"I don't want your money. Come on, now, didn't this man tell you to say something to me?"

"No—at least he may have done, but I've probably forgotten it," parried Bray. "I was a bit drunk at the time."

The man's wary expression changed to one of anger.

"You're makin' a plain fool of me with your *Gazette*. Get out of my shop if you can't do better than waste my time!"

Bray accepted the rebuke. That the man was engaged in some illicit business he felt sure. But he knew too well how impossible it was to get into such affairs without an introduction or "cover". He passed out of the shop with Creighton.

"Well, I pinched a copy of the paper while you were in there with that unpleasant-looking merchant," said Creighton.

"Good man! We'll hang round here for an hour or two to have a look at our friend's customers."

The customers confirmed his suspicions. Certainly most of them were poor people who fitted in with the scenery, but with them came a mingling of well-dressed men and women, who had a faintly furtive air. Three of these emerged openly carrying the *Gazette*. The two detectives returned to the station and went into the tea-room to have a look at their capture.

They opened the paper, scanned every line, turned it inside out, warmed it, and squeezed a lemon over it. It was inscrutable. Its bourgeois aspect and perfectly orthodox appearance gave no loophole for suspicion. It was everything it purported to be—a typical copy of a typical French newspaper of the moderate Right.

"And it cost us £20 and a day's work to get it," commented Creighton bitterly.

CHAPTER X

APPOINTMENTS OF ROYAL PERSONAGES

CREIGHTON returned to Thameshire. Bray was left with the copy of *La Gazette Quotidienne* and a stubborn feeling that somehow, somewhere, he would be able to find a connection between the cocaine found in Glasgow, that shop with the curious demand for French papers, Gauntlett's Air Taxis, and the murder of George Furnace.

He had read and re-read the newspaper until he had almost every word of it by heart. He had spent hours over the advertisements, because it seemed to him that a clue might be hidden in some apparently innocuous "small". Bray flattered himself he had a good nose for a code, but he could detect none here.

"I wonder if a journalist could see something I've missed?" he thought, gazing blankly at the paper. The idea of "journalist" suggested to him Archie Brown, crime reporter of the *Journal*, and associated with Bray on more than one tangled mystery. He could generally rely on finding Archie in Bride's, the Fleet Street coffee-house, about lunch-time, and he dropped in there now.

"Hallo, what are you doing in here?" exclaimed Archie as he caught sight of the policeman. "This looks bad. Is the dope distribution system of London centred at Bride's?"

"No, I came here to meet you, as a matter of fact."

"Really? How sweet of you. Or could it be that you want free advice?"

"I came here for the company, of course," answered Bray. "But I do happen to have a little problem for you, Archie. Here is a French paper."

"So I perceive, Holmes. And I deduce from the title that it is the *Gazette*. This was Romain's little hobby, I believe. Or did he sell it recently? I can't remember."

Bray outlined the circumstances which suggested that some message might be concealed in the *Gazette*. He mentioned no names, but Archie's eyes brightened. "This sounds a fruity mystery! Are you going to give me the story?"

"Sorry, I can't, because it's not entirely my pigeon. But if you can help me, I'll put you on to the local bloke who's running the thing and leave you to ferret it out in your well-known style."

"H'm." Archie turned the pages over rapidly with lean fingers, then he tapped the table with his tortoiseshell spectacles. When these were on, his pale narrow face had looked insipid. The removal of the glasses revealed a pair of bright, intelligent grey-green eyes in which all the expression of the face seemed concentrated.

"Look here, Bray, you talk of a message being concealed in some way. What do you suspect? I mean if there is a message by some third party it must be in the advertisements, but I take it you've tried them?"

"Yes," admitted Bray. "There are only ten smalls, and they're completely ordinary."

"Right. Well, then, the only other way a message could be got across would be by some displacement of type—in which case there must be a compositor or stereo man in the pay of the dope organization—or else by a code-word or message in the news—in which case they've tampered with a sub or a proof-reader. Do you suspect they've gone as far as that?"

"I see what you mean. Frankly, I'm completely in the dark. It might be done in either way. I haven't the vaguest idea who is in the conspiracy, or even if there is a conspiracy."

"That makes it rather difficult." Archie resumed his glasses and read the paper with slow attention. Starting at the first page, he followed it item by item to the last. Bray watched him anxiously. It was perhaps a hopeless task, and hardly fair to Archie to ask him to pick up a clue without some pointer.

Archie finished his lunch with the newspaper propped up in front of him. He gave a grunt and skimmed through it once more. Then he pointed to a paragraph.

"Here's something that arouses my suspicious nature. This three-liner stating that it is expected the Crown Prince of Kossovia will be able to visit the All-French Cycling Competition on Thursday."

"Suspicious?" replied Bray, puzzled. "Good lord! Why on earth?"

"Because the Crown Prince of Kossovia was in South America when that paragraph was written, and therefore couldn't possibly be back in France in time to attend any function which takes place next Thursday."

"But don't journalists make mistakes?" asked Bray.

"Repeatedly," declared Archie. "But not about the movements of Royalty of a country so closely connected politically and economically with France as Kossovia is."

Bray looked at the paragraph. "What message suggests itself to you?" he asked. "It's a short paragraph."

"The sentence may be in cipher, in which case, as you're probably better at cipher than I am, I leave it to you. But if it's not cipher, and it certainly sounds lucid enough, then I fancy the Crown Prince of Kossovia is a code-word for some person and the cycling competition a code-word for some place which the person is supposed to visit on the date mentioned."

"That's probable," admitted the detective. "Unfortunately, it doesn't help us much unless we know the code."

"You suspect dope distribution in this, I gather? Well, might the place be the centre where these people who buy the papers have to go for dope?"

Bray shook his head. "I don't think so, because this paper goes to towns as far apart as Bristol and Glasgow, and there couldn't be one centre for all of them."

"Perhaps it's a different paragraph for each centre?" suggested the journalist. "For instance, the mention of Kossovia might mean the message is intended for Glasgow dope-fiends. A message for Bristol addicts might be signalled by the movements of Mr. Einstein, and so on with other news personalities."

"That's possible. But we're still up against the difficulty that it's a purely arbitrary code, that we can't possibly decode it except by pure luck."

Archie got up. "Look here, come with me to the Junior French Correspondents' Club. I know the secretary, and they probably have the *Gazette* filed for the last few months."

Archie took Bray down a queer alley and up some winding little stairs to a room in which lurked a bearded man with a depressed air and the widest black silk ribbon in his pince-nez that Bray had ever seen. He seemed to take Archie's request as a matter of course and turned up a dusty pile of *Gazettes*.

"Thanks, Georges," Archie said to him. "Bernard, I suggest we try the theory that these messages appear on definite days in the week. That *Gazette* you got was Monday's. Let's look at an earlier Monday."

Archie unfolded some papers and dashed through their contents with the avid rapidity of the journalist.

"What about this?" he said with a sudden cry of triumph. "In the same column of short paragraphs and at the top, as the last message was. An announcement that the Princess Royal of Iconia is expected to open the Marseilles Fair on Wednesday."

"By Jove, it's a queer coincidence! Could it really be anything to do with the other message, though?"

"Here's another Monday's *Gazette*. Oh, boy, listen to this! 'The Hereditary Duchess of Georgina,'" translated Archie "'is indisposed and will be unable to attend the State opening of her Diet on Monday, as was intended. The session has accordingly been postponed to Tuesday.'"

Now really excited, Archie was making the *Gazettes* fly in all directions.

"Here's another. Still in the same place, at the top of the column of short news items. They all seem to come on the first Monday of a month. 'The Archduchess Edna is arriving at Nice on Wednesday.'"

Surrounded by scattered papers, the two men gazed at each other jubilantly. "Obviously, a royal personage is the key-word," exclaimed Bray. "You've spotted it, Archie. But what the devil do you make of it? It seems enchantingly vague."

"I think that the royal personage and the place are both merely 'cover'. I suggest the only important thing in this message is the date," answered Archie. "All it means is that the supply of drugs will be available in the usual place, or in the usual way, on the date mentioned. Evidently in the case of the Hereditary Duchess some hitch occurred, and it was necessary to alter the date from a Monday to a Tuesday. It's a delightfully simple code, because you can always drag Royalty into the news, and the Crown Prince of Kossovia blunder was pure carelessness."

Bray looked despondent. "I'm afraid you're right. So it can't really help us very much."

"It suggests one very odd point, though," Archie reminded him. "Why the devil do they use this extraordinarily clumsy apparatus of a foreign paper to deliver their message? It means, of course, that they've got a friend on the *Gazette* staff, presumably the man who edits that particular column. But, even so, why rely on a French paper? The obvious thing to do would have been a 'Personal' in *The Times* or the *Daily Telegraph*. A very silly message would have done: 'Babs. Meet at the usual place on Thursday. Hector', for instance. It would have been just as effective as the *Gazette* business and much cheaper and less suspicious."

"I take it you are suggesting I ought to visit Paris?"

"I fear so." Archie turned to the bearded man who was writing quietly at a desk. "I say, Georges, do you know anything about the *Gazette*—anything to its discredit particularly?"

"A rash question to ask about any French paper," said Georges, removing his pince-nez to tap his teeth with them. "But its political activities are no more and no different from those of most papers of that particular *bloc*. A little subsidy, no doubt. It changed hands a few months ago, if that interests you."

"Yes, I thought I remembered Romain having sold it. Who was the buyer?"

"That I do not know. Ferrand, their correspondent here, says the rumour is it was bought by some rich American who lives in Paris. But he admits this is only a rumour."

"Thanks, Georges." Archie waved a casual farewell. "Give my regards to Paul if you see him. There you are, Bernard. That's something to bite on. Now where does this ghastly net of intrigue have its source?"

"Baston," Bray told him. "Inspector Creighton is in charge of the case. But for Heaven's sake don't let on that I put you on his track. You found it out yourself, remember."

"I shall be as discreet as always. Baston? I can't remember any murder there." Archie wrinkled his brows. "Our local correspondent must be pretty dead. We've never had a bleat from that quarter."

"Well, it's all yours, my boy. But keep my name out of it."

"Of course. I don't wish to be flung into the *oubliettes* of Scotland Yard, to be tortured by nice policemen in dress suits. Cheerio. I must be getting back to work."

*   *   *   *   *

Creighton, while his London colleague was trying to discover the import of the newspaper they had pursued to Glasgow, was busy on trails leading more directly to the murder of Furnace.

Creighton himself was not, of course, satisfied that the innocence of Gauntlett's Air Taxis had been proven even negatively. On the contrary, his suspicions had been awakened by the sudden appearance of Miss Sackbut at Sankport. Moreover, he thought it still more strange, in the light of his new suspicions, that it should have been through Valentine Gauntlett that the revolver had been found embedded in the aerodrome surface. His mind had recurred to this because on his return from Glasgow he had found a letter from the Home Office expert confirming Creighton's belief that this revolver had fired the bullet which had killed Furnace.

Creighton, therefore, was really back at the old position. Irrespective of drugs or letters from Furnace, Miss Sackbut was the only person who had the time and opportunity to shoot Furnace. It was still necessary to prove motive. He had, he admitted, been relying on the drug distribution for this. But as far as Bray was concerned—and Bray had been his main hope—this had proved impossible to follow up. Therefore he needed some fresh evidence to connect the two incidents. He still believed there was a connection. At this point Creighton decided to go down again to Baston Aerodrome.

He ran down in his baby car and was just about to go into the club-house when the Bishop came towards him with all the appearance of flying from some real and urgent danger.

"Creighton! Talk to me! Lead me aside! Save me from that accursed woman!"

The Inspector observed the unmistakable figure of the Countess of Crumbles on the skyline, and understood much.

"Why, come to that, my lord, I *should* like a word with you!"

"Walk rapidly away with me," said Dr. Marriott agitatedly. "That woman is determined to get me on her Executive Committee, and I am equally determined not to join. At the same time, I have promised Miss Sackbut not to offend Lady Crumbles, although, upon my soul, I shall find it exceedingly difficult to comply with that promise." The Bishop was looking really frightened, and Lady Crumbles was now almost within hailing distance. She showed every sign of being about to hail.

"Lady Crumbles is very difficult to dodge, my lord. She was a patroness of our last Policemen's Theatricals, and I had some experience of her."

"I am absolutely determined to avoid her," said the Bishop decisively. "There must be some place at least where she will not pursue us. I think I shall go and wash my hands.

"No hot water!" exclaimed the Bishop a little later. "That's what happens when Miss Sackbut goes away. Well, well! Now, Inspector, you have kept very close during the last few days. Have you no clues? Or is it policy? Far be it from me to attempt to force myself into your confidences, but, none the less, I do feel entitled to be apprised of any really grave discovery in view of my original part in detecting the affair." The Bishop hesitated, then he smiled at the Inspector. "To be perfectly frank also, I have other objects in asking you. I have been thinking over the whole case more often than I care to admit, and various interesting possibilities occur to me that it would be as well to explore."

"Well, in a sense we've got further, and in a sense we haven't," answered Creighton cautiously. "Now, my lord, you've got some medical knowledge, as we know, and a deal of observation, as you've shown. You've met most of the members here. Would you say that any of them were drug addicts?"

"Good gracious me!" exclaimed the clergyman, dropping a nailbrush in his surprise. "I certainly should not! A most healthy lot of youngsters, and though certainly I might sometimes wish they would drink a little less and be somewhat less boisterous, I saw not the slightest evidence of any degeneracy. On the contrary. Dismiss it from your mind, Inspector. But what suggested it in the first place?"

"Undoubtedly the motive for the murder is tied up in some way with drugs," asserted the detective. "Furnace was blackmailing someone before he died; we have proof of that. He took a sample of a certain powder to be analysed shortly before his death and it proved to be cocaine. He accounted to the analyst for his possession of it by a fatuous story. As you see, this blackmail at once provides a motive for the murder, and we are trying to establish a connection between Furnace, this club, and the drug traffic. We thought at first that there might be some method of aerial distribution, but our first researches in that respect have been fruitless, I am afraid."

"These are large accusations, Inspector, against a man of Furnace's unblemished record," said the Bishop in his most solemn manner. "On what grounds do you suggest that he was a blackmailer?"

"For the last two years his income has been swelled by large, irregular payments in cash which cannot be accounted for in any other way."

The Bishop considered this carefully. "That is something, but not everything. On what grounds do you suppose this was accounted for by blackmail?"

"Because of his interview with the analytical chemists. He obviously came on this powder accidentally, but in a way that aroused his suspicions. His suspicions proved well founded. Yet he did not reveal his knowledge to the police, in spite of his promise to do so. Therefore he must have been making use of that knowledge for some unlawful purpose—namely, blackmail."

"Excellent reasoning."

"Thank you, my lord."

"Unfortunately, it has a flaw which renders it fallacious."

"Ah?" said the Inspector, a little nettled at the ecclesiastic's positive tone.

"You say he had been drawing blackmail for two years. You say he only took this sample—in ignorance—to the chemist's a few days before his death. Therefore this occasion was the first time he knew it was cocaine, and there could be no connection between the two. Therefore the drug had nothing to do with the blackmailing, so far as we know. Therefore doubt is thrown even upon the hypothesis that the source of the money is blackmail."

Inspector Creighton blushed. "Believe it or not, my lord, I completely overlooked that. Completely! Good gracious me! Really, you have a remarkable brain."

The Bishop waved the hairbrush, with which at the moment he was sleeking his greying but abundant hair, in a gesture of disavowal. Then he looked sharply at the policeman with a sudden distrust. But there was no hint of mockery in the Inspector's impassive face. "Logic is still part of the equipment of a theologian," said the Bishop. "The flaw in the syllogism was obvious."

The Inspector gave a despondent sigh. "That brings us back to where we were then, doesn't it? And very difficult it makes it too."

"It does." The Bishop considered it a good time to administer a kindly rebuke. "Particularly as I feel you are completely on the wrong track. Inspector, whatever the appearances, Miss Sackbut had no part in this."

"Of course not, my lord. I am sure no one would think so," answered the policeman with a hurt expression.

"I am not such a fool as I look," said the Bishop impatiently. "It is obvious to a mean order of intelligence that you not only suspect Miss Sackbut, but suspect her alone."

The Inspector hesitated. "It's very difficult," he said more humanly. "You see, I can't get away from the fact that the only person who had access to Furnace between the time the body was out of the hands of those three and the time that it came under your supervision was Miss Sackbut."

"Isn't that almost a point in her favour?" pressed the Bishop astutely. "After all, surely no murderer would murder someone when it was a proven fact that she was the only person able to do it?"

"I'm not so sure. The other circumstances of the murder suggest that there was a desperate need for Furnace to be finished off. And desperate needs don't wait for alibis."

"We still have no inkling of the desperate need," the Bishop reminded him. "Even the possibility of Furnace having discovered a plot which caused his crash is ruled out by the Air Ministry's evidence."

"*I* don't rule it out, expert or no expert," answered Creighton irritably. "Otherwise, the whole business is absolutely inexplicable."

"I feel it is that, anyway. There is, also, another point which I must say you seem to have overlooked. So far you have established five possible murderers." The Bishop raised his plump hand and spread the fingers. "One, two, and three: Randall, Vane, and Ness (but if so they must have worked in co-operation); four: Miss Sackbut; five: myself."

"Oh, my lord!" protested the Inspector.

"Five: myself," insisted the Bishop. "At all costs let us be logical. But you have forgotten one other possibility. It occurred to me when I was reviewing the case in my mind at a time when, I admit, I might have been better occupied."

"And who is that, if I may ask?" The Inspector's eyes were very watchful.

"The person or persons who *may* have come upon Furnace between the time when the 'plane crashed and the ambulance arrived on the scene."

"That's a fact! I must say I never thought of that. You do have some ideas, my lord. But there's not much time, is there?" Again the Bishop looked at the policeman to see if he was being sarcastic, and again encountered the blank wall of Creighton's face.

"Quite enough. Let us assume the person who planned the murder was watching its effect concealed at the far end of the aerodrome. Furnace crashes. The person rushes up to see that all is well. He sees there is some sign of consciousness. So he murders Furnace and makes his getaway. Or possibly he conceals himself. Upon my soul," said the Bishop, temporarily carried away by his imagination, "the murderer may have been watching us at the very moment we were dragging Furnace out of the 'plane!"

The Inspector nodded. "I like that theory, my lord. But, you see, it brings us back to the same difficulty. What was the scheme which brought a perfectly sound aeroplane out of the air at the murderer's feet, as you might say, dead against what the Air Ministry allows to be possible?"

Dr. Marriott waved the objection aside. "I leave that to you. But, you see, Miss Sackbut is by no means the inevitable suspect. I do assure you, Inspector, that no girl who can do a half-roll off the top of a loop as neatly as that girl could be guilty of such a crime. I, sinner that I am, cannot even land a Moth."

"Each to his trade, my lord. No doubt she would make a precious poor hand of a sermon, now," answered the Inspector solemnly, "or at detecting the flaws in a—syllogism, was it?"

"Possibly, possibly; but certainly not so bad in her way as flying is in mine."

The Inspector, however, was pertinacious, and refused to allow the Bishop to change the subject. "You still haven't given me your opinion, my lord. Do you think that someone did kill Furnace in those few minutes?"

The prelate smiled blandly. "Well, well, that's a difficult decision. What do you think of Bastable?"

The Inspector was momentarily baffled by the twistings of the other's mind. "Bastable? Oh, he's very hard-working and respected. Been the police surgeon for years. Very well liked locally."

"A worthy man, yes, certainly. But just a *little* bit of a fool, I fear, Creighton, and too slap-dash in his methods. These busy G.P.'s so often are. It's not my business, of course, except to suffer people of his kind gladly, as the Apostle advised, but if I were in your position I should get further medical advice on that bullet wound in Furnace's head—if it's not too late, that is. Isn't there some central organization?"

"The Home Office?"

"Ah, that's it. Yes, the Home Office. Now, if you were to get them to consult with Bastable … It might be difficult to do it without hurting his feelings. Perhaps you could raise some fresh point you need medical advice on? Of course, don't say I suggested you should do so."

Creighton looked at the other shrewdly. "That's your opinion, is it, my lord? Well, I think I can do it easily enough. H'm, very interesting. Thank you."

"Not at all. I hardly know why I suggest it," answered Dr. Marriott airily. "Well, I think we might venture out now. The Crumbles peril should have gone now. How I dislike that woman, Inspector; clean against all Christian charity! Dear me, I shall be late for the navigation classes. A very interesting subject, navigation, Inspector. But a very intricate one!"

CHAPTER XI

SCOTLAND YARD IN PARIS

BRAY had been given an introduction to Monsieur Jules Durand, of the Paris Sûreté. Durand's prosaic name is associated with some of the most wildly romantic trials of French criminology, and Bray appreciated the honour when, on sending in his letter of introduction, Durand himself came down to meet his British *confrère* and showed him into his pleasant little office.

The Frenchman placed his time and attention unreservedly at the disposal of his distinguished colleague. He hoped Monsieur Bray would do him the favour of being his honoured guest during Bray's stay in Paris.

Bray accepted all this with thanks.

"And now, dear friend, what criminal have you tracked to our city?" Durand, bulky, but with a neat little moustache, and pink-and-white features as smooth and delicate as the face of a wax doll, pushed across a cigarette-box. Then he lay back in his chair to listen to his colleague with the reverent concentration of a devotee of music. "I seem to remember your name in connection with one or two famous drug-traffic cases?" he murmured. "Were you not commended by Russell Pasha in a recent report?"

Bray was flattered, being unaware of Durand's quick call through to Records on receipt of the letter of introduction.

"It is on a drug-traffic case that I am in Paris now," he admitted. "I believe that this French newspaper I have here is being used to give messages about the drug traffic to British addicts.

How or why such an elaborate device has been employed I cannot understand. In fact, I have come over to investigate just this point. The cuttings I have pinned to the paper explain the story, I think."

Durand silently took the copy of the paper and the cuttings. When he opened it and saw the title, however, he was unable to repress a little exclamation.

But he said no more and read through the cuttings. Then he looked up with a grin. "A strange affection for Royalty! Snobs, these criminals! What do you make of it? A code of some sort, of course, but a rather unusual one."

"Undoubtedly a code, and I believe it to mean nothing more than that the drug is available at the usual place on the date mentioned in connection with the Royalty."

"And you hope to find out more over here? I am puzzled, my friend. *La Gazette Quotidienne* is a paper of the utmost respectability, neither Socialist nor Royalist, and much read by civil servants and teachers."

"Didn't it change hands recently?"

"You seem to know much already. It did. Naturally, such things are of importance to us; perhaps even more important than in your country, so we will know all about it." He lifted his telephone. "Charles? The *Gazette Quotidienne* dossier, if you please. Monsieur Bray, I hope if you continue your investigations you will use the extremest discretion. I know you will, of course, but I mention it because in the affair of a newspaper these enquiries are delicate here. They would have the ear of our superiors, you understand, if they wish to complain."

"You needn't worry," Bray reassured him. "I shall make my enquiries entirely independently, and it needn't even be known that I consulted you."

"Excellent. Ah, here is the dossier. It was two years ago that this change of ownership took place. Well, here we have something interesting. It seems we do not yet know who the real proprietor is. It has been bought by Maurice Roget, who is a *notaire* of whom we know nothing but good, but it is plain that he is the agent of another man. In fact, I see from our notes here that he has said so in conversation with the staff, and has even stated that the principal is a rich American."

"That's the story I heard over in England," admitted Bray. "It is self-evident he was rich to have bought it, and as even to-day Americans are often rich, it doesn't really help us much."

"Not necessarily rich," qualified Durand. "The control of the *Gazette* is vested in a fairly small *compagnie anonyme*, but the bulk of the capital was provided by debentures. Roget has only bought the *compagnie*, which might not have been expensive. In any case, French newspapers are on a much smaller scale than yours, with their fabulous circulations and insurance against twins. Besides, although the *Gazette* has been established so long, it is one of the smallest Parisian dailies."

"We're up against another mystery here, then. Bit curious, isn't it?"

Durand smiled. "Perhaps—perhaps not. There are many mysteries in Parisian journalism. But it does not follow that they are concerned with the drug traffic."

"Now, look here, Durand, I suppose you are on friendly terms with the members of the Press?"

"Profoundly so."

"Can you give me an introduction to some journalist who knows most of them? I leave it to you whether you introduce me to him as an English journalist—a part I could, I think, sustain with a foreigner—or whether you tell this man the truth, but to the staff of the *Gazette* I certainly wish to appear as a journalist."

"I understand. I know the very man—André Clair. I will tell him the truth—it is better—and he will help you more."

André Clair, a lean, fragile-looking exquisite, with a gay wit, proved more than helpful. Bray explained that he was particularly anxious to meet the man who looked after the suspect column in *La Gazette*. Clair decided that would be, unquestionably, Molineux, the social editor, for the column, as could be seen, was mainly social and personal news. Molineux was often to be found at the Café Hongrois. Clair would take Bray, and if Molineux was there the introduction could be effected as by chance. The rest he would leave to Bray.

Clair seemed thoroughly to enjoy the whole affair, and his start of surprise on seeing Molineux was almost too good to be true, as was his little panegyric on the virtues of his *confrère*, Bernard Bray.

Bray's French, though sound, was not really good enough to join in the pleasant badinage which Clair was gaily exchanging with Molineux, studded as it was with political personages referred to only by their nicknames. Instead, he devoted himself to studying Molineux, who was a tall, gaunt-featured, fair-haired Norman type. Of course, the physiognomy of a foreigner is always difficult to read, but Molineux did not look anything of a criminal. On the contrary.

Bray's chance ultimately came when Molineux was chaffing Clair about some mis-statement in his dramatic criticism. Bray joined in, as light-heartedly as his French permitted.

"Even *La Gazette Quotidienne* is not always impeccable. I noticed in mine, as I came over three days ago, that the Crown Prince of Kossovia was to open a cycling championship to-morrow, but he has the ill grace to decide to stay in South America."

Molineux laughed. "I absolutely refuse responsibility."

"Come, come, Jules," said Clair, taking the cue, "you can't. I know that column is under your care because you have been so truly kind as to publish in it little paragraphs about an actress friend from time to time."

"And this is the thanks I get!" smiled Molineux. "But it is true. You see, I have a proprietor with queer whims. He sends me little batches of paragraphs—about his friends, no doubt, or people he hopes to make his friends—and all these have to go in, at the top of the column. And who is better entitled to dictate such matters than the proprietor?"

"But at least one corrects the proprietor's errors," suggested Bray. "Or can he do no wrong?"

"That is the drollest part of it. Once he stated that some tiresome woman, the Hereditary Duchess of Georgina, I fancy, was to do something on a date I knew to be wrong. I altered it to the right one. My God, the trouble that caused, the panic, in fact! I have never heard such language as Maître Roget used to me—passed on, it seems, as it came hot from the proprietor on the London-Paris telephone. Since then those paragraphs go in without query."

"An odd fish, your proprietor," said Bray. "What is he like?"

"I haven't the remotest idea," said Molineux carelessly. "He is almost a legend. He is always on the point of coming to the office to visit the staff, but he never does. He is a rich American, we are told, but who he is and what is his name are matters I am as ignorant of as you."

After he had finished his *déjeuner* and bade farewell to the two journalists, Bray went for a leisurely stroll in the Bois de Boulogne to think. He was baffled by what he had heard. Assuming Molineux spoke the truth, it was not a case of a member of the staff being tampered with from the outside. On the contrary, the responsibility for that receded to the proprietorship itself. Some colour at least was lent to this by the fact that the proprietor was unknown even to the Sûreté, and had taken careful precautions to remain in the background. The rich American sounded a myth. He was the sort of person to whom eccentricities might be more safely attributed in Paris. But then why this fantastically complex and expensive machinery to publish a message which could have been put in *The Times* for fifteen shillings? And why, and how, suborn a Parisian *notaire* with a reputation?

Of course, Molineux might have been lying. He might have suspected Bray, even known his name as a detective, though that was extremely unlikely. If he had, however, it would be plausible that he had tried to clear himself by throwing the blame on an innocent but obscure proprietor. Yet Bray hardly believed that. The explanation had come so simply and instantaneously, without a change in tone or expression.

After all, now he came to think it over, perhaps the new explanation was not so fantastic. For while it was extraordinary to imagine that a dope organization should have gone to the trouble of tampering with the staff of a French newspaper merely to send messages to English customers, it was more understandable if in some way the proprietorship was already mixed up in the game. But how?

It was a lovely day and the air of Paris was going to Bray's head. He was beginning to feel dangerously untrammelled of the official restrictions which sat so heavily upon him in England. He therefore decided on a step he would never have dared to take in London. He decided to interview Roget under an assumed personality.

The lawyer's name was, he found, in the telephone directory, and he presented himself with assurance. To the clerk who interviewed him in the ante-room of the suite of offices occupied by the *notaire* he said curtly: "I come on business connected with the Crown Prince of Kossovia. That should be sufficient for your master."

It was. It secured him instant admission to a puzzled little man with the lined forehead and lips of the lawyer, a physiognomy that transcends national boundaries.

"To what can I attribute the honour of this visit? Are you a member of His Royal Highness's suite?"

Bray nodded. When it was necessary to depart from the way of honesty, he still believed in telling as much of the truth as was practicable, and he now said: "I am an enquiry agent. I have been in the British Police Force. My name is Bray—Bernard Bray."

"None is finer than the British Police Force," said Maître Roget pleasantly.

Bray bowed. "Thank you. I came primarily about this." He produced from a wallet the *Gazette* cutting relating to the Crown Prince's activities. "You will see it states here that His Royal Highness is to open a cycling championship to-morrow. He is, however, in South America, and it is plainly impossible for him to do so."

Roget looked suitably apologetic after glancing at the cutting. "I am very distressed by this error. As you will appreciate, these mistakes will occur with all newspapers. If you will have the goodness to communicate with the editor-in-chief, the mistake will be rectified in to-morrow's issue."

Bray bowed again. "If that were the only purpose of my visit, the task would have been carried out by one of the Prince's equerries. No, monsieur, the matter is serious." Bray lowered his voice. "You will appreciate that an announcement of this nature, which will induce many people to expect the Prince, but without success, may compromise his popularity in this country."

"Surely not!" smiled Roget.

"But yes. His advisers cannot help supposing some malicious influence is at work here."

The lawyer looked genuinely startled. "Monsieur! A journalist's error! Surely you are taking too grave a view?"

"Not without reason, I assure you. Preliminary investigation has convinced me that the paragraph was not written in your office, but came from your proprietor."

Maître Roget smiled weakly. "My compliments to the British Police Force. You are very acute. It may be the source of the paragraph, although I was not aware of it. But I assure you there is no element of malice."

"Who is your proprietor?" pressed Bray.

The lawyer's lips closed firmly. "I regret to say that I cannot communicate the name of my client without permission."

Bray managed an expressive shrug. "It is very strange. The Prince's advisers will hardly be satisfied."

"I am desolated, monsieur. But the mistake was made in all innocence, I assure you. May I suggest that a statement to the effect that the Crown Prince is still in South America, despite erroneous rumours to the contrary, should be inserted in our next issue? Perhaps even a column article on the Crown Prince, appreciative in tone? The Prince's Press agent could write what he liked."

Bray felt he was getting no further. In spite of his preconceived ideas, he was impressed by Roget, who showed every sign of being what he purported and was reputed to be, a lawyer of good reputation and practice. Moreover, it was quite plain that Roget's client, if such a person existed, had been absolute in his demands for secrecy. If, on the other hand, his client was a myth, then Roget would be even less informative.

"Naturally, such an *amende honorable* would be a token of good faith," answered Bray cautiously.

"I will ensure it this instant," exclaimed the lawyer, brightening, and went into the outer office.

Bray glanced idly about him, and fell to looking closely at the papers on Roget's desk. One in particular caught his eye—a letter from England sent by air mail and marked "Urgent".

He hesitated a moment. A fatal moment, for at the end of it he swept the letter into his pocket with hardly a protest from his conscience.

Shortly afterwards Roget returned. "I have seen to that. Express my extreme regrets to the Prince's secretary. Ah, monsieur, as you say in your own idiom, 'it is not all jam' being responsible for the conduct of a newspaper. None of my other trusts gives me one-tenth the trouble."

With a rather guilty feeling as his conscience stirred, Bray returned to his room in M. Durand's flat and carefully opened the letter. Inside it was an enclosure, addressed to "M. Maurice Grandet, The Foreign Publisher, *La Gazette Quotidienne*. (Private and Personal.)"

The enclosure, which was heavily sealed, was accompanied by a letter. It was in English, and read:

101, *Banchurch Street,*
London, E.C.4.

Dear M. Roget,
    Please see that these instructions are delivered into M. Grandet's hands this afternoon in the usual way.

Yours sincerely,
Theodosius Vandyke.

Bray made a note of the address, which looked like that of an office in the City, and then proceeded, with the same regrettable lack of compunction, to lift the seal of the enclosure with a hot knife. The message he read was brief enough.

The next consignment to be on Friday.

The Chief.

Before he went down to dinner he strolled out to a newsagent and arranged for a copy of *La Gazette Quotidienne* to be delivered to him next morning. He then retired to his room and began to think hard. "Consignment" irresistibly suggested the drug he was searching for. But how could it be despatched when he had already ascertained the impossibility of doing this? Perhaps some other method of distribution was used. At least, it seemed that Roget was the channel of some mysterious communication between the paper and some persons unknown, and that the proprietor was not a myth. Who, then, was Theodosius Vandyke? Was it a *nom de guerre*? Or was he the proprietor, or the man's secretary? And was "The Chief" the same person? Or was he yet another member of the organization? And did his pseudonym mean that he was the head of the organization?

He examined the curious paper on which the inner message was written. It was an orange-coloured paper, and when Bray held it up to the light he noted an elaborate watermark which could hardly be the makers' trademark, and suggested to him that it might be a kind of guarantee of the authenticity of an important message and therefore known to all members of the organization. The letter to Roget, which was typewritten on ordinary business paper, was of little use, but he wrote out at once a telegram to his assistant, Sergeant Finch:

Make enquiries about occupation age address past history nationality Theodosius Vandyke 101 Banchurch Street E.C.4.—Bray.

Bray opened his paper eagerly next morning, and at the top of the now familiar column he saw, with a quickening of interest, that H.R.H. Prince Francis of Dayreuth was leaving Cannes on Friday.

Durand teased him with his preoccupation at breakfast, and Bray looked grave.

"The fact of the matter is, Durand, that I ought to be moving from here."

"My dear friend!" said the Frenchman reproachfully.

"Yes, indeed, sad as it will be for me. But my presence may well be embarrassing. I have committed one illegal action in this pleasant city of yours, and I am turning over in my mind more illegal ones. It would be annoying if there were complaints made and it turned out that the person complained about was the guest of that shining light of the Sûreté, M. Durand!"

Durand laughed. "Yes, it might be awkward. But perhaps it can be avoided. What is your problem?"

Bray told him.

The Frenchman did not seem at all perturbed by the theft of the letter from Roget's desk. "A bagatelle. But what were you proposing to do with the letter afterwards?"

"I was thinking of restoring it, sealed up again, of course. I could visit Roget on the pretext of expressing the satisfaction of the Crown Prince's *aide*, and leave the letter behind then. It is obviously important that it gets to its destination, so that no suspicions are aroused."

"And what further crimes did you contemplate?" asked Durand.

"I had in mind to break into this precious publishing office somehow and try to find the stuff on the premises. Obviously Grandet, whoever he is, is in the thick of the business."

"But I do not see why we of the Sûreté should not get a search warrant ourselves, on information received from you."

Bray looked a little embarrassed. "It is very kind of you, Durand, but that is just what I don't want. To be perfectly frank, the English end is the only one I'm interested in. It won't help me if we break up the French organization and leave the English end intact. I can follow this dope from France to England if the French group is left undisturbed. But first I must get some assurance that it really is here, and some inkling how it gets through to England."

Durand thought for a moment, the play of his famous brain almost visible on his delicate features. Then he smiled. "I have it, my dear Bray, to perfection! A scheme that needs finesse, courage, and tact, but you have all of these. Listen!"

Bray listened and was enchanted.

*   *   *   *   *

Bray, looking a little slovenly in old flannel trousers and a tweed jacket, was soon directed to the publishing office of the *Gazette*. This, it appeared, was separate from the editorial offices. He went up to the trade counter and asked boldly for Grandet.

The office boy told him confidently that M. Grandet was not accessible to strangers, but Bray sent in a message that he, Robinson, had a letter from England which could only be delivered personally into Grandet's own hands. The office boy presently returned to take him to Grandet. This meant climbing several stairs and walking down a long corridor, through a door marked "*Abonnements Étrangers*", and into a dusty little office.

Grandet was an impressive individual at first sight, with a broad white face and a mane of silver hair that gave him a leonine aspect. Close inspection revealed very thin lips, a weak chin and the pinched, decided nose of the selfish egoist. Bray placed him as the first really criminal-looking type he had struck in his efforts to establish a dope organization in connection with *La Gazette Quotidienne*.

Grandet looked at him with close attention, and then took the envelope Bray offered him, which had been the enclosure in the letter to Roget.

He examined the seal carefully, and this for a moment made Bray anxious, but he felt sure that his and Durand's joint efforts in this respect had been good. Grandet, too, seemed to be satisfied and tore open the envelope without remark.

Between them, Durand and Bray had altered "The Chief's" laconic message. Plenty of room had been left between the signature and the message, and it had thus been possible to add a few words with a typewriter of similar make and ribbon colour. Scrutiny with a lens would reveal a difference in alignment, but it was permissible to suppose that Grandet would not carry suspicion to that length. The message now read:

The next consignment to be on Friday. Robinson, the bearer of this note, is to travel with it. He knows everything and can be trusted.

The Chief.

Grandet read the note and then opened a drawer and removed from it a sheet of orange-coloured paper, identical in appearance to that which bore "The Chief's" message. He held the two sheets of paper to the light, one on top of the other, evidently to confirm the perfect register of the watermarks. This proved the accuracy of Bray's guess that the watermark was a kind of guarantee of authenticity.

He now gave Bray a perfunctory smile and extended his hand. "The message is late, Mr. Robinson. The notice to subscribers has already appeared in *La Gazette*, and I am surprised that the circulation department was not informed first."

"There were difficulties," said Bray with a studied vagueness. "It was considered advisable, for some reason I do not know, not to send the message through the usual channels."

"I see. I am disturbed to hear it. It is strange this idea also, for you to travel through with the consignment." Grandet's uplifted eyebrows invited further explanation.

"There is reason. There is just a possibility of an attempt at robbery—not by the authorities, you understand, but by enemies."

Grandet made a clucking noise. "That is regrettable. I trust the Chief will deal with the matter. It is not a danger we want even to risk. You will be armed?"

Bray nodded.

"You must report here at two a.m. on Friday. I shall not be present, but my assistants will be. One will wait for you outside. He will see you into the van, and then our department's responsibilities will, I hope, be over."

"Certainly," Bray reassured him.

"While you are here, I had better take you in to see my assistants, so that they will recognize you on Friday."

"You are admirably cautious, monsieur."

"It is necessary in the foreign publishing business," said Grandet dryly. "This way."

Grandet led him to a flight of stairs marked with injunctions of privacy. They went up these and came to a door on which was a small notice:

Bureau de la Poste Aérienne Défense à Entrer

Grandet gave a peculiar knock and opened the door, which, Bray noticed, it was necessary for him to unlock first with a key he took from his watchchain. Four men were inside, in trousers and dirty shirt-sleeves, whom Bray instinctively placed as the dregs of the Paris underworld.

He looked quickly and unobtrusively round him. A shelf on one wall was burdened with a row of large stone jars. Scissors, paste-brushes, brown paper, string, and copies of *La Gazette* were strewn about the floor. Almost immediately Grandet introduced him to the smallest of the four men. This was a fellow with a little bristly beard and one glass eye which looked heavenward with a pious fixity contrasting somewhat oddly with the fierce cast of the rest of his features.

"This is Mr. Robinson, Leon," said Grandet. "He is a representative of the firm. He will travel with a consignment to England to-morrow. He has been sent to us by headquarters. Look at him carefully. He will meet you at two a.m. on Friday. Put him into the van and leave the rest to him."

The man looked at Bray with his sound eye and nodded. "Very well, Grandet. And, look here; about the German consignment to-morrow—is that definite?"

"Certainly," said Grandet. "You will have to work hard to get it through in time. You were ten minutes late with the Swiss packages this morning."

"The printers were late," grumbled the little man.

"That is hardly an excuse. It is an extremely small consignment. Remember this is a newspaper, and newspapers are always punctual about consignments. It is not only myself—you know the High Command is ruthless about efficiency, and rightly so. We have a reputation for our foreign publishing, and shall probably get a complaint from the Chief to-morrow."

"Cattle," muttered Grandet a little later to Robinson, who had maintained a discreet silence, as they went down the stairs again. "A pity we have to employ them. This way out."

When Bray got home, he found a long telegram waiting for him from Sergeant Finch.

Called on Theodosius Vandyke's office. This appears to be little more than an accommodation address. No one there. Charwoman told me office is rarely used. Porter said Vandyke is pleasant-spoken young man believed to be American. Seems to be rich. When he wants secretarial help he gets it from a bureau. Turns up not more than once a week and then only for an hour or so. Address not known. Landlord referred me to M. Roget notary of Paris as Vandyke's agent. This end you will look after I suppose. Vandyke calls himself an importer in

'phone book but not known to any of credit enquiry agencies.
Please advise me if further investigation required.

"I'll attend to that myself when I get back to England," Bray told himself that night.

He had acquainted Durand with the success of the plan, and the Frenchman was now inclined to be worried.

"Supposing they were to get into touch with the Chief between now and Friday and discover your fraud. It might be extremely dangerous!"

"There is hardly time," retorted Bray. "Besides, everything seems to point to communication with the Chief being one-sided. In any case, I must take my chance."

Durand looked at him with a worried frown. "At least let me put an agent on to watch you when you meet."

"Thanks awfully, Durand, but if they do anything it will be when I'm actually travelling with the stuff. And your agent won't be much use then!"

On Thursday evening Bray sent a further telegram to Sergeant Finch.

Find out all you can about Valentine Gauntlett head of Gauntlett's Air Taxis. Also Captain Randall the well-known pilot who is Gauntlett's partner. Criminal record or associations of Gauntlett if any particularly important.—Bray.

This done he slept, and rose at the unearthly hour of 1 a.m. to dress and keep his appointment. Its hooter silent in deference to Paris's bye-laws, his taxi swept like a ghost through the streets.

He dropped it round the corner and walked to the office door, where the glass-eyed little man was waiting beside a van.

"I have arranged with the driver," he said to Robinson quietly. "Jump in."

The van reversed, turned, and the light from a lamppost shone on the scarlet and yellow colours of Gauntlett's Air Taxis.

Then Bray climbed in, and the French driver—a youngster with dark eyes and an ingenuous smile—sped like a demon through the quiet streets out to Le Bourget.

CHAPTER XII

INEVITABILITY OF SELF-MURDER

INSPECTOR CREIGHTON looked at Dr. Marriott with an air of stupefaction on his honest face which the ecclesiastic thought almost too good to be true.

"My lord, you amaze me, really you do! You seem to know more about this business than I do!"

The Bishop of Cootamundra endeavoured to look modest. "Ah, has my little suggestion proved fortunate? That interests me. What is the result?"

Inspector Creighton opened a drawer in his desk and pulled out a folder.

"Bastable agreed to consult with the Home Office expert," he explained. "I raised some small point as an excuse so as not to hurt his feelings. A query about the force of impact of the wound. … Then I dropped a quiet word to the Home Office man. He spotted something at once." Creighton looked at the Bishop impressively. "The revolver wound was made before the blow on the head was received!"

The Bishop nodded. "The possibility had occurred to me some time ago, and that was why I raised the point. It is the only hypothesis that makes sense after all."

"I'm glad it makes sense to you," exclaimed the detective. "I'm blessed if it does to me. For the Home Office fellow swears that it was the revolver bullet that killed Furnace, so that he must have been shot dead just before he hit the ground! No wonder he went such a bump against the cockpit dashboard. He would have been as limp as a sack. He must have been shot dead in the air. But how?"

"Not very difficult, surely?" ventured the Bishop.

"Not difficult—with him alone in the air and not another aeroplane near! Why, it seems to me impossible!"

"Only too possible," said the Bishop with a quiet smile. "I fear you have the whole story now, Inspector. You remember the letter Furnace wrote to Lady Laura?"

"I do. And very misleading it was too."

"On the contrary. It was the simple truth," answered Dr. Marriott gravely. "Furnace, poor fellow, did kill himself. He shot himself in the air. A touch of imagination that, which one must admire, although one reprehends the essential cowardice of the act. It was a suicide which was the airman's equivalent of the Viking's funeral: death in a crashing 'plane. He shot himself in the head, and fell back, pulling the 'stick' back with him. The machine stalled, and then span. In the spin the revolver doubtless fell out of the machine. If you make a search of the fields you will probably find it."

"I did find it—fallen in the middle of the aerodrome," admitted the Inspector.

"You see?" said the other triumphantly. "Additional proof! Well, he span into the ground, dead, and his forehead struck the dashboard, accidentally obliterating the original wound."

"Then there was no murder?" said Creighton with an air of disappointment.

"No, I am glad to say," replied the Bishop. "None. Have you the Home Office expert's estimate as to the time between the bullet wound and the dashboard wound?"

"Yes, here we are." Creighton picked up a few folio sheets of neat typescript. "He says one must have followed within about two minutes of the other, perhaps less. The blood had no time to coagulate before the head struck the dashboard. That, of course, is what led Bastable wrong, to give him his due. The Home Office man said that only microscopical examination of the tissues revealed what had happened, and any doctor would have made Bastable's mistake. But, of course, these doctors hang together so much anyway, and he may just have been saving Bastable's face. Bastable more or less admitted that he'd made a very hurried examination of the body as the whole thing seemed so obvious."

"Well, at any rate that is final," remarked the Bishop. "We were watching the machine, and we should certainly have seen if anyone was flying near enough to shoot him just before the crash."

"Certainly, my lord. But if you'll excuse me, aren't you leaving some loose ends? I mean, I shan't feel happy in my mind unless I clear up the matter of that extra money made by Furnace, for instance. And that cocaine."

"I refuse to regard those loose ends as important, Inspector," said Dr. Marriott firmly. "Still, how does this do? Furnace is making money for certain services rendered. He knows them to be illegal and consequently he gets heavily paid for them, but he does not know what their illegality consists in. However, just before his death he becomes suspicious, and, after investigation, finds they are connected with the drug traffic. Now lots of quite decent men think it perfectly legitimate to do illegal things—to cheat the Revenue, for instance. I can't feel very indignant about it myself when I get my income tax assessment. But there is something abhorrent about the drug traffic, with its trade in demoralizing human souls and drawing them into a slough of degeneracy. A decent man, such as I think Furnace to have been, may well have been horrified to find that he had concerned himself in such a filthy business. But he may have thought himself too deeply involved to be able to get out of it. And so he killed himself."

"Ay, that's about it," admitted the Inspector, as he turned it slowly over in his mind. "It all fits in."

He felt a little sorry that the fine case he was working on had turned out to be not much more than the verdict at the inquest stated it to be, but there would be satisfaction in presenting the Chief Constable with a solution in this tangled case that cleared up everything. Not everything, though, because there was still the matter of the cocaine that Furnace had found. There were drugs at Baston, how or why he did not know, but it was a matter that had to be cleared up. If only his little trip to Glasgow with Bray had solved the mystery!

"If there is nothing more, Inspector, I must be getting back." There was real misery in the Bishop's voice as he added: "There is a meeting of the Executive Committee to the Baston Flying Display, to which I now belong."

"I am sorry to hear it, my lord," said the Inspector simply, "but I saw it was bound to happen. I know Lady Crumbles!"

CHAPTER XIII

INTERESTING CONTENTS OF A NEWSPAPER

BRAY arrived at Le Bourget Aerodrome, and the van drove over the tarmac up to the scarlet and yellow biplane which was waiting for them, its two propellers flicking over with a quiet gurgle. A faintly familiar figure stood beside the biplane's nose, wearing a leather coat and grey trousers. As Bray came closer he recognized it. It was the same woman whom Creighton had tried to dodge at Sankport Aerodrome, Miss Sackbut he thought the name had been. She stared at him while the van-driver explained that he was to travel with the 'plane. Then she called to him.

"Hi, haven't I seen you before somewhere?"

"I don't think so," said Bray, hoping that the recognition would not be mutual.

"Funny, I thought I had. Where are you going, in front or in the cabin?"

"In the cabin," answered Bray without hesitation, and Miss Sackbut made no protest. The van was being unloaded. He watched carefully, but they put nothing but bundles of newspapers in the 'plane.

Was this the "consignment"? He felt oddly baffled, afraid that the fiasco of their Glasgow trip would be repeated.

Meanwhile Sally spoke.

"This is the second time I've had to do this damned early morning trip for Gauntlett," she explained confidentially. "Thorndike piled up in a car in Paris last night. Tough luck, wasn't it? I always seem to be the ministering angel in these affairs. I don't know why Gauntlett doesn't get a B licence himself for emergencies, he's had enough flying experience."

"What is the weather going to be like?" said Bray politely.

Sally eyed the dawn growing on the eastern sky. Layers of vapour were drifting in front of it like horizontal trails of chimney-smoke. "A bit sticky, I'm afraid. Damned early time to start off in doubtful weather. I shall take the long Channel crossing all the same. This compass is fairly decent and I trust these engines."

She looked at her watch. "We'd better be getting off now. ..."

Bray climbed into the cabin. The seats had been removed to make room for the bundles of newspapers which were scattered on the floor, but he piled one package upon another and made a seat of it.

The creaking rumble from the undercarriage faded into the shout of the engines as the grass sped past, fell away, tilted below the left wing-tip, and then fell away again. They were flying over the neat fields of France, still shadowed by the retreating fog of night.

The coastline, with the silver and gold edging of the Channel's low tide, opened ahead after about an hour's flying, with the sun, now risen, on the right. But Bray was oblivious of the view. He was carefully cutting the bundles of newspapers and examining their contents. His back was to the pilot, in case she glanced in at him through the window at the back of the cockpit.

He opened one and then gave a little gasp. ...

He took out two or three newspapers and folded them carefully into his inside pocket. Then he tied up the package from which he had taken them.

Meanwhile the Channel had dropped behind them, together with the chalk hills of Kent, cut off abruptly, like a relief map, and with a similar artificial regularity in their curves. Almost before he had time to work out the bearings of his discovery, he found himself staring at the letters SANKPORT on a green field, as they banked in a tight circle and slipped over the edge of the aerodrome towards the hangars and bumped over the ground to the Customs Office.

It was this part that interested Bray, and he stayed to watch it. Two Customs men came out, and with the most perfunctory of glances at the contents, scrawled their approval on them. Suddenly Bray realized how glaringly he had neglected the obvious. Of course, it was only necessary to have one pair of confederates, and wait till they were on duty to run the stuff through. … Bray thanked Sally for his trip and went into the waiting-room to 'phone for a taxi to the nearest station. He had breakfast in Victoria and then walked to New Scotland Yard. Here a message was awaiting him, marked "Urgent"—to come up at once and see Superintendent Learoyd. "Urgent" was not used lightly in the Yard, and he went up to the Superintendent's without waiting to take off his hat or coat.

Superintendent Learoyd was more troubled than Bray had ever seen him. Such a panic could only be aroused from "Up Above", and so it proved.

"Look here, Bray, what's this business about investigating Valentine Gauntlett's life to find if he has any criminal associations?

Your man, Finch, has been nosing around, and he said you told him to do so."

"They were my instructions, sir," answered Bray, surprised. "While I was in Paris following up a certain line of investigation, evidence came my way which seemed to throw considerable suspicion on Gauntlett. So I wired the usual message."

The Superintendent exploded with a kind of hissing noise, his grey moustache blowing away from his lips. "You delightful idiot! Do you realize who Gauntlett is?"

"No—since I gather from your tone that he is somebody important," replied Bray a little resentfully. "I know he is head of Gauntlett's Air Taxis, that's all."

"Oh, Bray, Bray!" implored the Superintendent. "Please read the Social and Personal column of *The Times*! Lord knows what trouble you may get us into. Valentine Gauntlett is our new Home Secretary's nephew. And we've been poking round at his house and so forth trying to find his criminal associations! Ye gods, if the Big Chief heard of it!"

"The Home Secretary's nephew!" echoed Bray, and the Superintendent was gratified to observe an expression of real and not perfunctory horror on his subordinate's face. Bray had not thought of associating Lord Entourage, formerly Sir Joseph Beatson, the pillar of Evangelicalism and Temperance and Anti-Gambling, with Valentine Gauntlett, but now he vaguely remembered that Entourage's sister had married some South African millionaire whose name began with a G. It probably was Gauntlett.

"Yes, the Old Man's nephew!" repeated the Superintendent grimly. "Can you conceive a more unlikely criminal! Do you realize he was left a couple of million in trust by his father? He even does a job of work, which shows he's a steady sort of fellow in spite of his wealth. Any more impossible candidate for our attentions I can't imagine."

"I'm afraid I'm going to give you a shock, sir," said Bray gravely. "My attention was directed to Gauntlett's Air Taxis because I found that his 'planes were distributing in this country copies of a French newspaper which had some connection with a dope organization. It took me a long time to trace the connection, but I found it—in Paris. I travelled over this morning on a Gauntlett Air Taxis 'plane, pretending to be a member of the organization. I took this out of some of the bundles of newspapers carried by that 'plane. It's just a sample. They were all the same."

After one glance at Bray's serious face, the Superintendent took a copy of that day's *La Gazette Quotidienne*. He opened it, and almost at once noticed that a sheet of newsprint had been pasted over the centre fold to make a kind of bag which bellied suspiciously. He split the belly with his fingers, and a shower of white powder fell out and sifted on to the worn carpet of the Superintendent's room. The Superintendent looked at Bray.

Bray nodded. "I'm afraid so. Dope! We'll have it analysed to make sure. But there can't be much doubt, can there?"

"I'm afraid not," admitted the Superintendent.

"And that's not all. There seems to be a murder mixed up with it down at Baston."

The Superintendent looked dismal. "Ye gods, Bray, this is going to be the most ghastly scandal! We've got to go through with it, but we must go carefully. Tell me the whole story as you know it."

Bray settled down in his chair and accepted a cigarette. "It's the story of the most complex international dope distribution organization I've ever heard of. Its source seems to be Paris, but who its head is I don't know. It appears to be a man who goes by the name of Vandyke, who, I fear, may prove to be Valentine Gauntlett. But it may not be so. For all I know as yet, Vandyke may be a tool for someone higher up."

"How does a newspaper come into it?" asked the Superintendent.

"They've chosen a newspaper for two reasons, as I see it. It gives an excuse for an international distribution by air, with the minimum of handling, for a parcel of newspapers is the kind of thing that can be rushed through without any query as to why there is a rush. Secondly, the advantage of the newspaper as a vehicle for a drug is that it can be bought openly by any kind of person without suspicion and that it can itself carry messages to the customer. For instance, of the various Customs men who come on duty at Sankport Aerodrome, two have been bought by the gang. No doubt this has been done in all the countries where the dope organization operates. Consequently the drugs can only be smuggled through on the days when these men happen to be on duty together. This day is known a short while beforehand, however, and a simple code message in the newspaper gives the date. No doubt it is a different code message for each country. So far I have only discovered the English message, which appears on the first Monday in the month, and always contains a reference to some royal personage. The subscriber then knows when the dope is to be contained in his daily newspaper and takes great care that he gets it on that day. On any other day it is a perfectly ordinary and respectable newspaper."

Superintendent Learoyd looked helplessly at the torn newspaper and nodded.

"The use of aerial newspaper deliveries has other advantages, of course," went on Bray. "It cleans the whole business up so quickly. The drug is in the hands of the customers all over Europe by the afternoon of the same day."

The Superintendent agreed. "That's smart; very smart. Our main hope in this drug traffic is that the stuff passes through so many hands and takes so long to reach the consumer. These people have got over that. But was it really necessary for the gang to buy a newspaper?"

"I think so," answered Bray. "The essence of the scheme was the delivery by air. But the only way you could make regular delivery by air without exciting suspicion is by delivering newspapers. No other goods are distributed by private charter regularly, and it would only ask for investigation suddenly to start delivering say, cigarettes by air, for it is obviously an uneconomic method. Once you admit the necessity of using newspapers, and actually concealing the drug in the newspapers, it is necessary to be in control of the publishing department at least. In fact, control of the newspaper is almost inevitable. And as they only bought the control, and not any other charges, it probably wasn't expensive. I suspect other reasons for buying the newspaper as well—reasons which explain why it was done from Paris."

The Superintendent pursed his lips. "Oh, I see. Politics. That makes it difficult, doesn't it?"

"I'm afraid it does. But we've always suspected it, haven't we? You remember that with the help of the League's Narcotics Bureau we proved conclusively that an enormous consignment of white drugs was being despatched to Paris from Macedonia every month, and we traced the O.K. to let it through to a certain politician not in the Ministry but possessing influence. *La Gazette* supports that politician through thick and thin, and I'm afraid——"

"That that was the price of the support? Quite. These things happen on the Continent," said the Superintendent with a lofty British pride. "But you remember we didn't worry much, because so long as it didn't get to England, it didn't concern us. But now that we find it is getting over here, it's serious," he reflected. "I say, Bray, what about finance? The expense of running this organization must be colossal?"

"Yes, but so must the revenue. I don't know how it works, but I rather expect that each drug addict pays a subscription to the paper. It might be one hundred pounds a year—it might be five hundred. We don't know. For this he gets some kind of token, possibly a card, possibly a password which is changed every so often. This entitles him to become a customer of one of the agents, of which no doubt there are a dozen or so in England, three or four in each large town. These agents are probably paid an annual capitation fee per head, according to the number of customers. Even if they were only paid ten pounds a head, there is no reason why it should not be extremely paying to be an agent, say, with a couple of hundred customers and no expenses.

"Then there is the cost of the central organization," the Superintendent reminded him.

"Yes, but the paper has a perfectly solid and respectable history," answered Bray, "except for its support of one politician, and it probably pays for itself. There is the foreign publisher, Grandet, and his four assistants to be looked after. They must be paid well as they handle the drug from the bulk to the distribution. Then there is the bribery of the Customs officers in each country—a pretty heavy item. And finally the expense of the aerial distribution. This must be the worst drain, but if they have several thousands of customers, as they seem to, they must be dealing in revenues of a million or more."

"All the pilots and van-drivers would have to be bribed heavily. That can't be cheap."

"No, it's a heavy expense. What is worse from the gang's point of view is that there are a large number of people who could give away the secret. It's the one defect in the plan, but inevitable, I suppose, in such a large-scale organization. And what an organization it is!" said Bray enthusiastically. "It really staggers one to think of the efficiency. The dope comes in in tons from Macedonia to the publishing office of the *Gazette*. The stuff is stored there, and almost every day it is slipped into copies of newspapers—for Germany one day, England another day, and so on. Before nightfall it's in the customers' pockets, scattered among towns hundreds of miles away. It makes ordinary business look inefficient!"

"H'm, yes," grunted Learoyd. "They're very dependent on their Customs men."

"Perhaps, but with so vast an organization as the Customs, and so much money at the gang's disposal, it's not surprising they can find two bad hats among them in a whole country."

"Supposing their two men got moved to another aerodrome?" queried the Superintendent.

"Quite simple. They find some excuse for the aeroplanes to make that their new port of entry. It's easy enough to change. I've found that an aeroplane from abroad on private charter can clear at any Customs airport, from Lympne to Manchester."

"It certainly sounds a foolproof system. How did we get on to it?" asked the Superintendent curiously.

"Pure accident," admitted Bray. "It looks as if one of their pilots threatened to squeal. Doing a bit of blackmail, I fancy, and pushed it too far. So they shot him and tried to hide it up. It got past the coroner as an accident, but Creighton, of the local constabulary—quite a smart man—found something fishy about it and investigated, and came across cocaine. Then he got on to me, and that started the whole business."

"Queer! It's the sort of accidental way these things do start. Now, Bray, you know the position, what do *you* think should be our plan of action?"

"It's probably the same plan as you are thinking of, sir, but for different reasons—going slow. We've got all the minor people in the organization in our hands. We could get them any time. First we must take the names of all the Gauntlett pilots and van-drivers engaged in the newspaper delivery, and one of the straight Customs men can make a note some day of the people these newspapers go to, when he is examining them. We already know the two

Customs men who are bribed. We can get all the warrants written out and ready.

"But I suggest that we don't do anything until we can pull in the big men. I'll write Durand of the Sûreté to-night so that he can do the same, and we'd better get in touch with our liaison men in Germany and Switzerland, and anywhere else where Durand finds the *Gazette* is distributed by air, so that the police there act in concert with us. These small fry don't matter much. When the time comes, we can sweep them all in together in a really big killing. What is really vital is that we catch the big men, particularly the Chief, who is a murderer as well, and I think that means sitting back a little."

"Do you think you can scare one of the small men into giving the Chief away?" said the Superintendent thoughtfully. "One generally can, you know."

"They may not know who the Big Noise is," objected Bray. "But I can try, of course. I'm not sure that it mightn't best be done from Creighton's end. You see, these little men, when they hear there's a charge of murder in the air, may get the wind up, which they wouldn't on an ordinary dope prosecution. I shall have to work in with Creighton in any case, because Baston Aerodrome must have a pretty close association with headquarters, even if Gauntlett isn't the Queen Bee. But I suspect he is."

"It'll be pretty ghastly for us if he is," said the Superintendent slowly. "It's bad enough for Durand, because he'll have to fight against this politician bloke who gets the stuff into the country for him. But the nephew of our new Home Secretary! Gosh!"

Bray hesitated. "You don't suspect … I mean it's not possible is it…?"

The Superintendent shook his head vigorously. "Of course not. Good lord, Entourage wouldn't buy a cigarette after hours to save his life! But what on earth possessed a man with money and reputation like Gauntlett to get mixed up in an affair of this kind?"

Bray shrugged his shoulders. "Excitement, I suppose. It's difficult to account always for what makes criminals criminal. It's generally a case of 'we needs must love the lowest when we see it', I think. Shall I go down to Baston?"

"Yes. But have a talk with me first, after you've got all your facts in order. I'll get our plan of action drafted and the arrangements with the French and foreign police generally all mapped out. We must take care that nobody hops it while we're waiting. It's going to take a lot of men, of course, but it's worth it. It'll be the biggest round-up of my time, at any rate. Is there anything you want done right away?"

"Yes, sir, I'd like Finch to get a few photos of Valentine Gauntlett from the news agencies and take them down to the people at Banchurch Street to see if they identify him as Vandyke. Let me see, he won some air race which ended at Baston the other day. There's sure to be a group of the prize-winners taken at the end of the race."

"Right-ho. I'll look after that. Sorry to have to take the main conduct out of your hands, Bray, but you see it's an international matter now. You'll get the credit. Bung down to Baston as soon as you can, there's a good chap. I'll wait in this evening till you're ready for handing over everything here to me, so that I can settle details with the Chief. I leave it absolutely to your discretion what you do down at Baston, subject to the usual reports. Do you get on with Creighton all right? It's technically his territory."

"He won't make any difficulty," said Bray decisively; "he's a decent old bird. I'll tell him enough to make him realize how important it is, and drop a hint that he'll get a share of the credit in the main round-up when it comes. In any case he's already brought us in by consulting me, you know, so there's no difficulty there."

"Good; and look here, Bray, if they murdered someone to prevent a squeal they must be pretty tough. So look after yourself."

Bray laughed and went. The Superintendent looked after him and sighed when the door closed.

CHAPTER XIV

END OF AN ENGINEER

"To think that all this should have come out of an accident on an aerodrome!" exclaimed Inspector Creighton, in the tones of one who has seen a ten-foot djinn rise out of a medicine bottle.

Bray had told him in brief outline of the organization that was behind Gauntlett's Air Taxis, and Creighton had listened with delighted attention. "Well, our trip to Glasgow wasn't wasted expense after all! I must tell the Superintendent that!"

"How have your investigations into the murder gone, Creighton?" asked the Scotland Yard man, with no great expectations from the answer.

"Far enough to prove it's no murder at all!" answered the other with relish.

"What! Look here, are you certain of your ground?" said Bray with a start.

"Perfectly. The Bishop and I worked it out together. It is the only possible explanation. These are the facts." Creighton held up one thick finger. "According to the Home Office expert—here's the report—Furnace was shot dead two minutes before he was wounded by the blow from the dashboard as his aeroplane crashed. Now that apparently admits of two possible explanations." The Inspector tentatively elevated two additional fingers. "One explanation is that he was shot at by a passenger or by someone flying near, and that the aircraft fell, out of control, and crashed, with its pilot already dead. But this explanation is positively contradicted by several circumstances. There were people watching the 'plane, and they are prepared to swear that no one was flying near it. There couldn't have been a passenger or he would have crashed with the aeroplane."

"Or escaped by parachute," suggested Bray.

"And been seen by everyone," countered Creighton triumphantly. "Moreover, if anyone else had been in the aeroplane, Ness, the mechanic, would have noticed him. No, the idea of a passenger is impossible. And even if the murderer had been flying near Furnace unobserved, I do not see how he could have shot him neatly in front of the temple. It would almost certainly have been a slanting shot from the back or the side. No, everything shows the impossibility of another person being involved." Creighton lowered two fingers and left the third in sole possession of the argumentative field. "That allows us only the second explanation, the one which explains everything. Furnace shot himself, and almost immediately the aeroplane crashed, and he fell limply against the dashboard as it struck the earth."

Bray looked at Creighton for a moment, an ironical smile on his clear-cut features.

"It explains a great deal. But it doesn't explain the most important point of all—the starting point of your investigations."

"You mean the cocaine? It seems to me to fit in all right. Remorse or fright would be motive enough for suicide."

Bray shook his head. "No, I'm not referring to the cocaine. There is a little matter of post-mortem *rigor*. The Bishop and Bastable both told us that *rigor* had not set in when they saw the body, and they both assure us this could only mean that Furnace was still alive when he was taken out of the 'plane—and for some hours afterwards."

"But it doesn't make sense!" groaned Creighton.

"No, it doesn't," admitted Bray happily. "But it makes an interesting problem. The man was killed a few seconds before the crash, yet a few hours after the crash he was still living! No, Creighton, it's not as simple as we hoped. Whether it is accident or design I don't know, but the circumstances are such that the murder is an impossibility, and yet it is equally impossible that he was not murdered."

"I don't know what to think," confessed Creighton. "The medical evidence seems to go clean against the weight of the facts."

"That's not altogether fair," pointed out Bray. "It's fairer to say that one half of the medical evidence goes against the other half. If only Bastable hadn't arrived so late, and been so cocksure he knew what had happened, and such a blithering idiot anyway, he might have noticed something which would help us. Post-mortem stains, for instance. But we've got to go on what we've got, and as far as I can see it's a gamble. You're just as entitled to your suicide theory as I am to my murder theory."

"I'm not so pleased with it now," confessed Creighton.

"And I'm not pleased with my murder theory," retorted Bray. "But it does offer us some starting point for an investigation. My present feeling is this: let us continue to act as if we believed it to be murder and try to scare some of the people involved into opening-up on the dope business. Do you agree?"

Creighton considered. "I don't see for why we shouldn't. But who are we going to scare?"

"Tell me who's on the permanent staff of the aerodrome who might be implicated."

"There's Miss Sackbut. We're certain now she's in it as she carried the dope on your journey. I suspected her all along on different grounds, and seeing that she knew Furnace I think we can count her in. Probably she corrupted Furnace in the first place."

"Frightenable, do you think?"

Creighton shook his head mournfully. "A tough body. I shouldn't like to take the job on."

"Neither should I," admitted Bray, his mind harking back to the bright, direct stare and firm chin of his pilot on the Channel crossing. "Who else?"

"Gauntlett. But of course we count him out."

"Good lord, yes! Leave him alone. He's the last person we want to scare at the moment!"

"There's that little red-headed mechanic, Ness," said Creighton thoughtfully. "Ground engineer they call him. He knew Furnace well, and they often used to go together on these flights for Gauntlett, on which we now know dope was carried. What about him? I should think he could be intimidated?"

"Good! Send for him, don't you think? It always scares them more. They get worked up coming to the station."

Creighton got through to Baston Aerodrome and, when he had Ness on the end of the line, summoned him peremptorily to the police station.

"No doubt you'll know as well as I do what we want to see you for," he ended with sinister emphasis. "Come along as soon as you can."

Creighton hung up the receiver with a satisfied smile on his face. "Dead silence at the other end! I think I might describe it as a horrified silence! He'll be along pretty soon, I fancy."

Ness was, in fact, announced soon after. Apparently he had only waited long enough to take off his greasy overalls, for his clothes were soiled and there was a smear on his nose.

"Sit down, Mr. Ness," said Creighton quietly. "This is Detective-Inspector Bray, from Scotland Yard."

Ness started, and controlled himself with a visible effort. Bray watched his tongue shoot out and lick his lips. "What do you want to know?"

"We want to know everything, Mr. Ness," answered Creighton jovially. "We know most of it already."

"What do you mean? I don't understand what you are talking about." Ness looked determinedly at his boots.

"I think you do. Oh yes, I think you do." Bray's lips twitched at the appalling portentousness of Creighton's tone.

A long silence followed. Bray watched Ness's knees shake slightly. The mechanic controlled them at last and managed to light a cigarette.

"Do you know what 'accessory after the fact' means?" asked Creighton.

"Eh?"

"It has this implication, that anyone who helps a murderer, even by concealing his crime, shares some of the guilt. You understand, I think, Mr. Ness? You know that Major Furnace was murdered. Possibly even *why* he was murdered. But you have not told us."

"What are you getting at?" whined Ness plaintively. "You don't suggest I murdered Furnace, do you?"

Creighton gave a sly smile. "That would be a matter for a formal charge. At the moment we are only aware that you know much more about the matter than you originally told us. Inspector Bray has come down here with a good deal of fresh information, and my own feeling certainly was that we ought to arrest you without delay and charge you with the murder of Major Furnace. The main reason why I haven't warned you is because if you can give us a plausible explanation we will let you go. Otherwise I am afraid we cannot let you leave this police station, and the law will have to take its course." He paused. "We know, you see, that Major Furnace was dead before the crash."

Ness turned a sickly green and dropped his cigarette. His mouth began to tremble and he was unable to stop the rapid twitching of his lips, which fascinated Bray for a moment.

"I hadn't anything to do with his murder! I swear to that!"

"I'm afraid we can't believe that, on your bare assurance."

Creighton and Bray exchanged a pleased glance. Ness was badly scared. When the process had been carried far enough, it would be possible to press the man to give information about the dope-running business. The fact that the police knew about this might alone be enough to precipitate a confession from the man they saw before them, white and shaking. Their calculations were totally upset by his answer.

"I knew nothing about it until after it was done! I swear it! Look, I was at the pictures all the evening before. You can confirm it," he said eagerly. "I went with three other people from the aerodrome. They'll be able to tell you. I'll give you their names."

Creighton looked staggered. "What on earth has the previous evening——" he began, when Bray stopped with a warning glance.

"When did you know he was dead?" Bray asked the ground engineer.

"When I came back in the evening"; he shuddered. "Oh, it was horrible! And then when Vandyke told me I'd got to help him get rid of the body, I nearly threw my hand in. If I hadn't been certain I should be treated the same way as Furnace, I'd have done it!"

"So it was Vandyke who killed him?"

"No. Vandyke was in Baston with me. It was the Chief."

"Who's the Chief?" said Creighton at once.

Ness looked at him wonderingly. "I don't know. Nobody knows. I don't think even Vandyke knows. The Chief shot him and told Vandyke how to clear it up."

"Who's Vandyke?" asked Creighton after a glance from Bray.

"Don't you know who Vandyke is?" The engineer's shifty eyes fixed foxily on Creighton's face. "I believe you're trying to draw me out! I don't believe you know anything!"

"Yes, we know, young fellow," said the policeman sternly.

"You don't! You're trying to trap me!" His mouth worked nervously. "You tricky——! I'm damned if I'll fall for it! I don't know anything, see? I don't know anything, damn you!"

"Come on, now," said Creighton gruffly; "you can't get away with that!"

"I can! Tell me who Vandyke is, and I'll tell you more." The two policemen were silent. The engineer laughed hysterically. "See? You don't know, you double-crossing swine!"

Bray hesitated. The witness was slipping out of his control. Should he take a plunge on the information he already had? If only Finch had identified Vandyke! He might have done so by now. But the opportunity was already about to evade them, and he could not wait for Finch.

"We know who Vandyke is," said Bray carefully. "Valentine Gauntlett."

Ness looked at him for a moment in wonder and then burst into peals of nervous laughter. "You think Valentine Gauntlett is Vandyke! Gaud, that's rich! Why, you don't know a thing, you lousy crooks, and you're trying to bluff me that you do. Well, fine fools you look! I've just been pulling your leg, see?"

"We've got you where we want you, Ness!" shouted Creighton furiously, with an unconscious recollection of the films. "You've told us all we want to know."

"I deny it! I deny every word of what I told you! Prove it if you can!" The engineer had changed from despair to an impudent elation. "You haven't warned me and you haven't got a statement. I don't believe you know a thing about the murder. You're trying to bluff me, blast you! This is the last time you get me in a police station, with your damned knowing airs. Furnace committed suicide, and you're trying to make it murder to get promotion."

Creighton was livid with fury. He evidently meditated detaining Ness. He exchanged a look with Bray, who shook his head.

"Give him a bit more rope for a while," he whispered.

Ness was released by Creighton with an ill grace.

The ground engineer left the room with an ugly sneer, and Creighton ran his fingers through his scanty grey hair. "This tears it! What in hell's name do you make of this?"

"It blows your sweet little theory sky-high, Creighton. It wasn't suicide, at all events."

"But it doesn't make sense!" moaned Creighton. "How can a dead man pilot a machine? If he was shot the previous evening, how was he flying round the next day?"

"Are your witnesses of this flight really sound?" asked Bray reflectively.

"Gosh, yes! Half a dozen of them, and one of them a belted Bishop, or whatever they are."

"Then someone's wrong," insisted Bray. "Here, what about this? They shove the dead body into an aeroplane, let the darn thing take off with the controls lashed, and then it crashes?"

"I don't know enough about flying to say. It sounds improbable to me. I don't believe it's technically possible." Creighton meditated for a moment. "How about this? Supposing somebody else had crashed there, and the murderer happened to be on the spot and popped Furnace's body in place of the real pilot?"

"I don't think that's one of our best theories, Creighton," smiled Bray. "It demands a remarkable lot from coincidence. Besides, what's happened to Pilot No. One's corpse?"

"Yes, that's awkward," admitted Creighton. "It didn't sound very convincing when I said it. Do you think someone could have towed the aeroplane, with Furnace's body in it, above the aerodrome, and then cut the rope?"

"No," answered Bray decisively. "We can't get away from the fact that that machine was flying about in a way which excited no suspicion whatever among the experienced pilots who were watching it until the moment it began to spin. I don't think you can go beyond that."

Creighton began turning over the Furnace dossier. Then he gave an exclamation. "Look here. What about the Home Office expert's evidence? He says Furnace's crash took place very shortly after the bullet wound. He's quite positive about that. So Furnace must have been alive when he went up in the machine that morning. How about that, eh? Furnace is dead the previous evening, then the next morning dies again. Then is alive again a few hours later."

Bray reflected a moment. Then he smiled. "We've been damned fools, Creighton. That little fellow was feeding us with a lying story on purpose. He pretended to be scared in order to mislead us both. The cunning little devil! He was play-acting all the time. That means we ought to go by contraries. Valentine Gauntlett *is* Vandyke in that case. What about the Chief being someone nobody knows? Need we believe that either?"

"Another little invention, I expect," admitted Creighton. "Fortunately Ness doesn't guess yet that we know there's even a smell of dope in this business. They couldn't know that Furnace's visit to the analyst came to our knowledge, so we've one card left that will surprise them."

"Still, we're back where we were," Bray reminded him; "except that we know Ness is in the dope gang, and we guessed that before. Damn it, I thought for a thrilling moment that we really were on to something big there."

"Well, it's getting late. Let's have some lunch—and *no* shop! It may clear our brains. Do you golf, Bray?"

"'Fraid not. Too expensive in London. Do you fish?"

"Do I!" answered Creighton enthusiastically, "Why, I came back from a fishing holiday a month ago. Listen, you may think I'm only telling you the usual story, but on my last day, for a pool that the landlord told me was absolutely hopeless but I liked the look of, I tried a 'Scarlet Soldier', and in five minutes..."

*   *   *   *   *

(*One hour later*).

"...My dear Creighton, I swear that if I'd stayed at that place another week I should have gone out and got a rifle and shot that fish through the head as it lay laughing at me!"

The lunch had drawn to its close, and the two policemen were gossiping and watching the leisurely life of Baston pass the restaurant window. A blue figure walked questingly past.

"Hello," said Bray, "that constable there seems to be looking for you."

Creighton rapped on the window and attracted his attention. "Do you want me, Murgatroyd?"

"Yes, sir. Miss Sackbut has just rung up from the aerodrome. She says there's been a terrible accident to their ground engineer, Ness."

Creighton turned white, but said nothing. The two men reached for their hats.

"I brought the car along as I thought you'd probably want it, sir."

"Quite right, Murgatroyd. Drive us straight along there."

They got into the car.

"Stop at Doctor Bastable's," ordered Creighton. "We'll collect him if he's in."

Dr. Bastable was able to come and the four arrived a little later at Baston Aerodrome. Miss Sackbut, looking pale, met them at the gates.

"Is this never going to stop?" she asked Creighton reproachfully. "First George and then Andy! Surely there must be someone you can get at?"

Creighton did not answer the question. Instead he asked coldly what had been done.

"The body was left just as we found it," answered Miss Sackbut with a shudder. "There was nothing that could be done. You'll see why. I'd better take you there, I suppose."

Ness was lying about four hundred yards from the boundary of the aerodrome, and on the opposite side to the hangars. Bastable knelt beside the limp form for a moment but quickly got up again.

"Dear, dear! There's not much for me to do here. You can see for yourself. This unfortunate man has fallen from a height of several thousands of feet. The head's gone right into the earth. The skull must have been smashed at once."

"That's quick work!" Creighton whispered to Bray. "Someone must have found out Ness had been to see us. Poor devil! I suppose they thought he was going to squeal—or that he had squealed. They got him up in an aeroplane and threw him out. Pretty brutal sort of people we're up against, eh?"

"It's rather strange all the same," answered Bray. "I shouldn't have thought it was easy to throw anyone out of an aeroplane, anyway; and impossible if they were expecting it. And surely Ness must have been a little suspicious after his visit to us."

Bray shrugged his shoulders. "Evidently he wasn't. So they must have told him some plausible story to get him into the aeroplane."

Creighton noted in his book the position of the body and turned to the constable.

"Stand by, Murgatroyd, for a little. I'll 'phone up the station and get some more men to come along. The body will have to be photographed; then it can be taken to the mortuary." He turned to his colleague. "We'll go back to the aerodrome, Bray."

Creighton 'phoned for some more men from the manager's office, and when he had concluded he turned to Miss Sackbut with a business-like tone which might, quite unfairly, have been mistaken for callousness.

"Now, Miss Sackbut, how was this discovered?"

"Lady Laura discovered it," answered Sally dismally. "She'd just flown over from her private aerodrome at Goring. She burst into my office and said that as she was gliding-in to land she'd seen something queer in the next field. She didn't like the look of it. So we went over and found him. Poor Andy!"

"Where is Lady Laura?"

"In the bar."

"I'll go through," answered Creighton, motioning Bray to accompany him.

Lady Laura was sitting at a table drinking a glass of brandy, her lips like slashes of blood against the dead white of her face.

She looked blankly at Creighton for a minute or two before she recognized him.

"Nasty!" she said with a shake of her head. "Nastier than I ever want to see again. I was a fool to go over and find out what it was. I guessed it was something horrible. Poor little man!"

Inspector Creighton sat down opposite her.

"Do you mind if we ask you one or two questions? Or would you prefer to wait till you feel better?"

"No! Anything to take my mind off that sight. What is it? How can I help you?"

"As a pilot you can help us a good deal. We are assuming you know Ness didn't fall but was deliberately thrown out of an aeroplane. Murdered. ..."

"That's what Sally thinks," admitted Lady Laura soberly. "What a ghastly death!"

Creighton nodded briefly. "Now the question that occurs to us is: How could a pilot get rid of a man in mid-air? You see, we don't know enough about flying to say. As a pilot you could tell us. Would he loop, for instance?"

"Good lord, no!" answered Lady Laura decisively. "That would keep your passenger in his seat. Centrifugal force, you know. No, the only way of doing it that I can see is to roll over on one's back suddenly and stay there for a little. But I don't think that can have happened in this case."

"Why not?"

"Because any man of Andy's experience would do up the safety-belt automatically, directly he sat down in the cockpit. That would hold him in."

"But would every aeroplane have a safety-belt?" asked Bray.

"Certainly," she said positively. "It's a statutory requirement. Here's another point: What type of aeroplane would it be?"

Creighton looked surprised. "We haven't the remotest idea. Does it matter?"

"Yes. It couldn't be a cabin type, for instance, that's obvious. Come and look at my Leopard Moth afterwards and you'll see that no one could fall out of that."

"I suppose it would be the ordinary two-seater things—Moths, aren't they—that the club uses?"

"No, it couldn't be those either," she explained, "because the centre section of the wing is always just above the passenger's head, and he would be kept in by that. At any rate he'd be able to grab it as he slid out and cling there."

Creighton looked despondent. "Are you telling us you think it impossible? Because it has happened, you know."

"It is possible, but it seems to me only with an open two-seater low-wing monoplane. There aren't many of those about, you know. Gauntlett's Air Taxis have got a Klemm and a Hawk, either of which would do."

"Perhaps you can help us with a fact that has puzzled me," interjected Bray. "Wouldn't it be an extraordinary risky thing to do it, so near an aerodrome?"

Lady Laura shook her head. "Not to-day. The clouds are very low. I was hedge-hopping all the way from Goring. You've only got to rise to about two thousand, I should think, to get out of sight of the ground. Somebody might have seen Andy falling, of course, but the chances are against it. You can see for yourself there's hardly anybody at the aerodrome. The visibility has been too bad for instructional flying today."

The two detectives looked at each other, and, after thanking Lady Laura, walked over to the hangars.

"An intelligent girl," said Creighton. "I don't know why one is surprised when a good-looking woman has brains.

"A low-wing monoplane," he added. "Do you know enough about these noisy contraptions to recognize that?"

"I think so. I know that's not one, anyway," Bray answered, pointing to a bulky machine in the corner.

"Of course it isn't. That's the aerodrome mowing-machine," replied Creighton seriously.

"Is it? So it is. You seem to know more about these things than I do, Creighton," Bray chaffed him. "Look here, what about this scarlet-and-orange object? I feel sure that's a low-wing monoplane. Anyway, if it isn't, it's the sort of thing we want, because it's obvious there's nothing to stop you falling out if it turns upside down."

"Except the safety-belt," the other reminded him. "That's a teaser, you know. How on earth could the murderer persuade Ness not to do up his safety-belt? Even little Red Riding Hood wouldn't be such a fool as to fall for that."

Bray was bending over the aeroplane and looked up triumphantly. "Wait a moment, though; look at this! Here's a belt in the rear seat. I assume this canvas business *is* the belt. But the belt's been taken out of the front seat, and that's usually the passenger's seat I believe. Look, the fastenings have been absolutely wrenched out."

Creighton looked round, and saw a youth with a spanner in one hand regarding them curiously. "Are you anything to do with this show?" he asked.

"I'm an apprentice," answered the youth.

"Well, can you tell me why this belt's missing?"

The youth stared at the missing belt with widened eyes.

"It looks as if someone's wrenched it off."

"Of course they have. But when?"

"Must have been to-day. I went up in it yesterday, and it was there."

"That's something," said Bray. "Has the machine been up to-day?"

"No, sir."

Bray went round to the nose and laid his hand on the exposed engine cylinders. "Feel these cylinders," he said to the apprentice.

The boy did so. "Crummy, that engine must have been running fairly recently!"

"How long ago, do you think?"

"Couldn't have been more than a couple of hours," answered the boy decisively.

"Where were you a couple of hours ago?"

"In town, sir."

"That's not much help then. Whose machine is this, by the way?"

"Gauntlett's Air Taxis, sir. They don't use it much except for joy-riding over the week-ends."

"Right-ho," answered Bray. The boy trickled off with a backward glance of pleasantly thrilled horror. Bray stared at the aeroplane, whistling gently to himself.

"Any ideas, Bray?" said Creighton.

"Fingerprints on the stick-control thing," suggested the Yard man.

"Good idea. I'll get Murgatroyd on to that. He ought to be in the club-house by now."

Murgatroyd was there and was despatched to test the aeroplane for fingerprints while Creighton and Bray examined the various people on the aerodrome for information. Miss Sackbut had been in her office and seen nothing. The instructor had been taking a navigation class, and neither he nor his pupils, which included the Bishop, Thomas Vane, and two or three other club members, had noticed the scarlet-and-yellow monoplane take off. In fact, it is doubtful if they could have done so, as their window did not look out directly over the aerodrome. Mrs. Angevin had been sitting in the bar.

At the mention of Mrs. Angevin's name Creighton hesitated.

"The Bishop told me something about a violent quarrel between Furnace and Mrs. Angevin shortly before he was killed," he said to Bray. "Do you think she could be mixed up with it?"

"Might be," answered the other thoughtfully. "We can't prove anything, can we, if she says she was sitting in there? What about the bar-tender?"

"Well, the bar itself was closed, although the room is sometimes left open for members to sit in. So she was by herself."

The two policemen sat down with somewhat gloomy thoughts. Both had a guilty feeling they should have anticipated the present fatality. "Here's Murgatroyd!" said Creighton, jumping to his feet. "Perhaps he's discovered some fingerprints."

Murgatroyd's report was, however, negative. The grip of the control column had either been carefully wiped or else the last pilot had worn gloves.

"Damnation! No luck anywhere!" exclaimed Creighton irritably.

CHAPTER XV

SIMULATION OF A SUICIDE

INSPECTOR BRAY was walking thoughtfully round the edge of the aerodrome when he encountered Lady Laura. She was wearing white overalls and a white flying helmet, and Bray was struck anew by the contrast between the calm efficiency of her flying and her fragile, almost porcelain, beauty.

He was about to pass by, when Lady Laura stopped him with a gesture. "Have you found your low-wing monoplane yet?" she asked.

Bray nodded. "Yes. The safety-belt in the passenger's seat was missing."

Lady Laura's wide blue eyes looked straight into his. "Whose aeroplane was it?"

Bray hesitated. "It belonged to Gauntlett's Air Taxis," he said after a pause.

"Oh, their Klemm, I suppose," she commented. She turned her head and looked out towards the edge of the aerodrome, where a school aeroplane was taking off. "Do you think there is anything connecting the two things—George's death and Andy's?" she asked, with a not very convincing attempt at casualness.

"We think there is," answered Bray gravely.

"I'm not asking you all this without a purpose," went on Lady Laura. "Tell me, is it quite definite that George was killed? The Bishop tells me he thinks George killed himself, and naturally I have thought so ever since I received that letter from him.

But from something Creighton said, I gathered that you people felt fairly sure it was murder."

Bray studied Lady Laura's famous profile carefully. She had been with the Bishop and Miss Sackbut when Furnace had crashed, and again she had discovered the dead body of Ness. Her sharp eyes might well have discovered some fragment others had overlooked. He decided to be frank.

"I personally am certain that Major Furnace was murdered, Lady Laura," he said, "but we are not at the moment in a position to decide how the murder was done. He was shot and he crashed. That is all we can be certain of."

"You must be able to tell from the medical evidence how long before the crash he was shot," commented Lady Laura shrewdly.

"A matter of seconds," answered Bray.

Lady Laura nodded. "I rather feared it," she said in a low voice. "So he was shot while in the air?"

Bray smiled with a hint of patronage. "That is the obvious suggestion. But you see, it is ruled out because he could not have had a passenger, and no one saw another aeroplane anywhere near him. That is why we are unable, at the moment, to understand how the murder took place."

Lady Laura looked at him. There was a trace of irony in her smile, the answer to the suggestion of patronage in his tone. "I appreciate that. All the same, I see no reason why he should not have been shot just as the medical evidence suggests."

"If you can suggest any means whereby a pilot in full view of the ground can be shot dead without the murderer being seen, then I will agree with you!" answered Bray, a little annoyed.

"Certainly I can," she said calmly. "Have you studied the contour charts of this aerodrome and the surrounding district?"

"I can't say I have," he smiled. "No doubt Sherlock Holmes would not have overlooked such an essential point, but I forgot it."

Lady Laura pulled out a sheaf of maps from the pocket of her overalls and sat down on the running-board of a car parked near the edge of the aerodrome. Bray sat down beside her. She opened the map and indicated the aerodrome with the point of a pencil.

"Here's Baston Aerodrome. As you can see from the shading, it is a plateau on three sides, but when standing on the aerodrome you don't notice how rapidly the ground falls away because the beginning of the slope is hidden by the fringes of trees in the meadows beyond. It used to be a favourite joke of club members to dive straight down past the edge of the aerodrome into the dip of land and fly round there for a little while out of sight. To anyone on the aerodrome it looks exactly as if they had dived straight into the ground and crashed. In fact, when I saw the aeroplane vanish on the day George was killed I thought that it was some silly pupil doing the same thing. Then I realized it was George, and of course it was a thing he would never do."

Bray studied the map, a puzzled expression on his face, and then stood up to look at the aerodrome and the country beyond.

"I can understand all that," he said at last, "but for the moment I don't quite see how it would have made it any the easier to kill Furnace in full view of people on the ground."

"George was flying a club machine," said Lady Laura slowly. "There are two club aeroplanes, both of exactly the same colour scheme. When they are too far away for their registration marks to be seen it is impossible to tell one from the other."

"Good God," exclaimed Bray, "that opens up possibilities, certainly! You think that the aeroplane we saw crash——"

"Was not George's aeroplane at all. It was the murderer's," answered Lady Laura with a quiet smile.

"Let's work this out!" exclaimed Bray excitedly. "I believe we've really got it! Furnace goes up for a flight before anyone is on the aerodrome except Ness, who is in the game, anyway, and doesn't matter."

"Oh, is he?" murmured Lady Laura. "That explains the one thing I couldn't understand."

"The murderer sees his chance and follows in another club machine, either as passenger or piloted by someone else who is also in the game. He flies alongside Furnace and shoots him. Would that be possible?"

"Oh, quite," answered the girl positively. "If Furnace had just gone up for a flight to enjoy himself and to throw the aeroplane about, he would be quite ready to let another aeroplane formate beside him, particularly if he recognized the pilot. He would let him get quite close."

"Right," said Bray. "Then Furnace is shot while he is turning to look at the other aeroplane. Hence the wound is in front. Of course, the 'plane crashes, out of control, into the dip you have just shown me. Then the murderer flies round again, just as if he were Furnace, until he sees that there are plenty of witnesses on the aerodrome so that he can safely stage the last act. Perhaps Ness took care to tell them that Furnace was in the machine they saw?"

"He did," confirmed Lady Laura.

"Then, as far as I can see from what you tell me, all the murderer then had to do was to spin down over the point where Furnace had crashed and, as soon as he was hidden in the dip, correct the spin and fly along the valley, and so away. It would be quite easy for him to return, in the resulting confusion, and put the aeroplane quietly back into the hangar, I suppose?"

"Yes, that is my idea," admitted the girl. "But I ought to tell you that it would have to be a fairly good pilot. The dip of the ground doesn't leave much room to come out of a spin, and then the pilot would have to hedge-hop round the plateau to get away afterwards. But it is possible. I shouldn't mind having a stab at demonstrating, if you are doubtful."

"It's very sporting of you, Lady Laura. But I don't think we need ask for that yet." He grinned. "You seem to have found in two minutes what we couldn't find in two weeks."

"Oh, I've been thinking about it pretty solidly for the last few days," said Lady Laura seriously, rising from the running-board.

"You didn't, I suppose, happen to notice the club aeroplane coming back after the crash?" asked Bray, without any real hope.

"Yes," was the quiet answer.

"You did! Who was the pilot?"

"What an awful business this is," muttered Lady Laura miserably. "It was Dolly Angevin."

"Mrs. Angevin!" exclaimed Bray.

"Yes; and that was why, when you told me that Ness was killed in a Gauntlett Air Taxis' aeroplane, I wanted to know more."

The detective was puzzled. "I'm afraid I don't quite see the connection."

"Well, I suppose you would hardly have heard the club gossip, but, Good lord, everyone knows it here. Poor Dolly has a desperate crush on Valentine Gauntlett. It's pathetic, of course, because he's ten years younger than she is—at least. Probably more."

Bray turned over the evidence in his mind. Everything seemed to fit in. Gauntlett was implicated in Ness's murder through Mrs. Angevin, which is what they would have expected. If Gauntlett had influence over Mrs. Angevin, it was not so surprising that she should have been dragged into the affair. Bray remembered, with growing excitement, that Mrs. Angevin had been the only person found on the aerodrome after Ness's crash who could offer no check on her movements. She had said that she had been sitting in the deserted bar, but there was no one to confirm this.

It was, of course, hard to believe that a woman could coldbloodedly carry out two murders and yet seem a normal woman. But then, in Bray's experience, murderers generally seemed normal people, and, he reflected, there must be something a little abnormal about a woman like Mrs. Angevin, who was prepared to undergo appalling risks for illusory rewards. Of course, the identification of Mrs. Angevin as the murderer was still extremely hypothetical. He felt no great confidence in it. Nothing like the confidence, for instance, that he felt in the method of the murder as suggested by Lady Laura. That seemed as certain as such things could be, for it fitted like a glove every fact but one of those known to them, and also accounted for the short time between the fatal shot and the crash. It is true that it still did not account for the most puzzling item in the medical evidence, the fact that *rigor* had not set in when the Bishop was watching beside the body, but here Bray was beginning to veer round to Creighton's opinion, which in turn had been inspired by a muttered hint from Dr. Bastable, that, after all, the Bishop, excellent man as he was, was not a fully qualified doctor, and may have been mistaken on this point. "*Rigor,*" explained Bastable, "is not always as marked as the layman supposes."

Lady Laura seemed to him to be looking very despondent as she swung her flying helmet gently by its strap. He looked at her curiously.

"You've helped us a lot," he said, "and we're grateful to you. Too often the general public think it's the business of the police to trace the wrongdoer, and that they needn't take the slightest trouble themselves."

"I don't consider myself a member of the general public in this particular case," answered Lady Laura, looking up. "You see, they killed George. I should have been sorry enough, anyway, that a man who loved me as George did, a man I didn't treat fairly—oh, I admit it now—was killed in that way. And it would be rather worse, because I sometimes wonder if George would ever have got into the trouble he spoke of in his letter if he hadn't known me. But the worst of all is"—she hesitated, and seemed to go on with an effort—"George meant more to me than anyone I'd met. ..."

She gave Bray a decisive little nod which seemed to close the conversation and walked away, as little perturbed outwardly as if they had been discussing a subject no more exciting than that of the weather.

Bray walked slowly back to the club-house. "Extraordinary creatures women are," he reflected. "Some women. She led this poor bloke the most awful life, and now she says she was in love with him all the time. And she walks about looking unutterably calm and faintly bored, and yet I do believe she's really upset and worried." He sighed philosophically and addressed his mind to the problem of Mrs. Angevin.

* * * * *

Meanwhile, in London, an apparently unimportant incident was taking place which yet, when Bray afterwards came to review the affair, was the most vital factor in clearing up the complications of this mystery in which Mrs. Angevin, Sally Sackbut, Captain Randall, Valentine Gauntlett, and Tommy Vane were so perplexingly involved.

The incident was this. The Bishop was a guest of the Transatlantic Society at their annual Anglo-American banquet. Beside him was a silver-haired American with the face of a wise child and those crinkles round the eyes which come from a cheerful disposition.

They got into conversation. ...

CHAPTER XVI

TROUBLES OF A TRANSATLANTIC FLYER

"MRS. ANGEVIN is aged forty-two," declared Bray, reading extracts from a sheaf of papers.

"She doesn't look it," commented Creighton gallantly.

"No, but she'll look sixty in five years' time," said the Scotland Yard man grimly. "When this sort of woman starts to go, it's an avalanche." He continued reading. "She is the daughter of a rural dean. That's pretty bad, but not the sort of thing you can use in evidence against her. She has been married twice and has been freed once by the Grim Reaper and once by the Probate, Admiralty and Divorce Division. She was the Guilty Party, as our grandfathers used to say." He turned over a few papers. "She always appears to have been doing something. Led a woman's ice-hockey team for a year, then crossed the Gobi Desert alone, and flirted for a time with Arctic exploration. Then she became really well known, at least as a pilot. Not a good one, I'm told, and weak on navigation, but makes up for it on guts."

"Is she clever enough?" asked Creighton thoughtfully. "Our murderer would need cleverness as well as guts."

"Not necessarily," argued Bray. "The brains might have been behind the scenes."

"You're still set on making Gauntlett the Chief," commented Creighton. "Well, I think you're probably right. Any convictions against the woman in your records?"

"Nothing serious. Dangerous driving, of course, and a narrow escape from a manslaughter conviction, but this type of reckless individual may always get involved in that kind of thing. They think it's their duty to drive about the streets like maniacs. Oh, there's a fine for assault when she bashed a fellow over the head with her ice-hockey stick for making some uncomplimentary remark about the sportsmanship of women players. It was perhaps excusable."

"Still, it shows a violent temperament," pointed out Creighton. "Anything else?"

"No. There's a rather odd gap of five years in her life when she went to America. Nobody seems to know what she was doing then. According to one account, she was violently pursuing a recalcitrant lover about the American Continent, and it is said he was the Angevin she subsequently married. But all this sounds to me like malicious gossip. She was probably quite mildly and peaceably earning her living in some inconspicuous occupation. So, you see, we know absolutely nothing which is really to her discredit."

Creighton agreed. "The main thing is, can we find anyone on the aerodrome who might have seen her take off before the accident? Lady Laura saw her land in the second club aeroplane a fair time *after* the accident, but of course that's not nearly enough. We must be certain of the time at which it left."

Creighton consulted his notebook. "There's just a chance Tommy Vane or Sally Sackbut may have seen it. They were both in the club-house at the time, Miss Sackbut because she comes on duty early, and Vane because he was having a lesson that day.

It's just on the lap of the gods that they might have seen the aeroplane."

"They're the two worst possible witnesses, you know," Bray pointed out.

Creighton looked a little surprised. "Naturally, Miss Sackbut is doubtful, because she is almost certainly in the dope-smuggling game. But what on earth is wrong with friend Tommy?"

Bray gave a slightly shamefaced look at his colleague. "I am afraid I have spent the last day or two gathering the club gossip. I had a lesson in flying from Winters, and it appears to have given me the freedom of the club. It seems that Tommy Vane, poor devil, has a hopeless passion for Mrs. Angevin. Odd, isn't it, but these young puppies often fall for a woman much older than themselves. I gather she isn't the slightest bit interested in him, but occasionally deigns to use him for minor errands. So there you have the eternal triangle in a new form. Tommy hopelessly pursues Mrs. Angevin, and she, resolutely but with equal hopelessness, runs after Gauntlett. Gauntlett, wise man, keeps himself to himself."

"You do seem to get information from people!" sighed Creighton. "It must be your languidly bored manner. They forget you are a policeman. They never forget it with me."

"Oh, no doubt they make the mistake of thinking I'm as big a fool as I look," answered Bray carelessly. "But you see the awkwardness of this weakness of Tommy's. If the young fool ever guesses that something he says may implicate Mrs. Angevin, he'll not say it. And he's a pretty tough young man, I fancy, for all his boyish airs. You ought to see him down double Scotches!"

"I have," answered Inspector Creighton grimly. "Well, we must handle him tactfully, that's all. You'd better put on your sweetest and most winning manner, Bray, and see if we can bounce him into some admission before he realizes what is happening."

Tommy Vane was found in the bar. He greeted Bray cheerfully and Creighton with more reserve. His pale, knowing face looked out with a faintly malicious grin over an auburn short-sleeved shirt, decorated with a vivid green tie. His flannel trousers hung in redundant folds and were so pale as to be nearly white.

"You look worried! Baffled sleuths seek bright boy's aid," he said brightly.

"Baffled about describes it," acknowledged Bray with an answering grin. "I don't know whether you can help us very much, but it is just possible that you may have noticed some detail which didn't seem important to you and yet may be important to us."

"Oh yeah?" answered Tommy. With disconcerting penetration he added: "In other words, you're not baffled. You've got some cute little theory and you want me to back it. Well, fire away. I'll always help a pal so long as it's nothing sinful."

"It all turns on the identification of Furnace's aeroplane," said Bray carefully. "We have attempted to trace every moment of its flight from the time it took off until the time it crashed. But there are certain inconsistencies in the accounts we have received. It has occurred to me that as Furnace was using a school aeroplane, it might be that some witness had confused it with the other school aeroplane, which was flying at or about the same time."

"Where do policemen get that wonderful literary style?" murmured Tommy. "Well, your guess was correct. Another school aeroplane was buzzing round at or about the same time. It took off immediately before Furnace went up, and landed some time after the crash."

"Ah, we must get an account of its movements and that will clear up the inconsistencies," said Bray, adding with apparent casualness, "Who was the pilot?"

"Dolly Angevin," answered Tommy readily. Then something in the glance exchanged by Creighton and Bray aroused a sudden apprehension in his eyes. "I say, look here, you don't suspect *her*, do you?"

Bray laughed and prevaricated. "If you can suggest any way by which a person who is flying peacefully round in an aeroplane can cause another to crash, in full view of half a dozen witnesses, without himself being seen, why, then, old chap, we do suspect her!"

Tommy, after a suspicious glance at his face, was satisfied. With a nod to Creighton, he left the room.

Bray and Creighton discussed for a few moments this evidence. "It's as good a confirmation as we could expect, so far," Bray ended. "Lady Laura's evidence shows that Mrs. Angevin landed after the crash. Now Vane states that she went up before Furnace took off. The next step is to have a little chat with Mrs. Angevin, I think."

The opportunity came in the afternoon. Mrs. Angevin betrayed no apprehension at the prospect of being questioned. On the contrary, she chaffed them gently as she sat back, puffing at a cigarette in an armchair in Miss Sackbut's office, which had been temporarily placed at the disposal of the detectives.

Meanwhile Bray studied her. He had been cruelly right about her age, for the lines in her carefully made-up face betrayed the imminence of large-scale ravages. But at least they were the lines not of sulkiness or bad temper, but of strain endured for some unfathomable reason of the woman's soul in a hundred desperately risky ventures. Her delicately modelled nose, her small chin, and her naturally crimson lips were daintily, almost softly, feminine. Her eyes made up for it by their resolute and masculine stare.

Mrs. Angevin stared at him now. "No one else been murdered, I hope? After poor Andy, one hardly knows what to expect next!"

Bray met the challenge in her stare indifferently. "No; nothing else—yet. We are still concerned with the first two deaths, and we think you can help us a great deal."

"Really! I can't imagine anyone here who could help you less!"

Bray made a pretence of consulting his notes. "It seems," he said, "that you went for a flight in a school aeroplane just before Furnace went up and did not return until he crashed. You may well have seen something that would help us materially. At least, you should have told us of the flight," he ended reproachfully.

"I could have," she answered carelessly, adding after a pause, "but I did not because I thought the matter was unimportant. You are wrong on one point. I did not arrive at the aerodrome until *after* the crash, and I went up immediately. It is a little habit of mine after an accident. I'm rather afraid of losing my nerve." She stared at him defiantly. "I'm a bit more timid than I care to admit. It was quite a short flight, and Lady Laura can confirm the time at which I came down, because I remember speaking to her as I stepped out of the 'plane."

"She has confirmed it," answered Bray gravely. "But the time we are interested in is the time when you went up. And here accounts seem to differ."

"I can't help that," retorted Mrs. Angevin indifferently. "I have told you the truth."

Bray produced a large blue-covered book from underneath his papers. "Here is the journey log-book of the aeroplane in question, given me by Miss Sackbut. I find that the entry for the date of Furnace's death quite clearly shows that you took the 'plane up for two hours."

"Let me look at it," said Mrs. Angevin suspiciously. She examined the entry and looked up with a bitter smile. "The entry is made by Ness. Very convenient. He is dead and can't be cross-examined."

"You are surely not suggesting that we forged this entry, are you?" interjected Creighton sharply.

Mrs. Angevin made no answer, but irritably stubbed her cigarette into extinction.

"In any case, we have other evidence," went on Bray smoothly.

"Whose?" asked Mrs. Angevin sharply.

Bray looked at Creighton. "I think we may as well have him in." Creighton went out of the room and Bray offered Mrs. Angevin another cigarette, which she refused brusquely. Her eyes were fixed impatiently on the door. When she saw Tommy Vane enter she gave a gasp. Tommy Vane gazed at her with an air of trustful confidence, his usually hard, pale-green eyes looking rather like those of a spaniel. He blenched when he received the full force of the bitter look of contempt with which she returned his smile of greeting.

"Will you please repeat what you told us just now about Mrs. Angevin, Vane?" said Bray cruelly.

Vane looked from the detective to Mrs. Angevin with an air of hopeless confusion. "Only that I saw her fly off just before Furnace went up and come down some time afterwards," he mumbled. Mrs. Angevin flushed and he hastened to add: "She was up in the air all the time, I can swear. She never came near us again, or near Furnace."

"I don't know why you should tell such an outrageous lie, Tommy," began Mrs. Angevin. Tommy shuddered. "Nor why you, Inspector, should want to encourage this absurd story. I do not see what bearing it has on the murder one way or the other. But the fact remains, I did not arrive on the aerodrome until after the crash. I met two people—first, Tommy, who told me about it, and Sally, who merely nodded to me." She turned to Tommy and stared him fixedly in the eyes. "Can you really sit there, Tommy, and deny that I spoke to you after the crash, before I went up."

Vane's eyes dropped. "You're right, Dolly," he murmured weakly. "I forgot. I got muddled. I remember quite well. Of course you spoke to me."

Mrs. Angevin glared triumphantly at the detectives. Bray looked at Vane, an amused smile on his face. "And you would be prepared to swear to this? Your first story was a fabrication, then?"

"I got muddled," insisted Vane woodenly, tearing his eyes with an effort from Mrs. Angevin's now expressionless face.

"But I remember now. The second club machine didn't go up until after the crash."

The two detectives did not press the examination. "May I pop off now?" asked Vane miserably.

"Please stay a little longer, if it doesn't inconvenience you," answered Bray with cold politeness. "Creighton, old chap, can you dig up Miss Sackbut?"

Miss Sackbut entered shortly afterwards with her usual air of brisk efficiency, and after a glance at Mrs. Angevin and Vane, suppressed any outward sign of curiosity.

"Can you help us on a small point, Miss Sackbut?" asked Bray. "As you know, we like to trace everyone's movements, and, as a matter of form, obtain some independent confirmation of them. Now, do you remember having seen Mrs. Angevin on the aerodrome just after Furnace's crash?"

Sally's brow wrinkled above her spectacles in earnest thought. "I have a kind of vague recollection. ... I can't be sure, it's so long ago."

Mrs. Angevin stared at her. "Surely you must remember, Sally? You were just beside the hangar and I walked past it. I was going to speak to you, but you looked so upset, and knowing from Tommy what had happened, I didn't. I only nodded."

"Yes, I'm sure I remember now," said Sally.

"Would you be prepared to swear?" asked Bray.

"Yes, I think I would," replied Sally after consideration. "Yes, I'd swear it."

Vane created a diversion by appealing in a high-pitched voice to Bray. "What are you trying to do to Dolly? Are you trying to make out that she had anything to do with the two murders? Why, I tell you again she didn't come on to the aerodrome until after Furnace had crashed, just as Sally says. And she was nowhere near the aerodrome on the day Ness died."

"Really," asked Bray quickly. "Are you sure that she wasn't in the club-house—sitting in the bar, for instance?"

Mrs. Angevin made a movement of protest, but it was too late. Vane had already answered. "Certainly not! I passed through there before and after the navigation lesson. She couldn't possibly have been in there because the door was locked both times, and it was only opened to let us through. After we had finished the navigation lesson they left it open, I think."

Bray turned to Mrs. Angevin. "In the light of Vane's new evidence, perhaps you can explain—just to make our records complete, you know—how this squares with your story that you were sitting in the bar all the time on that day?"

"My story is true," answered Mrs. Angevin, staring him boldly in the eyes. "Tommy is lying." The young man stirred uneasily in his chair.

"But no one, unfortunately, saw you in the bar?"

"Yes, someone did," answered Mrs. Angevin unexpectedly. What followed was equally unexpected and extremely painful. Mrs. Angevin's hard-bitten face seemed to screw up like that of a child. A tear forced its way between the creases. She brushed it away with a furious gesture. "Valentine Gauntlett met me there. Speak to him. Go on. He'll tell you a lovely story about me. How he had to tell me not to make him conspicuous by following him around." Another tear was visible for a moment. "Pretty good, eh, for a woman at my time of life? Baby-snatching, I believe it is called." She began to laugh horribly. "My God, I've been a damned fool! Men are all alike." Quite suddenly, before anyone could stop her or even guess her intention, she strode up to Tommy Vane—he was gazing at her with a kind of pitying horror on his face—and slapped him resoundingly on the cheek. "You vile play-acting little cad!" she exclaimed. Then, with a sudden sob which was the sincerest part of her performance, and seemed to wrench its way out of her spontaneously, she almost ran from the room. The whole scene was piteous and yet grotesquely comic, like a burlesque melodrama.

Vane stared after her, amazedly caressing his scarlet cheek. Miss Sackbut's feelings found relief in an expletive which in the ordinary way would have staggered Creighton, as he had been brought up to suppose that it was a word ladies did not know, much less make use of.

"That will be all, thank you, Miss Sackbut and Mr. Vane?" With a gesture Bray cleared the room.

"Very interesting," he said to his colleague, in the comparative calm which followed the exit of the three. "I'd better ring up Gauntlett before she has time to prime him with the story he must tell us."

Bray's first reception was an extremely angry request that he should mind his own business as to what he, Valentine Gauntlett, had been doing on the afternoon of Ness's death. After Bray had hinted that Mrs. Angevin had already made a statement, Gauntlett admitted that he had had a talk with her in the bar of the club at the time of Ness's death. Bray hung up with a puzzled frown.

"He confirms it, so there we are. Tommy's first evidence makes Mrs. Angevin look as guilty as hell. The fact that he denied it subsequently only confirms it, so to speak, because he obviously only denied it when he saw it implicated Mrs. Angevin. But, on the other hand, Mrs. Angevin has got two perfectly good witnesses in her favour. First, Sally, who says Mrs. Angevin did not arrive on the aerodrome until after the crash, and then Gauntlett, who admits to talking to her at the time when Ness was killed."

"Of course, they're not, in fact, perfectly good witnesses," pointed out Creighton. "Quite the opposite."

"Certainly. We know they're both in on the dope-smuggling business, and therefore presumably in league with Mrs. Angevin. But we can't prove it—yet. And until we can, and until we find some worthwhile motive for Mrs. Angevin's action, we haven't the ghost of a chance of a conviction."

"No; we'll have to let her play around for a while," admitted Creighton. "Do you think she's the Chief?"

Bray shook his head. "Head not cool enough. And yet, I don't know. It may have been acting. If so, it was jolly good acting."

Creighton shook his head. "There was something besides acting in it. I don't know quite what. What's the matter, Murgatroyd?" he asked irritably as the constable poked his head into the office.

"Are you free?" he asked. "Can I have a word with Inspector Bray?"

"Yes, what is it?" asked Bray, surprised.

"A Sergeant Finch from the Yard is enquiring for you, sir. Shall I fetch him in?"

"Yes, please." Bray turned to Creighton. "Finch may have news about this Vandyke bloke, you know. I hope he has been identified as Valentine Gauntlett. It will help us a lot if he has."

Sergeant Finch walked into the room with his accustomed ponderous and deliberate air, which deceived many who did not realize that behind the façade of walrus moustache and ruddy cheeks lurked the sensibilities of a psychological artist.

"Any luck, Finch?"

"I have and I haven't, sir." Finch slowly opened an envelope and laid a photograph upon the table. The two detectives bent over it. It depicted Valentine Gauntlett, smiling and clasping a trophy, being "chaired" by a group of Baston Aero Club members. "Both the porter and the charwoman were sure that this gentleman with the cup wasn't Vandyke, sir. But, to my surprise, they both identified this young man in the foreground as him."

The sergeant's finger rested on a grinning young man in a large scarf and an open-necked shirt.

Bray looked at Creighton for enlightenment and saw him gasp.

"Good lord!" Creighton said. "Vandyke! Why, it's that youngster, Tommy Vane!"

CHAPTER XVII

DIFFICULTIES OF TWO DETECTIVES

BRAY and Creighton met again in the afternoon of the next day. The intervening time had been spent by both in investigating the antecedents of Tommy Vane, now identified as Vandyke.

"I find he came to Baston about two years ago," said Creighton, who had been working on the local end. "Nothing appears to be known about his previous history. He occasionally gets letters from America, according to his landlady. He does nothing in Baston and he goes up to town three times a week. The landlady has always assumed that this was in connection with business, but she doesn't know."

"It can't be to go to that office in Banchurch Street," answered Bray, who had looked after the London investigations, "because he doesn't go there more than once a week as a rule. There must be some regular meeting of the dope organization in London. That means putting a man on to tail him for his next trip. In fact, I've a good mind to do it myself."

"Well, that's really all I can find out," went on Creighton, "except Miss Sackbut's statement. I told you about that yesterday. Lady Crumbles states Vane is a man called Spider something or other whom she met in Hollywood."

"Yes," answered Bray; "so when I got to London I sent the tele-photo of Vane's head and shoulders to the Los Angeles police, and I've got a cable back already. Quick workers, those boys! Here it is.

"Re your confidential cable 5639/B. T.V. Man is Frank Hartigan, alias Spider Hartigan. Well-known Hollywood extra for two years; nationality English; born 1907; height 5 ft. 8 in.; blue eyes, dark hair, mole right-hand corner mouth; discovered to be agent Chinese black drug smuggling organization, Los Angeles, and deported two years ago. Subsequent history unknown.

"He was on black drugs then—that's hashish and opium, you know," explained Bray. "Cocaine is a white drug, so it's not likely to be the same organization here as was operating in America."

"Still, it seems to place him either as the head of the dope-smuggling business here—or very near the head."

"I don't think he's the boss," said Bray positively. "The kind of man who'd be the boss would be someone with unimpeachable credentials, not a fellow who's been deported from America."

"A man such as the nephew of a Cabinet Minister?" suggested Creighton.

Bray nodded, his face grave. "Exactly! The real puzzle, of course, is this: if Lady Laura's theory of the murder is right—and I thought it was—then someone was in the air at the time of Furnace's death, flying a club aeroplane. Now at first we thought this was Mrs. Angevin, and Vane's evidence confirmed it. But now we know Vane is a member of the gang, and we can hardly believe he would go out of his way to convict one of his own people. On the other hand, Mrs. Angevin had in her favour the evidence of Gauntlett and Miss Sackbut, also believed to be of the gang."

"It is a hopeless tangle," admitted Creighton. "It points to Miss Sackbut and Gauntlett being innocent, if they're working against Vane."

Bray shook his head. "Impossible. After all, you can't get away from the fact that Gauntlett's Air Taxis is doing the dope-running and Miss Sackbut has helped in it. No; I can only think that Vane had to say what he did without consulting Gauntlett and Miss Sackbut, and so they were at cross-purposes yesterday afternoon."

"In any case," pointed out Creighton, "it seems to let out Mrs. Angevin, and if she's not in on the dope-running, she's hardly likely to be concerned in the murder. What do you think of Tommy's apparent passion for her? Fake, I suppose?"

"I'm afraid so." Bray looked thoughtful. "I fancy Mrs. Angevin saw it pretty clearly that afternoon. Hence the slap on the face. Poor woman! One can understand her feelings. I don't quite see Tommy Vane's object in playing her up—it seems to have begun before the murder—but it is obvious enough it's not a genuine feeling. What a diabolically clever actor the little swine is! I was utterly taken in by the convincing way he lied about her and then denied his lies in front of her so as to make them sound all the more truthful."

Creighton looked again at the cable from America. "And yet in spite of his record he didn't murder Furnace? Or Ness either, because he was attending a navigation lesson while Ness was being murdered. So we come back to the same old point. Who killed Furnace?"

"Ness was right about Vandyke not being the murderer," suggested Bray. "He was also right about Vandyke not being Gauntlett.

He also said that Vandyke wasn't the Chief, which is what we think now. Oughtn't we to assume that he was telling us the truth about everything?"

"H'm." Creighton looked sceptical. "In that case Furnace was shot by the Chief the evening before the crash. And Ness was killed by the Chief for saying too much to us. But in that case Lady Laura's theory, which is the only workable theory we've had up to date, has got to be abandoned. We've got to believe instead that Furnace was shot the day before, and yet crashed immediately after being shot, and yet crashed the following morning, which is nonsense."

"I'm afraid we've got to give up Lady Laura's theory," admitted Bray, "once we agree that Mrs. Angevin is innocent. For, apart from her, there doesn't seem the slightest evidence to show that the other school aeroplane was in use during the time when Furnace appeared to crash. On the contrary, no one seems to have seen it until Mrs. Angevin landed in it."

"Here's another idea," suggested Creighton. "Supposing Ness was telling what he thought was the truth, but suppose he was mistaken? Suppose he really thought Furnace was murdered the day before, but was wrong. Then we can continue to look round for some means of making Furnace crash in the morning."

"Well, that would rule out Vandyke as the murderer, and I still feel he *ought* to be the murderer," the Yard man reflected. "I'm afraid he's innocent, anyway, for Finch told me he established that Vandyke was in his office in London until late on the previous day, and Murgatroyd discovered that immediately on his return Vane went with Ness to the pictures. I admit that visit to the pictures looks like an attempt to establish an alibi, but we policemen are apt to forget that people do go to the pictures sometimes merely for amusement."

"Mightn't Furnace have been killed after Vane had left the pictures with Ness?" asked Creighton.

"I don't think so, because Ness suggested that the pictures were a perfect alibi for himself, and he wouldn't have done so unless he knew the murder had taken place while he was there. So you have either got to believe with Ness that Furnace was murdered the day before—against all the evidence—in which case Vane is innocent, or that he was killed just before he crashed, in which case again Vane is innocent. And Vane couldn't possibly have killed Ness, because he was having a navigation lesson at the time and, anyway, he cannot fly. We don't want to multiply our murderers if we can help it. Whoever murdered Furnace must be able to have murdered Ness. I'm afraid Vane gets off without a stain on his character as far as the murders are concerned, blast him!"

Creighton groaned. "All this is very logical reasoning, but we are back exactly where we started. How in the name of all that's holy was that fellow killed in the air. Wait a bit, though. We have been relying on the evidence of the crash given by the two men who found the body. They were Vane and Ness—both up to the neck in the dope-running. Pretty suspicious, don't you think?"

"I agree, but other witnesses saw the crash taking place," Bray pointed out. "Miss Sackbut, the Bishop, Lady Laura and Randall were on the spot immediately after the crash occurred. So I don't see how there could be any dirty business there. A crash is a crash after all. And, in the long run, we mustn't forget that letter of Furnace's which gives us a strong presumption of suicide."

The two detectives thought it over in silence.

"If only the Bishop weren't in it!" lamented Bray at last. "We can assume that Randall and Miss Sackbut are in the gang, but the Bishop we can't get over."

Creighton scratched his head. "Yes, he's an intelligent sort of bloke too. A good witness. Doesn't pretend to see more than he did."

"I suppose he is a real Bishop and not a fraud?" suggested Bray cheerfully.

"I went into that before the inquest," admitted Creighton in a grudging tone which would have surprised Dr. Marriott. "I was very suspicious of him at first. But he's perfectly genuine, and had only just arrived in England after eight years of absence. So unless when Bishop he acted as head of the Australian dope organization, and had come to England to report progress—which is unlikely—we must take his evidence as true. And I'm blest if I can see on that evidence how Furnace was murdered, either in the morning or the night before."

"Look here," suggested Bray eagerly, "here's an idea! Supposing Ness was *falsely* told by the Chief that Furnace was dead, on the evening before the crash."

"Why should he be told that?"

"To see how he would react. The Chief might reason that if Ness went yellow and threatened to squeal when he heard about it, the Chief could explain that Furnace was alive after all and that he was only testing Ness. If Ness accepted the situation, the Chief could go quietly ahead with the murder, knowing that Ness could be relied upon."

"H'm," said Creighton dubiously, "it's a bit extravagant. Now how did he murder Furnace the next day?"

"He didn't," answered Bray blithely. "While Ness believed Furnace was already a corpse, and while the Chief was getting ready to make him one, Furnace goes and kills himself, as per his letter to Lady Laura."

"God bless my soul, Bray, what an imagination!" exclaimed Creighton. "It depends a good deal on coincidence, doesn't it? And here's another objection. Surely when Furnace had killed himself, they wouldn't go on letting Ness think the Chief had killed him?"

"They might," argued Bray, "on the principle that if Ness believed himself accessory to murder he would be less likely to squeal than if he had merely helped in some dope-running. Or again, the Chief may have told Ness it was suicide and Ness may have disbelieved him."

Creighton smiled. "You win!"

"Oh, it's all very provisional," admitted Bray with an answering grin. "But suppose we let the theory stand for the moment. It gives us one suicide and one unexplained murder."

"Do you think Ness could have been a suicide too?" suggested Creighton solemnly. "That would clear the whole business up."

"For heaven's sake don't be sarcastic, old chap!" pleaded the Yard man. "You'll discourage me altogether. No, Ness wasn't a suicide, because someone must have pulled his belt fastenings away and someone must have piloted the aeroplane. We know it wasn't

Vane or Mrs. Angevin. What about the Gauntlett Air Taxis' people. Randall, for instance?"

"I've tried them, Bray. The pilots were all out on jobs, and Randall and Gauntlett were up in Glasgow after some big charter job. That's cross-checked by my people. The staff all seem to have been in their hut. The mechanics aren't all accounted for, but I don't think any can fly. No, I'm pretty sure the Chief crept on to the aerodrome and wasn't seen at all. It's easy enough. He found Ness in the hangars and decoyed him for a flight. But whoever the murderer is, I should think it's someone who's known on the aerodrome, otherwise it would be risky."

"I suppose so. But that might be any one of a hundred persons!"

"He's a pilot, anyway," pointed out Creighton.

"As I believe there are about ten thousand people who can fly in this country, it doesn't help us much," answered Bray discouragingly.

"Well, let's put our unknown murderer aside for a moment. Do we at least agree that Vandyke isn't the Chief?"

"I think so, Creighton. We ought to trust our own judgment and Ness's statement there. Vandyke is just one of the tools. After all, if the Los Angeles police spotted Vane, he can't be first-class at this dope racket. I think he was just picked up by the Big Noise as a useful tool, bearing in mind his record."

"Right; I agree," said Creighton. "Now can we simplify matters by assuming that Ness's murderer is the Chief?"

"Yes, provisionally," agreed Bray. "Ness evidently seemed to think that the Chief did his own murders, because he told us that the Chief shot Furnace. And, after all, if you have decided on murder, it's a dangerous thing to leave to subordinates, especially if the welfare of a flourishing business organization you've built up yourself depends on it."

"Wait a moment, though," exclaimed Creighton. "We've forgotten that we originally placed Gauntlett as the Chief, but Gauntlett was away in Glasgow when Ness was murdered."

Bray sighed. "Very well. Let's assume that someone other than Gauntlett is the Chief. After all, can we be so sure that Gauntlett *is* the Big Noise? Mightn't he just be C.O. of the English section by virtue of providing the distributing organization?"

"That sounds plausible. Let's assume there's still another man above Gauntlett. He's the man we have to get, both as murderer and brains of the organization. You agree to that, Bray?"

"Certainly," said the Yard man positively. "I suppose you feel as I do, that we ought to give them still a bit more rope?"

"Yes. The first step is to shadow Vane."

"I'm doing that," Bray told him. "There's just a chance he may lead us to the central organization."

Thus the conference ended, a conference which, in spite of the logic and exhaustiveness of its discussions, ended up somewhat wide of the truth. . . .

*   *   *   *   *

Bray picked up Thomas Vane as he walked along the prim avenue in which he lived. Vane was no longer dressed in any of the varieties of violent sports garb which he usually affected. He wore a neat lounge suit and a bowler and carried an umbrella and gloves. Vane, in fact, had already become Vandyke.

Bray had no difficulty in getting on the same train, and he did not anticipate any trouble in London, since shadowing is a fairly easy matter to an experienced man unless the victim is aware of it. In the latter case, at least two men are necessary.

Vane dodged round Victoria Station until Bray thought for a moment that he was being deliberately shaken off. But Vane was only buying a ticket to Waddon, and Bray, standing behind him, did the same. They got into different carriages, and Bray kept a sharp look-out to make sure that his man did not get out at an earlier station, that favourite and rarely effective trick of shadowed persons.

It did not, however, seem that Vane suspected anything. He got out at Waddon. Bray walked behind him and presently found that Vane's destination was Croydon Air Port. Vane turned in and went straight to the hangars. An aerodrome official saluted him. It appeared he was known there.

A few minutes later Vane emerged from the hangar, wheeling a small biplane by the tail. The engine was started up, and to Bray's chagrin the machine taxied out into the aerodrome and took off in an easterly direction.

"I've lost him! Damn!" muttered Bray. "Of all the impossible things to shadow, an aeroplane is the limit! But what in hell's name is Tommy Vane doing flying an aeroplane when he is supposed to be incapable of making a solo flight?"

He got into conversation with some of the engineers on the field, but learned no more than that Vane—known there as Vandyke—had frequently chartered a machine from the local air taxi service on a "fly yourself" basis. Vandyke was assumed to be an American,

as the first time he had tried to charter an aeroplane he had produced an American licence, but it was not considered acceptable
owing to certain clauses in the firm's insurance policy.

A fortnight later he had turned up with an A licence and had
mentioned he had passed the flying tests in Belfast. Vandyke had
told one of the ground engineers that he had a thousand hours'
flying experience. This, according to the ground engineer, was a
lot for an amateur, and he thought Vandyke was "shooting a line".
Still there was no doubt he was a competent pilot. He had, however, been rebuked by the Control Office for looping near the
aerodrome, and there was a general feeling that he was inclined
to "show off".

Bray rang up Creighton and told him of his experience.

Creighton seemed astounded.

"It's a very odd thing," said Creighton, "for Vane was supposed
to be one of the club's worst pupils. Yet apparently he is an expert
pilot and has been so for years. There must have been some idea
behind his pretending to be a novice."

"Search me! Anyway, we've lost him," answered Bray. "Not
for good, I hope. I don't think he knows we suspect him, which,
I suppose, is something."

"What are you going to do now?" asked Creighton.

"I'm going to see the Superintendent," said Bray firmly.
"I've been thinking it over going down in the train. You know,
Creighton, I think we're taking a big risk leaving it much longer.
If there's another murder, we might be held responsible through
not acting before. Much as we want to get the Chief, it's not a risk
we ought to run. If my Superintendent agrees, the Yard will give

the word for the round-up to take place to-morrow in all countries, and rely on being able to find evidence against the Chief in the documents we seize. It'll be a huge killing, after all, and I can't believe one of them won't squeal."

"If they know!" said Creighton sceptically.

"People like Roget *must* know," insisted Bray. "If Durand offers him the bait of his freedom, then surely to goodness he'll turn State evidence. I know Durand would do it. What does your Chief think?"

"General Sadler leaves everything in the Yard's hands. So do I. Good luck!"

"Thanks, Creighton. Jolly decent of you!"

Bray returned to Scotland Yard and had a long talk with Superintendent Learoyd.

"It's been rotten for the Chief, Bray," Learoyd admitted, worry plainly written in the set of his leonine face. "He spent hours with Lord Entourage. Of course, it may be political death to Entourage. He says he may have to resign. I don't think it's at all likely, but I understand the old chap's feelings. I'm quite sure he hadn't an inkling his nephew was a bad hat. Still, it's all over now. We're quite ready to go ahead at once. To-morrow afternoon, I suggest. The warrants are all prepared, filled in with names and addresses—Gauntlett, Randall, Miss Sackbut for luck, Vane *alias* Hartigan *alias* Vandyke, the two Customs men, all the English pilots and van-drivers, and the firm's clerks. Our gaols will be chock full!" Superintendent Learoyd looked through his papers and made a note. "Zero hour is two p.m. to-morrow, then. I'll confirm it to the other countries."

"Cheer up, Bray," he added, noticing his subordinate's despondency. "Damn it, you can't expect everything. Here we are, rounding up the biggest white drug organization known to our records. What does it matter if we can't lay hands on the Chief?"

"I know. I ought to be content. But the cold-blooded way he slaughtered that wretched little ground engineer got under my skin somehow."

CHAPTER XVIII

AWKWARDNESS OF AN AMERICAN

THE Executive Committee of the Baston Air Display rested for a while on its labours and was content.

It sat, as was its due, in the Distinguished Guests' Enclosure, to the right and left of the Lord-Lieutenant of Thameshire, who was disposed in an uncomfortable-looking chair and attired with Ascot resplendence. Mr. Walsyngham was also effulgent beneath a grey top-hat, and wore on his face an expression of bright interest. This disguised his extreme indignation at the fact that, although he had been staying at the Lord-Lieutenant's house for a week, he had been completely unsuccessful in getting him to subscribe to any of the shares of his new flotation, Planet Airways. Beside him, dressed in a battleship-grey toilette which unfortunately increased her resemblance to a tank, Lady Crumbles was engaged in conversation with Lady Laura Vanguard.

"My dear, have you seen the Bishop?" asked the Countess.

"No," answered Lady Laura off-handedly. "At least, only for a moment. He was walking quickly behind the hangars."

"My dear Laura, what did he want to go there for?" exclaimed Lady Crumbles.

"To avoid you, I think. You were just arriving, you know."

"What delicious things you do say, darling," replied Lady Crumbles acidly. "Well, I must find him before the afternoon is over. I want him to give the prizes away. I've put them out all nicely on the table there."

"Yes, I was just looking at them," remarked Lady Laura. "But how will the poor dear know which to give to whom? They've got nothing engraved on them."

"Engraving is so expensive, dear," lamented the other. "Besides, as it is for a charity, I hope some of the winners will give their trophies back and then the engraving will be a nuisance. I am sure they will if I speak to them."

"I am sure they will," admitted the girl.

"Still, it may be a little puzzling for the Bishop. Do you mind writing out the labels? Shall I tell you which are which?"

"I don't think it matters very much, darling," said Lady Laura sweetly. "Better leave it to me. Are you doing the judging?"

"I am one of the judges—yes."

"Well, I shall be simply furious if you don't give the first prize to my new 'plane in the *Concours d'elegance*. It's one of the new Dragon Sixes with the sweetest cocktail-bar inside the cabin. And full of gorgeous leather armchairs."

"Is it that big silver thing out there?" asked Lady Crumbles.

"Yes; isn't it ducky?"

"Well, I don't know how you do it, with income tax and everything," answered the other enviously.

"I wonder myself sometimes. There's poor Sally beside it. She does look worried! She keeps on driving about herds of those little girls in blue who seem to have suddenly infested our aerodrome."

Lady Crumbles peered shortsightedly at the aerodrome. "My dear, those are my Airies. Don't you think they're sweet?"

"I can honestly say I've never seen so many repulsive small girls," replied Lady Laura sincerely. "Sally spends all her time driving them away from aeroplanes on which they want to scrawl their initials."

"Dear, dear, the naughty little mites! Still, perhaps I'd better speak to their patrol leader. Do be nice to them, they are so keen and enthusiastic! Sally has promised to give the most useful ones some ginger-beer."

"I will, too, if you like," offered Lady Laura. "I'll have some gin put in it as well and make it a real party for the little angels."

"Laura, I hope and pray you are only joking!" gasped the Countess. "Please remember I am the President of the local Temperance Association."

Lady Laura was, however, already leaving the enclosure and went into the club-house without answering. Sally had returned to her office and was hurriedly checking off a list of entrants.

Lady Laura smiled at her. "Hello, Sally, can I help with that? I've just escaped from the Crumbles bird."

"No, thanks," answered Sally; "but, darling, if you want to be useful you might go and relieve Sir Herbert at the microphone in a moment. He's being rather a lamb, but I can hear him getting hoarse, and then he does have such fights with his aitches."

"Right-ho, I'll take him a drink. Oh, by the way, lend me some ink. I've promised to do the labels for the prizes. Tell the Bishop if you see him he's got to give them away. They're such cheap things, I should be ashamed to give them myself, but the dear will probably agree. Where is he, by the way?"

"He's with some queer American friend," replied Miss Sackbut. "A funny little white-haired man with a bulbous nose and the loveliest soft American accent. The Bishop's been a perfect angel on the Executive Committee, a kind of buffer State between the Crumbles person and myself, but I think he's feeling the strain a bit now."

"I'm rather surprised not to see the Inspector here," went on Lady Laura. "I thought he was a permanent fixture on the aerodrome. I suppose he has given the case up. Really, I think the police are awfully inefficient nowadays."

"Yes," said Sally thoughtfully, "they always have some excuse. Not allowed to question witnesses, and so forth. Heavens, how they've questioned me! Laura, be an angel and pop out and see if Waxy has started doing 'Falling Leaves' yet, because, if so, that's the end of his turn, so grab a couple of Airies by the ears and send them off to the Control tent to give the signal to let the 'Round the Houses' race begin. And then pop off to the microphone. Oh, and do you want your Dragon got ready to fly away after the *Concours*?"

"No, I arranged with Winters to do a flight-trial on it. I was going to borrow the club Moth. It's not in use to-day and I shall be returning it to-morrow. So put my big fellow in the hangar. I'm taking the ink with me."

"Right! Bless you, Laura," murmured Sally, her head bent over her entry list again.

Lady Laura emerged and found "Waxy's" green 'plane tumbling earthwards in the graceful fluttering of the aerobatic known as the "Falling Leaf".

After despatching two Airies to the Control tent with the necessary message, she hurried to the Announcer's tent.

The change-over was accomplished, but unfortunately Lady Laura's dulcet tones were amplified over the aerodrome to the waiting thousands at the moment when she told Sir Herbert to "get back to the Crumbles menace, but Sally has a drink waiting for you to help you to bear it". The Distinguished Guests' Enclosure thought it better not to hear this "aside", and in a few moments Lady Laura's voice was retailing the ordinary pleasantries of the announcer.

Five aeroplanes took off, wing-tip to wing-tip, roared shatteringly over the crowd, and jockeyed for position in a tight bank round the hangar windsock. The "Round the Houses" race had begun. ...

Meanwhile the Bishop, with his American friend, was engaged in evading his duties on the Executive Committee, as Lady Laura's sharp eyes had already noticed. She had been talking to Mrs. Angevin when they rapidly disappeared as Lady Crumbles entered the enclosure.

"I am sorry that we did not stop to speak to the lady after all these years," said his American companion.

"You will get a chance to do so later," assured the Bishop. "Quite frankly, not even for you would I run the risk of being caught by Lady Crumbles so early in the afternoon."

"I'll take your word for it, Bishop. It was strange, wasn't it, that we should have been placed next to each other at the Anglo-American banquet?"

"Yes," admitted the Bishop, "but even so, I should not have known we had a common friend in the woman if her father had not been sitting opposite us, which made you mention that you knew her."

"I fear he does not know what you and I know," said the American gravely. "I sometimes wonder whether I was right in entrusting you with that little secret. I am afraid it was the wine and your extremely winning personality, Bishop. Please do not on any account divulge it to a third person."

"I shouldn't dream——" The Bishop saw his friend stiffen, and broke off. "Good lord, what is the matter? You look surprised."

The Judge pointed. "That fellow Hartigan I told you of! There he is. He looks as wild as ever. A winning character, but head-strong."

The Bishop laughed. "My dear Judge, you must be mistaken. That's our youngest member, Tommy Vane."

"I may be getting old, Bishop, but I can still trust my eyes," said the American positively. "That young man is not so young as you think. And he's the Spider Hartigan I spoke of to you."

The Bishop smiled and shook his head. "I'm very sorry, but I fear you are misled by some likeness."

The disputed person was now within earshot. The Judge looked at him again. "Hi, Spider!" he shouted suddenly.

Tommy Vane turned and stared at the Judge. For a moment the Bishop saw him pale, and then, collecting himself with an obvious effort, he was about to pass on, but changed his mind at the last moment.

"Hallo, Judge," he said, extending his hand. "Glad to see you; but my name is Thomas Vane."

The Judge smiled benevolently. "Perhaps, but not always."

"I have long given up my stage name," answered Tommy Vane, who had rapidly recovered from any embarrassment he may have felt. "Why on earth have you turned up here?"

"I came on to England for a holiday," explained the Judge. "But it wouldn't have happened if I hadn't sat next to the Bishop here at a banquet the other day. We got talking, and I told him of that queer little ceremony at which I presided." The Judge dug him playfully in the ribs. "You've kept it very quiet. Of course, I told him in confidence!"

The young man looked angry. "You shouldn't have told him at all, Judge. Damn it, you promised at the time not to breathe a word!"

"So I did," admitted the American. "So I did. But then, Spider, you promised me that the silence need only be temporary, a matter of a year at the most. And it was more than two years ago. So that relieves me of the obligation. But don't worry," he added, as he saw the other's angry frown; "the Bishop is a clergyman, and I told him more with the purpose of asking his advice than anything else. I certainly don't propose to broadcast the fact."

"Thank you for that, at any rate," said Tommy Vane with an ill grace. "And what about you?" he asked the Bishop.

"Naturally, my boy," answered the Bishop blandly, "I don't propose to make it public, either. But in the circumstances you can't expect me to keep completely quiet about the whole affair. There are other interests to be considered, and I think you yourself must realize that there are certain persons I must tell, otherwise they have been misled in a way which is not fair, having regard to their responsibilities and duties."

The Judge, with innate tact, had already realized that the Bishop and Vane might be hampered in their conversation by his presence, and the Bishop's obscure circumlocution indicated that this was the case. He therefore excused himself and wandered off to watch the next event, which promised to be amusing.

"Look here," said Vane, "it's damned awkward your knowing. If it had only been the Judge I shouldn't have worried, as I think I could have persuaded him not to speak, in view of the promise he made. But I appreciate the way you feel, and I know you will do what you think right. But can you keep silent for just one day more? Let's move somewhere where we're less likely to be overheard."

"Why for one day?" asked the Bishop, weakening, as Vane drew him gently by the arm towards the refreshment tent.

"Because I promise after to-morrow to make the whole thing public myself," answered Vane earnestly. "But you can imagine how difficult it is for me as long as I have no job and no position. I'm just an out-of-work film extra. To-morrow, if all goes according to plan, I shall have an assured job and a definite position, and then I'm going to make a clean breast of the thing to all the persons concerned. Then I don't mind whom you tell. Do you understand? I'm sure you do!" he added with a smile.

"Very well," said the Bishop, responding to this reasonable appeal. "In the circumstances I don't think I can refuse. I will say nothing for another day at least."

"You're a sport, Bishop," exclaimed the young man enthusiastically. "I'm most awfully grateful. I don't know how to thank you enough. I say, will you have a drink with me?"

The Bishop laughed. "It is certainly hot. If you can get me some lemonade I shall be grateful."

After five minutes Vane returned with a glass of tired-looking yellow fluid. "Bit of a struggle, but I got it. Let's go and look at the race, shall we? You ought to have been in this one, Bishop."

The competitors were required to cover different stages of a course by aeroplane, car, donkey, wheelbarrow and fairy-cycle.

"I fear I am too old," said the Bishop after it was over. "Really, I had no idea Mrs. Angevin could ride so well. She got a positive gallop out of her donkey. I find all these displays a little tiring. To be perfectly frank, I should be exceedingly glad of a comfortable chair and a sleep."

"I am afraid the distinguished guests have got all the deck-chairs," replied Vane. "Why not go into their enclosure?"

The Bishop shuddered. "No! If I were to sit down anywhere, it would be in some quiet corner where there was no fear of Lady Crumbles finding me."

"If that's what you want, why don't you crawl into the front seat of the club machine there." Vane pointed to the scarlet-and-silver machine on the tarmac. "You can get well down with your head below the level of the cockpit doors and no one will trouble you. Lady Crumbles certainly won't. She never goes near an aeroplane, as she has some lurking fear that the thing will explode or that the propeller might come round and hit her." He paused. "It probably would if I were flying it," he added reflectively.

"That is really quite a good idea, Vane," exclaimed Dr. Marriott. "If I am not visible when the show is over, please dig me out, as I shall be expected to give away the prizes. Do please remember, for I feel so abominably sleepy that I shall certainly not wake without being called. And look after the Judge for me. I believe he's my guest," mumbled the Bishop, "but I feel so drowsy I can hardly remember. ..."

The Bishop had climbed into the front seat with the agility necessary for this task and curled himself into the cockpit as well as he could. For a time the roar of an engine being run up near him beat an uneasy staccato accompaniment to his increasing drowsiness. His hand came upon a flying helmet in the dashboard cubby-hole, however, and putting this on he shut out the offending noise.

Just as he was coming up for the last time in the waters of oblivion before sinking into their woolly depths, some strange insistent warning seemed to be struggling to clear the mists. It was as if a danger lurking merely as a shadow at the back of his brain could now be more clearly perceived. But it was too late. With a final gurgle, the Bishop sank helplessly, fathoms deep into slumber.

After a final glance to assure himself that the Bishop was sound asleep, Vane covered him with a rug. Then he strolled slowly off in search of the Judge.

The Judge, with an expression of childlike wonder on his face, was watching fabulous monsters, distended with gas, being shot down as they floated over the public enclosures by pilots armed with shotguns.

He nodded when he saw Vane. "Well, have you settled matters with the Bishop, Spider?"

"Oh, he's all right when you handle him nicely," said Vane carelessly. "Give him a drink and he'll do most things you want."

"Drink!" exclaimed the Judge. "He struck me as very abstemious at the banquet."

Vane smiled. "I expect he was, if he had to pay for the drink himself. The poor devil hasn't a bean."

The Judge looked startled. "Land's sakes, but I thought your bishops got fat pay-rolls."

"Ah, but when he was unfrocked all that kind of thing went," Vane explained. "He hasn't a penny to his name now."

The Judge looked genuinely horrified. "But I don't understand! What was he unfrocked for?"

"Oh, nothing much," said Vane easily; "just habitual drunkenness. I call it rather narrow-minded of them really, particularly as he doesn't get fighting-drunk, only sleepy-drunk."

"I find it impossible to believe," protested the Judge. "Such a charming man! Besides, what was he doing at the Anglo-American banquet if he is like that?"

Vane shrugged his shoulders. "As he'd paid for his ticket I suppose they couldn't really refuse him. Not without making a scene. In fact, that was probably why he didn't drink anything. The waiters were no doubt instructed not to serve him with wine."

"You really shock me!" The Judge's childlike eyes widened. "I cannot but believe there is some mistake."

"Come with me, Judge, and see," insisted Vane. "Believe it or not, but as soon as you left I stood the poor old buffer some drinks and he got as tight as an owl and crawled into that aeroplane to sleep it off."

Vane led the now horrified American to the aeroplane in which the Bishop was reposing. They both climbed on to the wings and Vane shook the ecclesiastic violently by the shoulder. He gave no response beyond an incoherent mumble.

"Land sakes!" muttered the Judge.

"How much has he borrowed from you?" asked Vane.

"Why, not a cent!" answered the American. "He invited me to come down and watch this display as his guest."

"By Jove, he must have got you fixed for a good killing," laughed the young man. "It's not my business, but I should look out. I mean, be careful when he asks you to play cards. Well, look here, I must buzz off, Judge. Glad to have met you again after all these years!"

Thomas Vane walked off hurriedly, apparently on some urgent business. His bright scarlet-and-blue scarf, wrapped once round his neck, with the ends flung over his shoulders, trailed behind him as he hastened on his way.

None the less he spared the time, a moment later, to glance over his shoulder, and saw with satisfaction that the Judge, a perturbed expression on his face, was walking slowly towards the exit gate of the aerodrome. Vane's knowledge of his psychology had been proved accurate. A moment later and the Judge had vanished through the gate.

Vane's smile of satisfaction changed to an expression which was extremely disturbing on so young and boyish a face. He was looking at the club aeroplane in which the Bishop was sleeping invisibly, and the expression on his face seemed charged with sinister possibility for that unsuspecting man.

Vane's attention was distracted by a shrill whine in the sky, of a note that indicated, to his experienced ear, a supercharged high-powered engine. There were no R.A.F. machines taking part in the display, and the noise certainly could not have come from any of the low-powered light 'planes which were competing in the new event, and which now, with sideslips and wild swishes of their tails, were attempting to come to rest in the middle of a tennis-court marked out on the aerodrome.

The source of the noise was presently visible as a low-wing monoplane flying towards the aerodrome. As it flew nearer it could be seen that the undercarriage was retracted into the fuselage, and that the lines of the 'plane were those of a high-speed aircraft. It came straight towards the aerodrome, shot diagonally under one of the competing light aeroplanes as it apparently hung stationary in the sky, and made the little 'plane stagger for a moment in its backwash. Then the stranger turned in a tight bank round the aerodrome.

Something about the aeroplane seemed vaguely familiar to Tommy Vane, but, his brow wrinkled in a puzzled frown, he failed to place it. The head of the pilot, partly masked by the reflections from the sloping windscreen, could be seen, but the features were indistinguishable. The 'plane came still lower, and, lifting a glinting pistol above his head, the pilot fired a Verey light. The red rocket-star fell in a wide curve with a dramatic effectiveness that made the spectators glance hurriedly at their programmes. But in vain, for the new machine was not mentioned in that list of events.

In the Control tent it caused acute annoyance. "D-GGXX," read out the Control official, scanning it through his field-glasses. "A German machine. Looks like a Heinkel. What the devil is he doing over here making a right-hand circuit and barging into our display? I've a damned good mind to report him to the Air Ministry."

"Probably some German visitor who heard of our show and thought he would pay us a surprise visit," answered Sally Sackbut mildly. "He doesn't mean any harm. Look, he's waving again. Now he's clearing off. Better leave him."

The German Heinkel (if it was one), after a final circuit of the aerodrome at a low height, had climbed like a rocket and was rapidly dwindling into the distance. The display went on, the landing competition ended, and two red machines took off for a display of crazy flying.

The Bishop slept. ...

Meanwhile Lady Laura had completed her duty at the microphone.

"Too exhausting, darling," she moaned to Sally. "And I haven't yet finished writing out those slips for the trophies." She produced some paper from her bag and began to cover them with her strong, sturdy calligraphy.

"It's awfully good of you, Laura, to help me all you have done," insisted Sally. "You are an amazing person really, beneath your social butterfly crust. You've been invaluable with this display, bless you. I really don't know why you don't go in for something that would make use of your gifts!"

Lady Laura laughed, turning round from the desk at which she was sitting to smile at Sally. "You're the first person who has credited me with ability," she answered. "Look, I've scrawled these cards very hurriedly. I must get back to Goring this afternoon. Make my apologies to Lady Crumbles for me, and while I remember it, I'm expecting a bloke to turn up looking for me. Give him this note and tell him he's arrived too late."

Sally took the envelope. "You're very ruthless to your admirers! What's his name, by the way?"

"He will be too shy to give it, bless the poor lamb," said Lady Laura with a smile. "But you'll realize it's he all right. So long, Sally. You're too good for this job, my dear."

With a wave, Lady Laura was gone. Sally walked to the window and saw her spin the airscrew of a club machine, jump in, and fly away in the pause between the crazy flying event and the next item on the programme, the parachute descent.

The parachute descent passed off successfully, and the crowded enclosures were duly relieved or disappointed to see the flash of silk as the canopy puffed from its pack and safely lowered its human burden to earth. The parachutist was driven triumphantly round the enclosure, and then the voice of Sir Herbert Hallam, once again officiating in the Announcer's tent, was heard. Evidently Hallam had been refreshed by his rest, for his aitches were well under control again.

"The next item will be a display by the pilots of Gauntlett's Air Taxis, who, with the entire fleet of this remarkable concern, will give a demonstration illustrating the utility and resource of modern air taxis. You will see the fleet lined up at the end of the aerodrome with the pilots standing by. At the other end of the aerodrome…"

As Sir Herbert amplified his theme, the crowd turned their eyes to the brave show of scarlet-and-yellow machines at the far end of the aerodrome. They had only a hazy idea of what was the precise nature of the event, and therefore a little burst of applause went up when a tradesman's van shot into the aerodrome gates, and was followed by two more. They drove straight across the aerodrome and stopped opposite the air taxis, whose pilots stared at them in some surprise.

Sally Sackbut had seen it, and rushed out of her office. She grabbed the first club member she could find.

"Hi, Tommy Vane!" she said. "Dash along and turn those blighted lunatics off! Find out where they came from and take their names for trespass. Run along now."

Tommy Vane jumped into his red Austin Seven and wallowed across the aerodrome, arriving just as Creighton was getting out of a van lettered with a baker's name.

The policeman pointed to him. "Take him first!" said Creighton to his assistant. "Thomas Vane *alias* Vandyke *alias* Hartigan."

Tommy Vane turned white as the heavy hand of a police constable fell on his shoulder. But it was only a momentary disturbance, and a moment later he smiled back with boyish joy as if the Inspector had made a joke.

"What am I charged with?"

"Possession and distribution of illegal drugs," said the Inspector shortly.

"I'm glad it's no worse," sighed Vane.

Creighton turned to the constable. "Keep a close eye on him, Murgatroyd. He's more dangerous than he looks. Now pinch all those pilots, everyone you can see in scarlet-and-yellow uniforms! Impound their aeroplanes. Get that man in the light flannel suit—it's Gauntlett himself. Pinch that bloke with the competitor's armlet and wearing an eyeshade. That's Captain Randall. He's down in the list too."

The Inspector consulted his notebook and turned to Bray, who had stepped out of another van. "We don't want anyone else for the moment except Sally Sackbut, the secretary. She'll be fairly easy to take. In fact, I see her racing across the aerodrome towards us now. I've given the cordon outside instructions that if anyone tries to make a bolt they're to be pinched, whoever they are, and you do the same, Murgatroyd, if you see anyone bolting. There's Lady Crumbles coming. Take my advice, Murgatroyd, and pretend you're dumb. I'm going over to the Announcer's tent, but don't tell her so." The Inspector hurried off.

CHAPTER XIX

METHOD OF A MURDER

"This is Inspector Creighton of the Thameshire Constabulary speaking," boomed the loud-speakers.

There had been signs that a panic might develop in the crowds in the enclosure, who had watched the little bunch of men in blue seize a dozen people and bundle them into the waiting vans. Inspector Creighton now did his best to create an atmosphere of reassurance.

"It has been necessary in the course of our duties to arrest certain people at the aerodrome to-day. It is nothing to do with the display now in progress, which no doubt will continue according to programme. Meanwhile, you are asked not to leave your enclosures until the display is finished. Police are waiting at all the exits, and they will not be taken off duty until we are sure that all our arrests have been successfully effected."

"But how can we get on with the programme when the flying manager has been arrested?" wailed Lady Crumbles, who had worn down Murgatroyd at last and extracted from him the whereabouts of the Inspector. "Oh dear, oh dear, oh dear! Four of my Airies are in hysterics with fear, and the Control tent people say they are not going to take any responsibility for the display without the flying manager, and she's under arrest."

"I am sorry, my lady," said Inspector Creighton firmly, who was able to deal with Lady Crumbles as an official although helpless before her as a private individual. "I am sorry, but we have to do our duty. You must rely on the other club members to help you out."

"What has happened? What are you arresting everybody for?"

"Drug smuggling," said the Inspector briefly. "And probably murder as well."

Lady Crumbles gave a little scream. "Good gracious me! Why *ever* did I allow them to associate me with this dreadful display. Drug smuggling! Why, even at this moment my Airies may be sniffing opium or whatever it is. That dreadful woman Sally Sackbut! I always mistrusted her."

"I don't think you need worry about the children, my lady," answered Creighton dryly. "They are hardly likely to be given any drugs unless they can afford to pay for them, which I think improbable. You would be helping us much more, if I may say so, if you would go outside and get some flying machines in the air to distract the public, otherwise they'll certainly be asking for their money back."

"Asking for their money back?" echoed Lady Crumbles, horrified. "Something must be done about it at once. Sir Herbert, have you any suggestions? Could you give a turn?"

Sir Herbert coughed. "My flying days are over, Lady Crumbles. But I don't see why our women's race shouldn't go ahead. Mrs. Robbins is 'ere, and Greta Forsyte, and Miss Gilberte. We shall 'ave to do without Lady Laura and Mrs. Angevin, as I believe they left a little while ago."

Inspector Creighton sighed as Lady Crumbles swept out. Then he left the Announcer's tent and walked towards the hangars. There was a room at the end of them formed by partitioning and provided with windows, and here Bray was already seated at a table checking off a list.

"We've got them all now," Bray told him. "Most emphatic protestations of innocence on the part of the pilots. Quite convincing, some of them. Really remarkable display of innocence in one case. But every one of them, as I saw from the records before I put them in the list, has carried drugs at some time. Valentine Gauntlett is breathing fire and slaughter and invoking his uncle's name. Randall seems, if anything, rather amused. Some of the other chappies are still protesting their innocence to Murgatroyd."

"Are you taking any statements here?" asked Creighton.

"There's no need to hurry about taking anything from these people who swear they're innocent. But that Vane fellow is worth having along here, I think. He's been saying some rather odd things." Bray turned to Creighton's assistant: "I say, Murgatroyd, if Vane still says he wants to make a statement, bring him along, will you? The other two tenders can go away. Right!"

"It's a damned awkward time to have to make the arrests," grumbled Creighton. "Lady Crumbles is furious. Fortunately the Lord-Lieutenant has left."

"It couldn't be helped," Bray pointed out. "It was essential the arrests should be as simultaneous as possible. Even as it is, Germany acted a little earlier than we did, and it might have caused awkwardness. I don't think it has, though, as we seem to have got all the important people."

"All?" queried Creighton.

"All—except the Chief," admitted Bray. "We're hoping the papers we impound will give us enough clues to find out who he is. I still have a sneaking feeling that this fellow Thomas Vane, or Vandyke … Oh, here he is!"

Tommy Vane had by now completely recovered the careless gaiety which was his habitual mood. He looked absurdly young, with his cropped hair and extravagant scarf. He sat down in a chair facing the two police inspectors.

"You wish to make a statement?" asked Bray formally, and warned him.

"I do," answered Vane.

"First of all, what is your real name and nationality?"

"I am British, the product of one of our leading public schools," answered Vane cheerfully. "Need I shame it by mentioning it? Poor but honest parents; or, rather, honest and hence poor parents. Army people. My name is Hartigan, later called 'Spider' Hartigan, because of a little trick I did in the States, crawling up and down a thin rope attached to an aeroplane. As to my other names, Theodosius Vandyke is my idea of what a rich young American might be called, and Thomas Vane, as you will please notice, is rather an ingenious version of the same names—same initials, for instance. Oh, my real Christian names are Claude Jeremy. Rather awful, don't you think? I'd prefer you to call me Spider."

Both policemen maintained a stolid expression on their faces. Tommy Vane shifted uneasily in his chair.

"I don't quite know how you got on our track," he went on boldly. "You seem to have been very thorough."

"Possibly more thorough than you think," commented Bray, watching him closely. "At the same time as the arrest here took place, round-ups were also made in Germany, France, Belgium, and Holland."

Vane shrugged his shoulders. "Well, of course, if one organization went *phut* the others were bound to follow. That was our weakness, as I always told the Chief."

"Who is the Chief?" asked Bray quietly.

Vane smiled. "All in good time. Where was I? Oh yes. I often used to point out the weakness of our organization to the Chief. But he insisted that it was holeproof. Now perhaps you had better begin my statement. I, Claude Jeremy Hartigan, being of sound mind and body—or is that only in wills? Anyway, put in the usual stuff—I declare that during the last two years I have been engaged in the nefarious practice of dope-smuggling. Nefarious is good, don't you think, or is it too literary for a police statement?"

"Will you kindly stick to a plain narrative?" said Bray patiently.

"I beg your pardon. ... Practice of dope-smuggling. ... Under the Chief I was the main executive officer and contributed no small part to the final shape of the scheme. The main outlines, I admit, were the Chief's. In any case, the most important point was that the Chief's political and social acquaintances were such as to make very easy the obtaining, without suspicion, of the central nucleus of our organization in Paris. By giving the Chief and the Chief's friends as references, I was able to impose myself upon Maître Roget as an eccentric millionaire and persuade him to act as my purchasing agent in the acquisition of *La Gazette Quotidienne*. The capital for this was provided not by the Chief or myself—we were both distressingly and revoltingly poor—but by a manufacturer of white drugs in Bulgaria whose goods, in turn, we promised to use exclusively. There is honour among thieves and criminals, and we kept this bond faithfully. By the way, did your French friends arrest Roget?"

"They did," answered Bray.

"That's too bad," Vane shook his head mournfully. "I should have thought Roget's reputation would have secured him from suspicion. He acted in good faith throughout, and no one will be more surprised, I am sure, than that worthy notary when he is told that the charming Mr. Vandyke—I went to some trouble to be charming—is a criminal." Tommy Vane smiled genially at the policemen. "The whole beauty of our scheme was the degree to which we used innocent people. It was safer and so much cheaper. It was, I believe, the main reason why we were never suspected for so long. I assure you that only five people connected with *La Gazette* dreamed that it was a centre for drug distribution. Those five people were Grandet and his four assistants, all men with criminal records, but so carefully segregated in their sub-department that no one was likely to come into contact with them. I trust you will be good enough to forward this part of my statement to the French police."

"I think I will," said Bray thoughtfully. "I seem to remember Durand saying something of the sort, although the evidence against Roget was pretty damning."

"Good. Poor little Roget must be cleared. Well, I suppose there is no need to go into the mechanism of the distribution in detail—you probably know it already. Its essence was the suborning of the necessary number of air Customs officials in each country, and an arrangement whereby the day when those officials were on duty was signalled to head office. The real touch of genius in the scheme was, of course, the use of air transport, so that the drug was in the hands of the consumer before the end of the day on which it left the centre. I hope you appreciated the neatness of that idea, and also the efficiency with which it was worked out?"

"We do appreciate it," commented Bray dryly.

"Ah, but you don't, not fully," expostulated Vane. "You have made the obvious clumsy error of thinking that it was a vast organization of bribery and corruption. But it wasn't. The really delicious part of it was that the air taxi people themselves were absolutely unaware of the nature of the cargo they were carrying!"

Bray and Creighton looked at each other with mutual surprise. "What! Do you mean to assert," asked Bray, "that Gauntlett's Air Taxis *weren't* a part of your organization?"

"Most certainly I do," answered Vane in surprise. "Our procedure in each country was to put the newspaper air delivery out to tender among the various air taxi firms. The best tender won it. This disarmed suspicion, because it meant we employed a firm which was known by the Air Ministry and the police to be perfectly honest!"

"But the risk! It seems tremendous!" exclaimed Bray.

Vane shook his head. "Only a tenth of the risk that would result if all the pilots and van-drivers were aware of the nature of their cargo. The secret would be bound to leak out then among so many. Besides, the difficulty of getting enough dishonest pilots would be immense. And the cost of the organization, if it were a dummy one, would be an impossible tax on the scheme."

"Yes," admitted Bray. "That point had puzzled us."

"There was no real risk. The drug was done up into bundles of newspapers, and each bundle was sealed. Would any pilot dream of opening them in the ordinary way? There was no danger that the cross-Channel pilot would clear Customs anywhere except at the aerodrome where our men were on duty, because he would know the other smaller aeroplanes were waiting there to distribute the papers to the provincial centres. The scheme was absolutely safe. *La Gazette* contracts were fought for eagerly by the air taxi firms of a dozen countries, and all that part of the organization was taken off our shoulders. We only had two responsibilities, apart from getting the dope into France. One responsibility was to arrange for safe Customs clearance at one regular aerodrome at more or less regular dates. This was the most expensive and difficult thing in the whole scheme and took us longest to arrange, and we never knew from one week to another when our two men would come upon the rota. The other responsibility was to provide a newsagent in each large town ready to act as a drug distribution centre. As Inspector Bray will appreciate, that is a fairly easy task. Provincial distributors, and lists of likely customers, can both be obtained in the world of white drug smuggling fairly cheaply. In our case they were kindly provided for us by our drug manufacturer without charge. So you see really the organization was much simpler than it seemed, and that was the main charm. Most of the work was done as a commercial proposition, by very respectable firms, experts in their line. All we had to do was to keep a general organizing eye on each national distribution."

"And where did you come in?" asked Bray.

"I came to Baston to look after the English side: hence my appearance as a novice member of the club. As Vandyke I went to Croydon regularly, chartered an aeroplane and flew to the Chief's headquarters for our conferences. I may say I adopted this method to shake off any roving policemen who might choose to follow me."

Bray flushed, but said nothing.

"There is no point in giving you the heads of the other countries," went on Vane. "Doubtless you have already got them. If not, well, you must look for them elsewhere. As you will have gathered by now, I don't propose to incriminate anyone besides myself in this statement."

"You persist that none of the pilots engaged in carrying the drugs was aware of it?" pressed Creighton.

"Most certainly," answered Vane positively. "That is my main point in making this statement. Gauntlett, Randall, Miss Sackbut, Downton, Thorndike—none of them has or had the slightest knowledge of what he or she was doing."

Creighton gave an unbelieving smile. "I am afraid that story is too tall to believe. If, as you say, the pilots knew nothing about it, and had not to be bribed, can you explain why Furnace, before his death, had to be paid additional sums beyond his ordinary salary amounting to more than a thousand pounds per annum? Moreover, how did he come to be in possession of a drug which he knew to be cocaine—knew because he had taken it to a public analyst?"

Vane's face became suddenly watchful. "Oh, you knew that, did you? I didn't realize it. Well, as it happened, Furnace was the one man who did find out—by sheer accident. He forgot to deliver one bundle, and some confounded impulse persuaded him to pull off the binding and have a look at one of the papers. Of course it was just bad luck that it happened to be one of the days when we were delivering drugs, and when he found a white powder in the newspapers he got suspicious at once."

"But he didn't have it analysed at once," Bray pointed out.

"No. Fortunately he mentioned it to Ness directly he arrived. Ness was my assistant in the English organization; I had bought him cheaply and he was useful because he knew the movements of the Gauntlett people and could keep a check on them. Well, Ness told me at once, so I got on to the Chief and I was given authority to buy Furnace at any price. It wasn't so expensive as it might have been, because I told him it was saccharine we were smuggling. He agreed to keep quiet for twelve hundred a year, and we paid it; but I was never happy, because he obviously suffered from ingrowing conscience. Furnace wasn't a fool, and something made him suspicious. I don't know what it was, but anyway the damned fool went to an analyst, and that blew the gaff. He began to get qualms of conscience and suddenly decided he was the most awful rotter the world had ever known. Brooded for days."

Vane sneered. "I think what really broke him was his love for a woman whom he felt to be too good for him, now that he had become a criminal. He got a fit of acute depression and span into the ground—after shooting himself, apparently. Why he shot himself first I don't know, but I realized what had happened directly you found he had been shot as well as crashed. Unfortunately I couldn't explain without giving myself away."

Vane looked defiantly at the two. "Well, that's my statement, Inspector, and I hope you'll let those pilots go!"

Bray and Creighton went into whispered consultation.

"Damned awkward," confessed Bray. "It might be right, you know. It would explain a lot. You remember we were puzzled by the fact that Gauntlett and Miss Sackbut didn't back Vane up over Mrs. Angevin's movements. I think we'll have to let Gauntlett, Sally Sackbut and Co. go for the moment, unless we find something to incriminate them in the documents we've got from Banchurch Street."

He spoke to Vane again. "If you think this statement is going to help you, my lad," he said roughly, "you're mistaken. There's nothing here about your organization we didn't know or couldn't find out. Now look here, don't be a fool. You're in a bad jam, why make it worse? Tell us who the Chief is, and we won't forget you. I can't make a definite promise, but you can trust to us."

"Get thee behind me, Satan," said Vane pleasantly. "I don't propose to tell you who the Chief is. And I think it is extremely unlikely that you will ever find out. As a matter of fact, I happen to be the only member of the organization except one German who ever came into contact with the Chief otherwise than by letter. No, let me correct that. Several members of the organization met the Chief, but in circumstances that would have made it impossible for them to realize who they were speaking to."

"We shall find the Chief all right, don't you worry," said Creighton positively. "Somebody will give him away, consciously or unconsciously. Why not do yourself a bit of good, since the thing's inevitable, and make our task easy?"

"My dear fellow," said Vane wearily, "that is one of the things that are definitely not done by the *pukka* criminal. I am sorry, but we cads have our code."

A silence followed, broken only by the steady writing of Sergeant Finch, who was acting as amanuensis. His task completed, he gave the statement to Vane, who read it carefully.

"The style is rather heavy," he commented, "and it shows no trace of any special sense of humour. Still, it is the best I can expect, I suppose."

He scrawled *Claude Jeremy Hartigan* in his bold eccentric hand across the foot.

He had not completed the initialling of the pages when Murgatroyd came in and quietly approached his superior.

"We've been having trouble with some fellow who says he's an American Judge," he explained. "One of our lads pulled him up when he was trying to make a quick getaway. He keeps telling some extraordinary story about a drunken Bishop who's trying to work the three-card trick. I can't make out whether he's dotty or just putting it on."

Bray laughed, and Vane, who, as the cause of it, could appreciate the humour of the Judge's bewilderment, ought to have laughed too, but he did not. On the contrary he lost for the first time his air of ease.

"I ran into that guy this afternoon. He *is* dotty all right," he said earnestly. "Sorry to disappoint you, but he's nothing to do with us. He was brought here by the Bishop of Cootamundra, but he's got some queer idea about him, and when the Bishop left him for a moment with me he suddenly decided to run away from the Bishop."

Bray looked at Vane closely.

"All right, Murgatroyd," Creighton was saying, "let him go after you've searched him, if his papers establish his identity."

Bray realized it might have been his imagination, but he thought he saw an expression of sudden relief pass over Vane's face at Creighton's words.

"If you don't mind, Creighton," remarked Bray. "I'd like to have a word with this Judge."

"Just as you like. Ask him to come in, Murgatroyd."

Judge Innes was flushed and a little dishevelled, but still capable of a generous flow of indignation.

"Are you the Captain?" he asked Creighton. "Is this your British justice, arresting an American citizen as he walks peacefully along? What's the big idea? What are you charging me with anyway?"

"You are not being charged with anything, sir," said Bray in his most mellifluous tones. "It was necessary for us in the course of our duties to arrest several criminals at the aerodrome, and a cordon was placed round it to prevent any of them making their escape. The public were asked over the loud-speaker not to leave the grounds until further notice. You were found attempting to do so, somewhat rapidly, as I understand. Hence the action of our officers."

"Well, if that's so ... still you have no cause to suspect me. I'm an American Judge over here on holiday, and the only thing that's the matter with me is my innocence, I guess. I got tied up with some old geezer who called himself a Bishop, but it turns out he was nothing much better than a confidence trickster. If it hadn't been——"

At this point the Judge's eye fell on Vane, who now stood looking out of the door of the room, over the shoulder of the policeman guarding it. Unfortunately, although his face was turned away, his scarf was visible and the Judge went up to him.

"Why, Hartigan, fancy finding you here! You can explain to these bulls—these gentlemen, I mean, about the Bishop. How I got sold by a guy like that! Is my face red?"

Bray and Creighton began to speak simultaneously.

"Why, do you know Hartigan?" they asked.

"Sure I do," answered the American. "I live near to Los Angeles, and I knew Hartigan well when he was at Hollywood. A very popular young man he was, and a great friend of my wife still, although he left us so suddenly—I don't know why. I only heard some silly rumours I didn't believe. Made his pile I expect, though I never heard there was much money in being a stunt man. Perhaps, though, he couldn't go on being one after his marriage."

"What exactly was his job?" asked Bray, rather less interested now that he knew how the Judge had come to recognize their prisoner.

"A stunt man," explained the Judge. "He doubles for the stars and does the difficult or dangerous things they won't do. Boy, but Spider was grand! Did you see that film about four years ago called 'Hell-Birds'?"

Bray nodded. "As a matter of fact I did."

"Say, but wasn't it great?" said Innes enthusiastically. "Those crashes! That piece where the airman hero goes straight up to ten thousand feet and spins into the deck and you can see him waving all the time? There doesn't look any fake about it and I can tell you there wasn't. This baby here did that, and had he a hair out of place afterwards? I'll tell the world he hadn't!"

Vane interposed angrily. "What the devil has all this got to do with how you knew me? I don't want my past bleated about as if you were my Press agent. You're a damned fool, Innes!"

The judge turned red with indignation. "Say, if that's what you think ..." He reached for his hat and was about to go. "You wouldn't think this boy here used to stay at my house for weeks on end and call my wife Mother, would you? All right, Tommy, I can take a hint!"

The two police inspectors exchanged a glance. Creighton nodded. "Will you please stay a moment, sir?" begged Bray. "This is more important than you think. Am I to understand that Hartigan, as a stunt man, actually had to crash aeroplanes—really crash them, not just fake photography?"

"Of course. Don't you know that there are dozens of stunt men doing that for every flying film, Captain? You come to Hollywood and I'll show you. All those spins into the ground are real. It's just a way they have of taking the bang with a wing-tip as the ship touches which saves them being injured. They get hurt sometimes, but they're well paid for it. You ought to read Dick Grace's book. There was a lad if you like! He had even you licked, Spider. Why, I've seen him put a handkerchief on the ground and then crack up and reach for the handkerchief while he was still in the cockpit, hanging upside down with the rest of the ship in pieces on the 'drome! He'd give you a crack-up within ten feet of the camera, Grace would, if you paid for it. But that spin of yours in 'Hell-Birds', Spider, was a sure fine thrill! Grace himself hasn't done better!"

"You damned maundering old fool!" exclaimed Vane, white with exasperation. "Do you realize I am under arrest?" His voice shook with rage. "Damn and blast you, what did you want to come over to England for, you confounded old hayseed!"

The Judge's face softened when he saw the young man's stricken face. He put his hand on his shoulder.

"Why didn't you tell me you were in trouble, son?" he said. "I'd have helped you, you know that, don't you? What is it, gentlemen?"

"Drug smuggling," answered Creighton briefly. "We have his confession here."

"Say, that's bad." He looked at Vane. "Were those rumours I heard about you down at the studio true after all then?"

Vane nodded. "Absolutely accurate," he said with forced lightness. "Uncle Sam eventually asked me to leave his country quickly, for the country's good."

The Judge looked upset. "Maggie will be sorry to hear that, son. She thought a lot of you. I'm sorry if I got you on the raw. Now, look here, don't be afraid of answering me. You want a good lawyer when you get in these jams—can you afford one? The first thing Maggie will ask me when she hears of your trouble is, did I help you? You know what she is about a thing like that," said the Judge with gentle tact, "and it'd be more than my life's worth if I couldn't answer her."

"I'm quite all right, thank you," said Vane coldly. "I'm probably a damn' sight richer than you are, since the slump."

The Judge smiled. "You're bitter, son, but I understand. Take my name, will you, Captain, in case I'm wanted? I'd like to give evidence for the defence about this young man's character."

Bray had been discussing something in a low voice with Creighton while the Judge was talking to Vane. He now seemed to have made up his mind.

"Will you wait here a little longer, Judge? There is something I would like you to hear; you can probably help us.

"Vane, or Hartigan," went on Bray, his young lawyer's face suddenly menacing, "I'm going to put to you a reconstruction of some of the evidence you have told us, and which I consider you have distorted for your own ends." The detective looked down at his notes and compressed his lips, as if what he saw there had finally decided him. "You declare that the shooting of Furnace was suicide. That, certainly, was the view we ourselves had arrived at, but it was severely shaken by the murder of Ness. Ness was not killed by you, Vane. We admit the strength of your alibi there. But I think you know who murdered him, and I think it was the Chief."

"Possibly!" Vane shrugged his shoulders. "Supposing it was. Does it get you much farther?"

"It leads me to the conclusion," went on Bray calmly, "that the first suicide *was* a murder after all. I must admit you have an alibi of sorts, and, to be perfectly candid, if Furnace was murdered, I see no way in which it can be proved whether you or the Chief murdered him."

"Indeed!" said Vane mockingly. "Perhaps on the facts of the case you can explain how he was murdered at all."

"That is what I am about to do. The Judge, unconsciously, has supplied the missing link which puzzled me in the chain of events. We know that the machine crashed, and we know that Furnace was shot a minute or two before the impact that wounded his forehead. My theory explains how this could be reconciled with murder. I assert that at a date which I cannot put later *than the previous day*, Furnace was shot. I do not think it was you who shot him, for you seem to have had an alibi for most of the preceding day, as did Ness. But you *might* have done it. The main point is that, difficult as it is to believe, Furnace was shot the day before the crash. That is the only explanation of the circumstance which has always defeated every other theory—which we have had to neglect or explain away in every other theory."

"The *rigor*, I suppose?" interjected Creighton.

"Yes, the *rigor*! It was not present when the Bishop watched by the body, nor again when the doctor examined it. When we discovered the bullet-wound in the head, we attributed the absence of *rigor* to the fact that Furnace had been shot a few minutes before the Bishop examined the body, and that the *rigor* had not set in even at the time when the doctor came on the scene. But when we went back to the theory that Furnace was a suicide, and shot himself just before he crashed, the *rigor* was again a stumbling-block, for by all the laws of physiology, with a normal subject like Furnace, the *rigor* should have been developing when the Bishop saw the body, and fully developed when the doctor attended to it. But it wasn't."

Creighton nodded. "Yes, Bastable was positive about that."

"There is only one possible explanation: Furnace was killed before the crash, long before—the preceding evening in fact. Why? Because that would mean that he had been killed so long before that the *rigor* had come and gone. You will remember that this was Bastable's first assumption—that the *rigor* had passed off by the time he saw the body. The Bishop's evidence made him suppose that the *rigor* had not yet set in. In fact, it had come on normally and had passed off normally. This means that Furnace had not been killed in the crash, and, knowing that the *rigor* takes up to twenty-four hours to pass off, one must assume he was killed the preceding afternoon."

"Good lord! Of course!" exclaimed Creighton.

"Now do you see my point?" said Bray triumphantly. "Whatever the explanation of the absence of *rigor*, it was incompatible with Furnace's suicide. For if the *rigor* had not come on when the doctor examined Furnace, as we thought at first, he must have been killed after the crash. But Furnace *wasn't* shot after the crash, according to the medical report.

"If, on the other hand, the *rigor* had come *and gone*, it meant that Furnace was killed some time *before* the crash, and that again was incompatible with the medical report that he was shot a minute or two before the impact. So that either explanation of the *rigor* involved contradiction, and yet I was unable to believe the suicide theory. It is true Bastable ought to have been able to fix the time of death, and he would have been able to do so had he made a careful examination when he arrived. It is true he arrived very late, and therefore it would not have been a precise time. But it would have been near enough. Unfortunately, but naturally, he accepted the story of the crash and only made sure that life was extinct."

"I had constructed various possible explanations, but none of them fitted. Judge Innes has provided me with the one possible explanation. Furnace was never in the aeroplane at all!"

"What?" exclaimed Creighton, genuinely startled.

Vane said nothing, but watched the detectives with a cold smile on his face.

"Furnace was shot the previous afternoon," went on Bray calmly, "and almost immediately was hit on the head with an instrument to simulate the effect of hitting the edge of the dash-board. This blow also covered up the traces of the bullet-hole, but in case the bullet was ever found the revolver was embedded in the soil of the aerodrome to give a possible explanation of suicide."

"Why shoot him at all? Why not kill him at once by a blow on the head?" queried Creighton.

"Because it is not easy to go up to a strong man and hit him a fatal blow on the temple, with the certainty that the blow will be of a kind to look as if it had been done in a crash. You can't use an ordinary 'cosh' or club because the resulting wound will be obviously wrong. Probably the Chief is a small man and not too skilful at physical violence. No, the shot is understandable enough."

Creighton reflected. "I still don't understand how the body was taken from the wreckage if Furnace was killed the previous day?"

"I do now," answered Bray. "Vane took up a club aeroplane and spun it into the ground so that its landing-place was out of sight of the aerodrome. I went wrong because, as a layman, I never realized it would be possible for a pilot, however skilful, deliberately to crash a machine with a reasonable chance of escaping with his life."

"Good lord!" interrupted Creighton. "Now I come to think of it, that agrees with the evidence of the Air Ministry's technical expert at the inquest. He said that the main force of the impact had been taken by the wing-tip, and he was surprised at Furnace being killed."

"Exactly," replied Bray. "It seems that this man Hartigan, who deliberately posed as the most foolish of pupils, is a pilot who made his reputation at Hollywood at that kind of thing. Isn't that so, Judge?"

Judge Innes nodded silently.

"Apparently Furnace suspected Vane of being a better pilot than he pretended to be," recollected Creighton. "I remember the Bishop telling me of a queer little incident when Furnace span the aeroplane and Vane was forced to right it himself. That would explain it. And Winters always told me Vane used to 'put on' his fear of flying. 'Showing off', Winters called it."

"Very well," went on Bray. "Vane crashes the machine harmlessly——"

"Not harmlessly," interrupted Creighton, "for I remember at the inquest one of the witnesses remarked that Vane had hurt his arm. They assumed he had done this when freeing the pilot from the wreckage. Obviously he had done this in the crash."

Bray nodded. "A good point. Then as soon as the crash took place, Ness rushed out of the hangars in the ambulance tender.

He must have been waiting for this, sitting in the driver's seat, with the engine running."

"Yes," said Creighton, "at the inquest he explained his promptness by the excuse that he had been overhauling the engine and that it was actually running at the time."

"He tore at full speed out of the garage, and beside him, not too easily discernible (for the driving-seat was enclosed), was a figure. That figure wore the flying helmet and mask and enormous coloured scarf and leather coat which were recognized sartorial eccentricities of Tommy Vane. But it was not Tommy Vane—it was the corpse of Furnace."

There was a low whistle of amazement from Creighton. The Judge looked tired and old. Tommy Vane was still smiling thinly.

"The rest was easy," said Bray. "Behind the trees the corpse of Furnace was laid on the ground, and Vane now put on the coat, scarf and helmet. The dashboard had doubtless previously been smeared with blood and hairs from Furnace's head, and possibly slightly battered, to give the appearance of having inflicted the fatal blow. The seat belt had parted when Vane crashed, and so the illusion was perfect by the time Randall, and later the Bishop, Miss Sackbut and Lady Laura, arrived on the scene.

"There was just one flaw. The chances against it were enormous, but there it was. The Bishop of Cootamundra had some medical knowledge, and he was watching by the body at a time when the *rigor* should have just been developing, and it wasn't present. That might have been explicable by a delayed development of the *rigor*, but when he spoke to the doctor he found that it still had not been present, and the doctor had, in turn, attributed this to an early development. That flaw wrecked the whole scheme because it brought about investigation. Creighton probed into Furnace's past and found that analyst's letter which gave us a clue to unravel the whole skein finally."

"Finally?" asked Vane mockingly. "Have you found out who the Chief is? As the Chief murdered Furnace—you are quite right about it, and I congratulate you—you are still as far away from the solution of the murder as ever!"

"I should have thought the Chief was a fiction of your imagination," Bray said quietly, "if it hadn't been for Ness's murder. But he *was* murdered. And you weren't there. And I think Ness's murderer killed Furnace. But I admit I'm still as far off finding the Chief's identity as ever, until I can go into the papers we've got." Bray looked at Judge Innes. "Can you help us? Do you know any criminal in Los Angeles with whom Hartigan associated?"

The Judge and Vane exchanged a look.

"I know no criminal in Los Angeles with whom Hartigan associated," Innes answered slowly. "And I seem to have done mischief enough already to a lad my wife and I were very fond of." He looked kindly at the young man.

Vane's mouth twitched, but he said nothing, and his eyes fell before the Judge's.

There was a knock upon the door. Murgatroyd came in with a telegram.

"For you, sir," he said, handing it to Inspector Bray.

Bray tore it open. Then he swore.

"The chief of the German organization, Graf von Fahrenberg, has got away! Apparently he was on the aerodrome and he slipped into a fast machine and escaped. Damn it, they ought to have known that as a war ace he'd try and make an aerial getaway!"

Bray drummed irritably on the table with his thin fingers. "They say the machine was heading for this direction, and may have had time to warn the organization here, as the Germans found it necessary to act a little before our zero hour."

"Good lord!" exclaimed Creighton. "Would that be the German pilot who swooped down on the aerodrome and shot off a red light just before we came? They told me about it in the Control tent. They were rather annoyed with him."

"Great Scott—of course!" said Bray. "But we got here in time. Or did we? Creighton, do you think he came here to warn the Chief?"

"Gosh, if he did! And the Chief's slipped through our hands!" The two detectives stared at each other in silent consternation.

"It wouldn't have made any difference, as we don't know who the Chief is yet," said Bray philosophically. "All right, Murgatroyd, there's no answer."

Murgatroyd shifted uneasily on his feet in front of Creighton. "There's just one thing, sir. Miss Sackbut is very worried about some note Lady Laura left with her that a friend of Lady Laura's might be asking for. She says will you take charge of it, as she's got to go to the station? All her friends were arrested, she says, so it's your responsibility." Murgatroyd handed over the orange-coloured envelope.

"What the devil does she think I am?" grumbled Creighton. "No name on the note, either," he added. "Just 'To be Called for'. How the hell can I know who will call for it?"

"Miss Sackbut didn't know herself, sir," said Murgatroyd, and grinned. "But I gathered it would be someone who's—well, sweet on Lady Laura, if I might say it without offence."

Vane laughed discordantly.

Bray, suddenly catching sight of the envelope, drew an audible breath.

"God Almighty, Creighton, what have you got there!"

With an excitement he could not control, he almost seized the envelope from Creighton and tore it open. He picked up the note which fluttered out and, before reading it, held it up to the light. Then he glanced at the contents.

Creighton was startled to see the expression of surprise which had come over Bray's face. At last the detective passed the little slip of orange-coloured paper to Creighton.

"Written on the gang's special notepaper," Bray said with an effort at calmness; "read it."

Dear Inspectors (the note ran),

I have left this note with Sally, unaddressed, knowing that sooner or later you will suspect me and it will come into your hands. Sally, of course, knows nothing about it.

Please excuse the theatricality of this last gesture of mine. It is the last, you see, and it is only human to want a certain amount of drama in the final moment of one's life. I don't know how you discovered the flaw in our organization. I'd rather not know, it might give me too low an opinion of myself! Luckily Count von Fahrenberg, a gentleman even in the last emergency, was able to get here to give me the agreed warning. I played for a time with the idea of fighting matters out to the end. After all, you had very little "on me", and the documents you have doubtless impounded will be of no use. All the same, there's something degrading in being hounded by the law, and baited by their watchdogs, in public, in open court, don't you think? You'll understand, Inspector Bray, even if Inspector Creighton doesn't! So here you are:

I, and I alone, shot Furnace and killed Ness and (*this at least is something to be proud of*) *devised the scheme of Furnace's crash. I'm not proud of the Ness business, but it was done in a hurry. I didn't know how much the little rat had given away. The suggestion I made to you about the murder of Furnace, and which with Tommy's help I foisted on Mrs. Angevin, was one of my earlier ideas for the murder, discarded, as being too risky.*

Inspectors darling, I've saved you a whole lot of trouble, will you do something for me in return? Let my husband Tommy down lightly. He was only doing what I planned, you see. Give him the note I enclose.

Laura Vanguard.
("The Chief").

A small folded sheet of paper which had fluttered out when the Inspector had torn open the envelope now caught his eye. He picked it off the desk, read the inscription and, after a moment's hesitation, handed it to Vane without unfolding it. Vane thanked him with a look.

Vane read it. He looked as if he were about to weep, and his face, youthful always, seemed now like that of a mere boy. But the next moment he gave a bitter smile, and the paper, crumpled between his fingers, fell to the floor. It was some time afterwards that the Judge, taking pity on the scrap fluttering about, torn and trodden on, picked it up. The Judge glanced at it once before he shook his head and put it carefully in his breast pocket.

It read:

> *Good-bye. Good luck.—Laura.*

The Judge added this last tender message of one of the most callous murderesses he had known to his collection of problems of psychology. He had come across many in the course of a life which had taught him much, without ever affecting a certain simplicity of his, alternating between childishness and profound wisdom.

"You knew they were married?" Bray asked the Judge, when Creighton had finished reading Lady Laura's letter.

"I did," he acknowledged. "They were married from my house. It's been like some bad dream, sitting here these last few minutes and learning gradually what sort of thing Hartigan got mixed up in and what this wife of his had done. They came to me in Hollywood to be married and asked me to keep it quiet. I did. Lady Laura's distinguished parents were reason enough, and I never thought much more about it. I will say that Maggie detested Lady Laura from the moment they met. 'A ruthless woman,' she would say. 'She may love Spider,' she told me, 'but that won't prevent her ruining him.' 'Oh, you may laugh, Silas,' she'd say to me, 'but she is the sort of woman who does ruin men—ruthless and cold she is, and cleverer than you've any inkling of.'" …

"Shut up, shut up!" screamed Vane, his self-control suddenly leaving him. His face worked hysterically: "Do you think I care a damn what you think of Laura, you lousy little yokel! She was the greatest woman I've ever known, really great, and you talk about her as if she were a pickpocket! Oh, don't stare at me all of you. Don't you realize that she's gone; she's flying away bravely perhaps into the sea, perhaps straight into a hillside. Perhaps even now she's crashed and dead!" He broke off suddenly with a sob and buried his face in his hands. "Oh, damn the lot of you!"

There was a silence in the little room. Innes went forward as though to pat the young man on the shoulders and then thought better of it. In the silence, the raucous voice of Sir Herbert Hallam could be heard drifting in the open windows from the loud-speakers. All listened with a kind of fascinated attention.

"Ladies and gentlemen, the display is concluded. I am sure you will agree it is one of the finest and most entertaining and most instructive that it 'as hever been our lot to witness. I am sure you will go away realizing what a wonderful thing haviation is and 'ow it affects our daily lives. I believe the day is not far distant when we shall all be buzzing across the Atlantic at four hundred miles an hour and popping in and hout of our back gardens in our little aeroplanes. Which just shows us what a wonderful thing haviation is, and I'm sure hall of you who've witnessed this very excellent show will agree.

"You were probably puzzled by the little incident that 'appened with the police, and I am 'appy to assure you that it 'as all been satisfactorily settled, and you will read about it in your papers to-morrow. Just another proof of 'ow aviation is haffecting our daily lives in all sorts of ways! Before you go I am sure you'll like to hear me record our thanks for the work put in by the pilots and voluntary staff, but above all by the Countess of Crumbles, who as horiginator of the scheme and Chairman of the Executive Committee 'as worked wonders, and I'm sure the Hairies, God bless 'em, will be set up for life. Thanking you for your kind support, ladies and gentlemen, good-bye. Put on a record, George, while I go and get a drink. ..."

A record ground out some desperate gaiety, and there was a mighty scuffle and murmur as the sheeplike crowd pushed and shoved out of its pens. Motors started up, tired children bawled, and 'good-nights' were bidden. The sun was already beginning to get near its setting, and one by one, with the roar of an opened engine, the visiting 'planes rose from the aerodrome and hurried for their home hangars before darkness fell.

It was Vane who broke the silence. He had moved from the chair and was looking out of the window of the room, which faced on to the aerodrome.

"Good lord!" he exclaimed. "Laura's Dragon is still out there!"

He opened the window and a policeman sprang forward to hold his arm, but he was only opening it to speak to Sally Sackbut as, escorted by a policeman, she passed by them.

"Where's Lady Laura?" he yelled. "Why hasn't she taken her machine?"

"She left it for Winters to try," shouted back Sally. "She borrowed a club Moth and went back to Goring in that."

Vane looked dazed. "Heavens, what an ironic thing!" he muttered.

"Why?" asked Bray. "Does it matter?"

"Matter!" said Vane dully. "Laura's going to kill herself in that 'plane—and I put the Bishop in there after I'd drugged him.

"Damned funny," he added, in the horrified silence that followed. "Our dear Bishop will have the honour of dying with my wife, while I am left behind. Pretty shaming, eh?"

CHAPTER XX

KIND CONSIDERATION OF A KILLER

THE little red-and-silver biplane had slipped away quietly from Baston Aerodrome. The oblong pattern of the flying field, with its car park looking like a swarm of beetles, and its mass of insect heads, and its aeroplanes poised on the ground with outspread wings like butterflies, had receded below the wheels. At the same time the weather began to worsen.

It had been fine all day, although the south-west wind and the oppressive pallor of the sky had always been threatening. Now clouds were coming up on the wind, and the fleecy lumps of haze tore past the wings, dissolving as they moved.

The biplane climbed.

"A bit sluggish," thought Lady Laura, looking at the rev. counter, which, however, showed full revolutions when she opened the throttle. They climbed persistently, and presently the aeroplane's shadow no longer chased it as they flew towards the sun, towards the bad weather, for they were muffled in the clouds.

The clouds soon parted and rippled below them like a loosely-woven counterpane. Roads, railways, streams, suddenly appeared sharp-edged across a gap in the billowing clouds. Or perhaps there loomed the firmly-rounded dark green of a copse.

The windscreen in front of Lady Laura spattered suddenly with beads of moisture and rain. Water began to trickle steadily, flying backwards in a curve from the trailing edge of the upper wing.

Soon the aeroplane was hung suspended in a world of its own. Below, a white sea of cloud rippled. Around it other clouds flew past, tattered, ragged, and allowed frequent glimpses of the sun which, when it appeared, painted the vague blue of shadow from the aeroplane in fantastic magnification on the grey screen of the more solid cloud-banks below.

Lady Laura looked round her, drinking in the sense of solitude which is one of the profound experiences of flying. ...

The Bishop, huddled up on the floor of the front cockpit, was sleeping heavily at first, but later in a fitful dreamfulness. In his dream he was pursued through endless corridors by some strange insect which assumed a different shape every time he saw it. He hurried across the floors of monstrous halls, plunged into caverns, and shot up lifts, but his retreat was continually cut off by the threatening cry of his pursuer and the dreadful buzzing of its wings. At last he was involved in utter peril, in which the nightmare had him at his mercy and was enveloping him with fold after fold of its convolutions. He awoke and found himself struggling with a rug in which he was wrapped. The menacing buzz of his attacker had become the peaceful drone of the aero engine. It came back to him that he had gone to sleep in the cockpit of an aeroplane which, therefore, must now be in flight. Meanwhile his head was almost split in two by a headache in which the Bishop, had he not been a temperate man, would have recognized all the symptoms of a "morning after".

He half stood up, turned, and saw himself looking into a face which, even behind the streaming wind-screen and gnome-like goggles, he recognized as that of Lady Laura. And as he looked at it, he saw an expression of horrified surprise flash over it. The figure gesticulated at him. He looked down and saw nothing but cloud.

Lady Laura was shouting, but the words were snatched out of her mouth by the slipstream and drowned by the roar of the engine. But at last he gathered from her gesticulations what she meant. He put his hand up to his head. He still wore the flying helmet that he had put on to diminish the noise of the engine while he slept, and he now plugged in the telephone and heard Lady Laura's disembodied voice.

"How on earth did you get in here?"

"I must apologize," answered the Bishop. "I felt extraordinarily drowsy and looked round for somewhere to sleep. I was persuaded by Tommy Vane to climb in here, and I must slowly have sagged down on to the floor. It was rather surprising that I did not foul the rudder-bar."

"Why didn't I see you when I got in?"

"Vane appears to have thoughtfully covered me with a rug, so perhaps it is not surprising that you did not see me. But I cannot understand why I was not wakened by an aero engine starting up a foot away from me. It seems almost incredible."

"You were drugged," answered Lady Laura succinctly.

The Bishop turned it over in his mind. "Drugged? But how? And why? I must confess my head feels rather like it. But I took nothing all afternoon, except—yes, let me see—a small lemonade from Tommy Vane."

"That was it."

"Surely you were joking? Why on earth should Tommy Vane——"

"Because you knew too much, Bishop." Lady Laura's voice was precise and cold—a still, small murmur in the telephone. "You had barged into that nuisance of a Judge person who had married us in Hollywood. We thought that would never come out. Tommy had done his best to hide it by pretending to make a dead set at Mrs. Angevin. But the Judge had apparently told you of our marriage. So with his usual wild impetuousness, Spider drugged you and put you in a safe place. Unfortunately, Spider always bungles everything when he does not consult me. He put you in this club Moth, intending no doubt to dispose of you at a convenient time, but in the note he succeeded in getting into my hand in the Announcer's tent, he omitted to tell whereabouts he had hidden you. So, you see, I have committed the stupidity of running off with the machine in which he put you."

The Bishop was unable to grasp for a moment what Lady Laura meant. The words mixed with the dizziness of his drug-dazed brain and danced about, full of all kinds of sinister implications.

"Dispose of me?" he faltered. "I am afraid I am still a little drowsy, because I simply cannot understand what you mean."

"It doesn't matter very much now," she said carelessly. "You see, everything's blown up. So it doesn't matter if our marriage does come out."

A sudden premonition filled the Bishop's brain with the same sensation of evil he had felt so many days before when standing by the body of Furnace. He shivered.

The aeroplane leaped and wallowed suddenly with a gust from the face of an advancing cloud, and Lady Laura was silent for a moment as she righted the 'plane. Then she spoke in the same cold voice.

"I believe the condemned criminal usually is expected to make a confession before he goes to the gallows to the clergy-man who is on duty for that purpose. I seem specially lucky— I've got a Bishop for my confessor. You see it was I who was the head—the brains—of the dope distribution organization about which Inspector Creighton has doubtless told you. Does it surprise you? You flatter me! It was I who found it necessary to shoot Furnace and devise a satisfactory way of disposing of his remains. Finally, it was I who killed Ness. Comparatively simple, you see, in his case, as he never knew who the Chief was. I merely asked him to come up for a flight with me, as I had bought a machine from Gauntlett and was troubled by a noise in the engine. We got up into a cloud, and while he was listening I did a half roll. ... Probably my husband had in mind a similar scheme for getting rid of you, but I certainly should not have been a party to anything so clumsy. One should never do the same thing twice. It is as inartistic as it is dangerous."

The Bishop was utterly unable to speak for a few minutes. "Have you no compunction whatever for what you have done?" he said at last.

The small voice hesitated. "Yes, I don't know whether I can describe exactly why I disliked shooting Furnace. Only I did. It was so revolting chiefly because the poor brute thought he was in love with me and, what was worse, even imagined I loved him! He was actually preparing to divorce his wife for me. Poor George, and he was so dreadfully ugly and stupid! He hadn't the least idea I was the Chief and wasn't even aware of my connection with the dope organization. He thought I was as brainless as the Society butterfly of the novelist, and as good as gold at heart." She laughed rather horribly. "Do you know, I really believe that what made him get restive more than anything else, when he found it was cocaine that he was carrying, was the idea that it might make him despicable in my eyes! Rather ironical, isn't it? Like the plot of one of those Russian plays, or Ibsen or something.

"That, of course, was what made it so dangerous. I got a letter from him in which he told me, what he'd already half hinted at to Ness in conversation, that he was going to clear out of his entanglements at any cost. Tell the police, in fact. And he still didn't know that I was responsible for his entanglements! I saw then that it was necessary to eliminate him. The truth was that he'd been a continual anxiety to the organization from the moment he found out that we were smuggling. I'd rather any of the other pilots, or even Gauntlett or Randall or Sally, had found out about the dope than Furnace. He had a queer sort of honesty that nothing would eradicate, I'm afraid.

"In his letter he talked about 'ending the mess', and it struck me that the phrase might equally be used for committing suicide, though, of course, anyone who knew George and his deep-grained pugnacity would realize that he would never, *never* commit suicide. However, it gave me the idea for my murder, and the whole thing went through without a hitch. But I really hated doing it. Honestly I did, Doctor Marriott. I made an appointment with George for the evening before the crash, alone, and I can't somehow forget the way the smile on his face at seeing me changed suddenly when I pulled the revolver out and shot him. ... Just for a moment ... but it was horrid." A disembodied sigh came down the ear-phones. "Well, there it is, and you see it was all no good. Just the tiniest little flaw, and the whole organization broken up! Luckily I was warned in time to get away, and I certainly don't propose to go through the business of a public trial. But you are a fresh problem."

"Why?" asked the Bishop.

"I don't believe in *wasteful* murder," she explained. "There is no reason for killing you now, and it would be rather inartistic to do it."

"Is it necessary to deceive even yourself?" asked the Bishop gently. "If your better feelings urge you not to take yet another human being's life, need you disguise from yourself that it is your better feelings that are prompting you?"

"Don't cant, for heaven's sake!" said Lady Laura shrilly. "And don't cherish the idea that anything you say will persuade me to face the mob and the public. No, I'm going to end things quietly and neatly. Don't you think suicide is justifiable in the circumstances?"

"Less than ever in these circumstances," said the Bishop positively.

"Would you try to stop me?"

"I most certainly should."

"Confound it! That means I daren't land somewhere and put you down or else you'd try to grab me or do something silly. How unreasonable you are!"

They flew on in silence for a time. The worst of the weather had passed, and breaks were now visible in the clouds below them, through which the Bishop saw at first the sandy outline of the coast and then the grey oozing surface of the sea. The sun was getting very low, and the clouds were beginning to be dyed with a spreading flood of orange.

The Bishop was endeavouring to arrange his thoughts preparatory to making a final struggle with the refractory mind of Lady Laura. His head sang with the after-effects of the drug, and the sudden revelations of the last few minutes gave him the impression of having been transported to a nightmare world.

"Perhaps you are right," said Lady Laura unexpectedly. "I'll go back and face it. I'm feeling so tired too. Reaction I suppose! Can you take charge for a little?"

"I have no controls here," said the Bishop absently, his mind puzzled by the strange change of mind on the part of the woman.

"You'll find the dual control stick in a clip on the cockpit side. Put it in the socket. The rudder-bar is already there."

"I see. I have the column in place now."

"All right. Don't touch it for a moment. I'll tell you when I want you to take over. Have you got your safety-belt fastened?"

"Yes. I did it up after that last bump."

The wings slid across the horizon as the machine turned back on its course, and the Bishop sighed with relief. He still found himself unable to grasp the reason for Lady Laura's change of spirit.

The wings straightened on the new reciprocal course, and they were heading for the coast again—for the point from which they had started out. The nose sank. Evidently they were about to go through the cloud, and presently its fleecy whiteness was all around them.

The Bishop could never recapture a clear sequence of the remainder of events. He only knew that suddenly the machine was on its back. The control column struck his knee sharply as it was tilted hard over. He thought he heard a cry behind him, and a momentary rustle. Hanging with his full weight on his belt while the aeroplane lurched and fluttered upside-down like a mad thing, he turned his head. The cockpit behind him was empty. . . .

But almost instinctively the Bishop was giving his main attention to righting the 'plane. He put the stick over and a little forward, with some dim idea of diving from the inverted position or rolling back. He apparently did the right thing, for, as he came through the bottom of the cloud, a couple of thousand feet above the sea, the machine righted itself and he was able to check it before it rolled again and hold it on a steady course.

The Bishop flew over the tossing and tumbling surface of the water, flew in continuous circles, clumsily but pertinaciously. But there was no sign of a human being there, no black, bobbing figure, not even an arm flung desperately in the air.

At last the Bishop decided to return and, with his back to the sun, flew steadily, close to the sea, until the coast of Kent, with its white slash of chalk, came into sight.

The Bishop had already resolved in his dazed mind what he would do. He kept steadily on, flying below the cloud until at last he saw to his right a great stretch of turf with the welcome white circle in its centre. Sooner or later, he had felt sure, he must strike an aerodrome. Here was one.

The Bishop shut off the engine and turned. He turned again as the machine glided parallel with the boundary of the aerodrome, and presently the ground was coming up to him. "The first check…" he muttered dizzily to himself.

Nearer. … Then, "Back with the stick," repeated the Bishop under his breath, his face set. "Back! BACK!"

There was a sickening drop, and the Bishop realized he had landed about ten feet too high. With a wrenching, splintering noise and a crash which shook him cruelly, the 'plane struck the ground and collapsed, heeling over on one wing-tip.

The Bishop undid his belt and began to walk, a little unsteadily, toward the hangars. He was met by the ambulance. With a strange feeling of unreality he saw Miss Sackbut step out and heard her exclamation of relief as she saw him.

"I am afraid I have crashed the second club 'plane," he said, walking waveringly towards her.

"It's not a crash if you can walk away from it," she answered, smiling.

"Where am I?" he said, putting his hand to his forehead.

"This is Sankport. Lady Laura flew over here on her way, but without circling, and although they couldn't see the registration letters, they recognized the club colours and 'phoned us. I was desperately worried when I heard from Creighton what had happened. Luckily he and Bray decided that we were telling the truth when we said we didn't know what had been happening under our noses. So he let me go and I jumped into a machine and flew out here. I've been out twice to try to find some trace of you, but I haven't been able to find a thing." She looked at the 'plane. "Where is Lady Laura?"

The Bishop bowed his head. "She was too clever for me even at the last. She—escaped. The coast-guards must look out for her body."

Sally was looking at him with a strange intentness. "When was this?"

"About half an hour ago."

"I think Tommy Vane must have known. For it was just half an hour ago when they were leading him away. Suddenly he gave a shout and broke away from the policemen who were holding him. God knows how he got free! He ran across the aerodrome and then, whether by accident or on purpose, I don't know, he ran into a propeller. … He was killed instantly. …"

He looked at her. He suddenly observed that her face was white with horror. The Bishop began to shake off the nightmare of his trip with Lady Laura and to realize again the existence of an exterior world.

"I must 'phone Creighton," he said; "stay here, Sally."

*   *   *   *   *

Next day he looked in to see Sally and found her on a deserted flying-field.

"Well, that's the end!" he said with forced cheerfulness. "The police have made a clean sweep of everything. The organization is broken up. I suppose things will resume their old placid way at Baston? You know, I expect, that my leave is nearly up, and I shall soon have to return to my diocese?"

To his surprise, Sally suddenly burst into tears. Never having seen her anything but pugnacious and imperturbable, it gave him a shock.

"The same old way! Do you think I can ever go on with Baston? I'm not fit to be left in charge of a club. And I thought that I was so clever and good at managing things!"

"But, Sally, you have done splendid work here," he faltered.

"What, when all the time I was helping a gang of criminals without knowing it, and letting my instructors be murdered and the club 'planes crashed, and the club's name be ruined! How can I possibly hold up my head again? If only I had had my wits about me all these terrible things would never have happened. But I'm just a little conceited fool." She searched dimly for a handkerchief and, being unable to find one, accepted the Bishop's large square of linen.

"My dear girl," he began again.

"I'm not a girl," she snivelled. "I'm over thirty—I'm thirty-five—and it is too late for me to do anything else. I don't think I'm really good at anything, not even flying. And I used to be so pleased with myself. . . . Oh, why did I ever come to this wretched place!"

This gave the Bishop an opportunity to make a suggestion which he had meditated for many days. Only his timidity and his knowledge of Sally's commitments with her club had prevented him from speaking before.

"I have come to the conclusion I shall never make a pilot," he said, indicating with a gesture the damaged machine in the hangar, which had been towed there from Sankport. "But as you know, I have a 'plane out in Australia and if I could have a pilot to fly it for me . . . In short, if you would accept . . ." He became confused. "I know you are fond of flying, and that's why I mention it, though, of course——"

"Oh, I should simply love to go out to Australia with you!" Sally said enthusiastically. "But although I would make quite a good aerial chauffeur, what about the scandal of a Bishop's woman pilot? Are you married?"

"I am not," he answered slowly; "but there would hardly be any scandal, Sally, if you were to do me the honour of accepting the proposal I am making. For, when you interrupted me, I was about to ask you to be my wife. . . ."

*   *   *   *   *

… Which explains why the Flying Bishop of Cootamundra (as he is known), and his wife, have a horror of detective novels.

"It reads all right in a book," the Bishop will explain, "but it's dreadful if you encounter it in real life."

THE END